CHASE

ALSO BY ZACK MASON

Killing Halfbreed
Shift
Chase
Turn

CHASE

Zack Mason

Dogwood Publishing
Lawrenceville, Georgia

Published by Dogwood Publishing
Copyright © 2011 by Zack Mason

All rights reserved under International and Pan-American Copyright Conventions. Published in the United States by Dogwood Publishing, a division of More Than Books, Inc., Georgia.

Library of Congress Cataloging-in-Publication Data is available upon request from the publisher.

Trade Paper

ISBN: 0-9787744-3-4
ISBN-13: 978-0-9787744-3-1

E-Book

ISBN: 0-9787744-4-2
ISBN-13: 978-0-9787744-4-8

Manufactured in the United States of America.

9 8 7 6 5 4 3 2 1

First Edition: May 2012

Cover Design by Matt Smartt

This book is dedicated to
God,
the Creator of Time and Author of all Adventure

-and-

to Sam & Hazel Lessley
who first inspired me with
a sense of the history around us.

Previously in *Shift*
(Book I of the ChronoShift Trilogy)

- Mark Carpen, a former special forces soldier, loses his children in a terrible car accident.

- The family of the drunken teenager driver who killed them sues Mark for everything he owns and Mark's wife, Kelly, abandons him.

- Mark turns his back on society and loses himself in the North GA mountains to live off the land.

- While wandering, Mark discovers an empty shed in the middle of the woods. Inside, are several watches — time-travel devices that latch onto the wearer's wrist and can only be removed at death.

- With the watch, which Mark calls a *shifter*, he can jump through time at will. He uses the shifter to acquire billions of dollars in a matter of months.

- Mark returns to the day of the wreck to save his kids, but a strange and powerful force firmly prevents him from stopping the accident, no matter what he tries, and he is devastated.

- A mysterious stranger, who also bears a shifter, recruits Mark to embark on certain time-travel "missions" for a company called ChronoShift. His name is Hardy Phillips.

- Mark soon meets and conducts missions with a second member of ChronoShift, Ty Jennings. The three men quickly become friends.

- Suddenly, Hardy and Ty disappear into thin air — their office abandoned.

- Alone, Mark uses his shifter to fight crime and tragedy on his own. He hires Savannah Stanford to do historical research and builds himself a time-travel "armory."

- Mark travels back in time and recruits younger versions of Hardy and Ty from the U.S. military before the two men have ever heard of time shifters. Mark gives them his two extra watches. Together, they form a new company and name it ChronoShift. It is unclear who actually hired who.

- Later, Mark saves Laura Kingsley, an exotic dancer, from a violent assault. He becomes infatuated with her, and they date.

- Laura is only interested in material gains. When she realizes she cannot dominate Mark, she breaks off the relationship. She then takes up with Hardy. Mark's fury over the betrayal causes Hardy to separate from ChronoShift

- Alexander Rialto, a senior agent with the IRS, begins to investigate Mark's tax history. After 15 years of continual investigation and frustration, Rialto finally discovers Mark's secret, but not before being fired from the IRS for persecuting Mark.

- A bitter Rialto kills Ty in the year 2027 and takes Ty's shifter for himself. He uses it to kill Hardy, taking that watch as well. Rialto then recruits for himself an army of time-traveling, ex-mafiosos whose primary objective is to destroy Mark Carpen.

- As *Shift* concludes, Mark and Ty have been captured by Rialto's men — Mark in Washington DC at the death of Abe Lincoln in 1865, and Ty in Dallas at the Kennedy assassination in 1963. Both are set to be executed and neither Hardy nor Savannah have any idea where they are.

Like Secret Codes?

The author has been given exclusive access to ChronoShift's website while it is under construction.

1. Go to www.Chrono-Shift.com
2. Login: 09071890
3. Click on "Proxy" and look closely to see if you can solve the code.

Chapter 1

April 30th 2013, Boston, MA

A series of electronic chirps from Hardy's phone interrupted what otherwise would have been a perfectly pleasant breakfast with Laura Kingsley.

Exotic beauty was the only way to describe her. The caramel tone of her skin was accentuated well by her chestnut brown hair, laced with streaks of blonde. She captivated his eyes and mind with the raw, physical attraction of her beauty.

Sure, she dyed her hair and wore contact lenses most days that transformed her eyes into sparkling violet amethysts, but who cared? It looked good. Her expertise in all things cosmetic came easily to her, even when she made spontaneous changes.

This morning, she'd chosen different contacts. Her striking purple pupils had been replaced by a bright emerald green.

She was *not* an easy woman to keep happy. If it weren't for the shifter Mark had given him, doing so would have been near impossible. She had expensive tastes.

Hardy Phillips lowered the piece of browned toast he'd been buttering and picked up the cordless.

"Hardy?" asked a familiar, yet timid female voice.

"Hey, Savannah. What's up? Did Mark decide he wants to speak to me again?"

"Sorry, no. It's not about that."

"Okay." He laughed to hide the hurt he felt. "What then?"

"I'm not sure, but I think something's wrong...seriously

wrong."

"What happened?"

"You know how you guys meet...er...they meet every Monday morning. Well, yesterday, neither Mark nor Ty showed up. There's no good reason for them to miss. You know that better than anybody."

"You know about the shifters?"

"I pretty much figured it out by myself, so Mark filled me in."

"I see. Well, you're right. If they didn't show up for the Monday meeting, something's wrong. I'll be right over. Fill me in when I get there." He terminated the call.

The Monday morning meetings had been designed to serve as an alarm system of sorts as much as a planning time. Since the three of them could shift to any hour or minute they ever needed, if one of them didn't show up as scheduled, it could only mean one thing.

"What was *that* about?" Laura inquired.

"Mark and Ty are missing. I've got to go and see what's going on."

"Mark's a big boy...surely he can take care of himself. Why should you go running off to help him when he's not even talking to you?"

"He's not talking to me because of *you*, Laura."

She knew that. Better than he did.

"So? You're still not his caretaker. It's time you forgot about him and formed your own company."

Hardy scowled. This was a side of her he didn't like. "I owe everything to Mark. If he wants to hate me, that's his prerogative, but I'm not about to let something happen to him. He saved your life too. Did you forget?"

She didn't respond except to shoot him a look that told him what she wouldn't be forgetting for several days was this conversation.

He didn't care. He'd bend over backwards to make her happy with superficial things like money, things that didn't matter, but he wasn't about to let a friend come to harm. She'd just have to get over it.

***

Concern lined Hardy's face as he strode into the office. He glanced sideways at the wall and winced. The last time he'd been here, Mark had thrown him against that wall and nearly choked the life out of him.

"How are you, Savannah?"

This was the girl Mark should be pursuing. She was perfect for him. More than just pretty, she was beautiful in a delicate, elegant way, and cultured to boot. Not at all like Laura. Laura's only good attributes were her physical ones. Hardy could be happy with that, and yes, he knew how shallow that made him.

Mark deserved so much better than Laura, but he was too blinded by his infatuation to see her faults. *He deserved someone like Savannah.* If she'd just let her hair down once in a while, maybe Mark would notice.

"I'm fine, Hardy."

"Fill me in."

She told him about the manipulated bank accounts and the discovery of a man named Smith who not only had a shifter, but was actively trying to harm Mark. Recounting how they'd searched for Smith and undone his sabotage, she showed Hardy the note that Mark had found in the bank vault when he'd last confronted Smith.

IN finite terlock

L-04-14-65 L.H.O.
K-11-22-63 J.W.B.

She explained they'd thought it was a reference to the Lincoln and Kennedy assassinations. Mark and Ty had thought

Smith must have been planning something around the assassinations, and since the note was their only lead on how to find the man again, they'd split up, Mark going back to 1865 and Ty to 1963.

"They split up?"

"Yes, Mark took Lincoln and Ty took Kennedy. Last I knew, they were just going to look around and see if they spotted Smith anywhere."

"Smells like a trap. Seems mighty careless of Smith to conveniently drop this note at that bank."

"It didn't occur to us at the time, but I guess you're right. I didn't get worried till today. They didn't show up at all yesterday, which can only mean..."

"Mark's never been suspicious enough. Yes, if they didn't show up, that's bad. We should be able to undo it though — that is, as long as this Smith doesn't get me too."

Chapter 2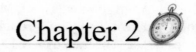

April 14th 1865, Washington D.C.

  Hardy decided to go after Mark first. Finding out what happened to him shouldn't be too tricky. If Mark were looking for this Smith guy, he would have visited Ford's Theater in D.C. the night of Lincoln's assassination. Even if Mark had visited a number of other different times or places, the only place Smith would know to find Mark to capture him would be at that theater near the moment of the assassination, and Smith *had* to be the one responsible for Mark's disappearance.

  On the other hand, if it turned out Smith wasn't responsible, it would prove impossible for Hardy to find Mark if he didn't visit Ford's theater that night.

  Dressed in upper-class attire appropriate for a Washingtonian of 1865, Hardy waited just outside the theater. He kept a close watch on anyone entering or leaving, especially the carriages pulling up in front of the venue to let people on and off. If Hardy were going to kidnap someone, he'd want to be able to whisk them away quickly. Smith would likely be thinking along the same lines.

  Around 10:15, a single muffled gunshot echoed from inside the theater.

  Such a humbling, hollow sound. Hardy knew what that shot meant for Abraham Lincoln.

A few moments later, Mark emerged from a side entrance followed closely by two rough-looking men dressed in black frock coats. The men ushered Mark toward a carriage which had been parked for several minutes by the curb.

Why didn't Mark just shift out to escape? He suspected they must have a gun on him.

Hardy dared not attempt a rescue here. There was a chance this Smith knew what he looked like, which meant he needed to stay out of sight.

Before Mark could enter the cab, one of the men chopped him on the back of the neck. The other caught his unconscious body and shoved it into the empty car.

Hardy followed them at a safe distance on a horse he'd rented from a local farmer. The inconspicuous carriage bearing Mark advanced at a slow pace as it left the city, rocking with each small hole in the roadway it encountered. To remain unnoticed, Hardy made sure he maintained a significant distance between himself and the cab, especially once their surroundings became more rural.

He would have to drop back even more if these guys went any farther into the country. The farther they went, the more Hardy and his mount would stand out.

One of those men was probably Smith and, if so, he would have a shifter. Hardy needed to find a way to free Mark before he got hurt, and he was having trouble imagining scenarios where that wasn't going to be a difficult feat.

He was definitely *not* looking forward to entering into a shifting duel with another time traveler. He needed to devise a plan that would get Mark out of there without being outdone by Smith.

The houses lining the road were growing sparser, enough so that he'd soon be noticed. It was camouflage time.

He wondered, if he were to push the shift button right now, *would his horse go with him?*

He knew Mark had shifted with Laura once just by holding her hand. There was only one way to find out. If he was wrong, he'd only have a sore rear to show for it.

He pushed the button...and thankfully, did not find himself in sudden free fall. As he'd hoped, both Hardy and the horse were now twenty minutes in the past.

He just loved this watch. It had some very nice features.

The carriage was behind him now, further back down the road. Instead of appearing to be following, he now rode a good distance ahead of the coach that held Mark. It was an excellent surveillance maneuver since it wasn't natural to suspect someone *ahead* of you of actually being in pursuit.

He stayed consistently well ahead of the coach until he noticed it turning off onto a side road out of the corner of his eye. He shifted once more, traveling back far enough to appear in front of the carriage again, but now on the side road.

When the car turned onto a narrow drive that led to a farmhouse, it was time to shift again. He led the horse to a grove of trees and staked it out behind a small knoll where it would remain unseen from the house or the barn.

He needed to shift to an hour before the carriage arrived so he could scope out the buildings while they were empty. Hardy remounted the horse before he shifted, thinking he might need him for a quick get-away.

After this last shift, however, the horse began to act funny. It spread out all four hooves and planted them firmly, looking at him with the most pitiful expression he'd ever seen on a horse.

It nipped at its flanks with a sudden desperation and then he thought it might be sick, but instead it suddenly broke out into a thick sweat. Rivulets of perspiration rolled down its coat, even along its face. He was worried that he might have inadvertently killed the animal, but after a few minutes, it finally began to recover.

Apparently, when shifting, large animals got nauseous faster than people. An interesting factoid to be filed away for a future date.

Perhaps he'd be better off not relying on this horse for a quick get-away after all. Come to think of it, he had just shifted a total of five times within a few hours, including the initial shift to 1865. He would be smart to camp out for the evening and let the shifter recharge before he attempted a rescue. If anything went wrong when he tried to free Mark, they might need to shift several times in a row.

While he felt sympathy, the miserable look on that horse's face had been kind of funny. What wouldn't be funny was if they got caught because the shifter shut down on him. Since he knew where Mark was now, Hardy would simply scope out the barn and farmhouse at his leisure, and then move away from the property to camp for the night. He would wait the standard twenty-four hours to let his shifter rest, or do whatever it was it needed to do to reset, and then go back.

***

Mark lifted his head. He'd just heard some commotion outside the rustic door. His arms ached, his legs were cramping, and he was tired of waiting.

Why don't they just get on with it?

Rialto, the man they'd known as Smith, had left at one point — at least Mark hadn't heard his voice for a while — but now he was back.

Mark strained against his bonds, but they wouldn't give. He was stuck. He couldn't even pull them close enough to his teeth to chew through them. His only chance would be to bust off one of the slats of wood to which he was tied, but that would require more time than he probably had. They could return any second to put a bullet in his head.

Suddenly, static hissed directly behind him, the type of hiss you only heard when someone was shifting in or out. Music to his ears. He barely had time to turn and register Hardy's face before he grabbed his forearm. Then, Mark felt himself shifting out.

The ropes had come along for the ride, but now they dangled loosely from his freed wrists.

The barn was gone. It had been night and was now daylight, probably early morning. Hardy must have shifted them to a time before the barn had existed.

They were in a narrow pasture surrounded by trees. About five feet to Mark's right was a grassy slope that descended into thick woods.

Warring emotions battled inside as Mark studied his rescuer. He would have much preferred it to have been Ty who saved him. The relief he felt was strong, but anger over the past swirled against it, clouding his vision.

Mark started to speak, but was interrupted by the sound of more electric crackles. Seeing the figures of two men phasing into their time right behind Hardy like something out of Star Trek, Mark dove straight into his former friend and tackled him. They rolled down the slope and into the forest.

Bullets spat up plumes of dirt where they'd stood just moments before. Knowing their best hope was to not break momentum, both men let themselves continue rolling down the slope as far as possible.

"Defense!" Mark called out.

Hardy understood immediately. They'd slowed sufficiently to control their descent, so both men dove toward each other, throwing themselves into a crouching position, back to back. Together, they had a full 360 degree view of the surrounding terrain. Hardy passed Mark one of his handguns.

The shots from the top of the hill had ceased, but neither man expected the attack to resume from there. Their attackers wore shifters like them. Any second, they could hear the electric static from a new shift, and from any direction.

If they heard that, they would have a fraction of a moment to respond, but if Rialto's men shifted into their time far enough away from their position, Mark and Hardy would never hear them coming. With one good sniper rifle, their enemies would be able to pick then off like fish in a barrel.

"We've got to get out of here," Mark breathed.

"No kidding," Hardy replied.

"What year are we in?"

"1834."

Mark began adjusting the settings on his watch. "All right, same day. Twenty years back. We shift on the count of three."

"Roger that."

"One, two,...*three*."

The woods shifted oddly in their vision, most trees shrinking, some larger, more mature ones appearing out of nowhere. One that had lain collapsed on the forest floor in front of Mark was suddenly upright and healthy. It was an effect that was still difficult to get used to.

Hardy looked at Mark. "What now, hot shot?"

Chapter 3

November 22nd 1963, Dallas, TX

Ty groaned. He wanted to lift his bloodied face up in defiance of his abusers, but he couldn't summon enough strength. He refused to let them think they'd broken his spirit.

Earlier, Ty had shifted back to the day of the Kennedy assassination in search of traces of their newly discovered nemesis, John Smith.

Unfortunately, Smith had turned the tables on Ty. He didn't know these men who had kidnapped him, so he'd never seen them coming. He and Mark hadn't even known Smith had henchmen working for him until now.

For all Ty knew, there could be an army of men out there with shifters on their wrists. What if Smith was just the tip of the iceberg?

These men hadn't divulged any info so far, not even their names. Smith was nowhere to be seen, and their apparent leader sported an odd, squarish patch of grey above his brow amidst what otherwise was a solid bush of jet black hair, so Ty mentally dubbed him Grey Tuft.

Grey Tuft had a shifter just like Mark and Ty's, but the other hirelings didn't. Which was a good thing. That would seem to indicate there was a limit on the number of time-traveling goons opposing them.

It was these other hirelings who beat him mercilessly now. He didn't think Grey Tuft even knew they were doing it. No doubt he was a cold one. He had made it clear he was going to kill Ty and bury his body in concrete so it would never be found, but in spite of the man's cruel tone, he didn't seem to have a lot of passion invested in the deed. To him, it was a job, following orders. A senseless beating requires anger.

These other two, however, were a different story. They were the hired help. Lowlife scum scraped up from the dregs of society. They hadn't dared lay a finger on him before Grey Tuft left the room, but once that door had closed, the racial slurs and blows flowed forth.

Ty now heard a new voice outside the room. He went limp, feigning unconsciousness, hoping to stop the beating so he could hear what was being said. The two goons kicked him a few more times in the gut for good measure and then retired to some chairs in the corner where they lit a couple cigarettes.

The voice outside the thick door bore clear authority in its tone. *Was that Smith?* Ty could barely make out the muffled words.

"...know what I said...plans changed...No."

"We should...at least..."

"Can't die...cause too many problems...clear?...Take him..."

"... the others?"

"No problem...just...him..."

The conversation stopped. The door opened. Grey Tuft entered by himself.

Peeking weakly through swollen eyes, Ty didn't see any sign of Smith or anyone else outside the door.

"You *idiots*! What did you do?"

Grey Tuft kneeled and turned Ty's face up, examining the extent of the damage. "You two are lucky he's alive or you'd be headed for a concrete grave yourselves right now."

"Wuz yur name," Ty slurred, spitting blood through his teeth.

"What's it matter?"

"Wanna know whoz gonna kill me."

"Torino. Vincent Torino, and there's been a change of plans, your highness. You ain't gonna die, but you still ain't gonna see the sun for a long, long time. Boss has got different plans for you."

He let go and Ty's head sagged, lolling from side to side. This time, he truly did fall unconscious.

***

August 14ᵗʰ 1834, Virginia Woodlands

"I thought we were prepared for this kind of thing," Rialto growled, glaring a hole through his men.

"Rialto — you, of all people, should know how difficult it is to pin down someone who's got a shifter."

"If you're prepared, it shouldn't matter."

"We were, but I couldn't stay with the guy 24 /7. Phillips shifted in and out within a one-second window and took Carpen with him. Even if we'd been in the room with our weapons ready, we couldn't possibly have gotten a good shot off in that amount of time."

Stanley Graves was sweating profusely, but more from the thick summer humidity than from any pressure put on him by Rialto. Killing another time-shifter was a difficult proposition, especially when the guy had friends capable of intervening. No, he didn't feel bad about Carpen slipping through his fingers.

"You don't fear me, do you, Graves?" Rialto asked.

"Huh?"

"If I ever have to show you why you should fear me, it'll be too late for that fear to do you much good. *That* I promise."

Graves involuntarily gulped. "Look, Rialto, we've got all the time we want. You saw how easy it was to capture their shift signatures with this tracker. We almost came in right on top of them last time, and we know they're sitting under those trees over there in 1814. These trackers Irvine gave you are amazing. We have the upper hand for sure."

Stanley Irvine, a physicist Rialto had hired to study the shifters, had successfully built several small portable devices that Rialto called "trackers." The trackers were encased in black plastic and slightly larger than a car fob. If a tracker was pointed at a person shifting between times, the handheld device could detect tiny fluctuations in the electro-magnetic field surrounding the person and interpret those fluctuations to give the exact date and time to which that person had just gone.

In other words, Mark Carpen could shift through time till he was blue in the face, but all Rialto had to do was point his little tracker at Carpen as he left and he would know to exactly which moment in time the man had gone. It was a powerful device, yet it ran on a simple watch battery.

"What's the plan, boss?"

Rialto slitted his eyes, staring at the copse of trees where Carpen and Phillips would be sitting — twenty years in the past. His enemies would be there for just a moment in 1814, but for Rialto, they were there perpetually. He could shift into their "moment" any time he wanted. There was no reason to hurry or be impatient. His tracker empowered him. He was the chaser. They were the ones on the run, frantically wondering which second would be their last.

"We could play shifting games with these guys for days, but we wouldn't accomplish anything without the element of surprise. Plus, they could get in a lucky shot. When we go after them again, we'll shift in at a distance so they don't hear us coming. If they shift out, we'll follow. If they don't shift out, we'll snipe 'em."

***

August 14th 1814, Virginia Woodlands

Silently, Mark and Hardy moved deeper into the woods. Mark raised two fingers to his eye and motioned sharply in two different directions. Hardy understood the hand signal. They would split up, moving in parallel, but staying about a hundred feet apart. If one of them ran into trouble, the other would be close enough to help, but far enough away not to get caught in the same trouble. Patrolling 101.

Being mid-August in Virginia, the brush was dense enough to provide good cover. They weren't visible to each other, but knew vaguely where the other was at all times. They continued stealthily until they reached a natural rendezvous point.

***

"Where are they?" Rialto hissed.

Graves pointed at a flash of black cloth between some bushes. "I think that's Carpen over there."

"Where's Phillips?"

"Not sure. Can't see him."

Rialto cursed. "These guys are in their element now," he rued.

"Why don't we go back to when they were under those trees together?"

"Because they were only there for a couple of seconds. Good chance they'd just shift around us and gain the upper hand if we're not successful with our first shots."

"What are we gonna do then?"

"We don't push it. We'll stalk Carpen, one of us on either side. Keep an eye out for Phillips. If you get a good shot at Carpen, take it, but if it looks like that's going to happen, prepare yourself *before* you take the shot. If Phillips sees Carpen go down, he'll shift back to take you out before you shoot.

"If we never get a good opportunity, we'll follow as far as we can without giving ourselves away."

Graves nodded and they split up, Graves continuing along Mark's right flank and Rialto circling around to the left. They didn't dare get too close. Carpen was highly trained in pursuits like this — and they were not.

Rialto saw him again. He whipped his rifle up hastily.

Carpen had momentarily exposed himself in a small clearing through which he had to pass in order to reach a large cluster of rocks. The rocks would make excellent cover, and he knew he had to take Carpen out before he reached them.

He hesitated.

He was too nervous. If he pulled the trigger, he might succeed and kill Carpen, but then Phillips would know. Phillips would shift back. Phillips would put a bullet in his head before he pulled the trigger, but that would only happen if Rialto pulled the trigger originally.

His hand shook with indecision. He cursed as Carpen made it to safety.

***

Hunkering behind some brush in an open space enclosed by the giant rocks, Mark had a clear view of both entrances to the central pocket where he was hiding. Over his head, a rock overhang would protect him if Rialto or his men tried to climb the boulders and attack from above.

Something moved in the brush by one of the entrances.

Mark readied himself.

It was Hardy.

Stealthily, Hardy entered the rock cluster and joined Mark in his defensive position.

"Anything?"

"Yeah, heard one of 'em behind me," Mark replied.

"How do they know *when* to find us?" Hardy hissed, "We shifted twice. That should have ended it. It's like they know where we went, but to the exact second."

"Rialto must have some kind of detection device that can tell where we shift to."

"Who's Rialto?"

"How *exactly* did you find me, Hardy?"

"Savannah."

"What did she tell you?"

"Showed me the note, told me about Smith, where you and Ty had gone."

"Where's Ty?"

"Not sure. He disappeared too. I came after you first."

Mark studied him. "Smith's real name is Rialto. That's all I know about the guy...other than the fact he's trying to kill us for some reason."

"Where'd he get his shifters?"

"No idea."

"You think maybe our shifters used to belong to him?"

"How should I know?" Mark pondered the possibility. "No...something's fishy. At one point, Rialto got hold of my old Wal-Mart shares before I'd cashed them in and burned them. It undid all the wealth I'd built, but it also made his shifter disappear from off his wrist. His ability to shift is somehow tied to every- thing I've built."

"So, why's he trying to kill you then? That would have to affect him too, right?"

"Don't know. If he's trying to kill me now, then whatever happened to allow him to get a shifter must have already hap- pened."

"Man, this time travel stuff is bending my brain."

"No joke."

"What are we gonna do?"

"If he can detect us when we shift, we'll just give our position away every time we do. We need to evaporate into the woods without shifting and put as much distance between them and us as we can. If we can lose them, they shouldn't be able to detect our shifts any more."

"Agreed."

"Let's split up. We don't want to give them an opportunity to take us both out in one fell swoop."

"Good call."

"Head toward D.C. Meet me in front of the White House at 8:00 PM tonight."

***

"Climb that rock and see if you can get a shot," Rialto ordered.

Graves ran to the rocks and scrambled to the top. He straightened, ever so slowly, and scanned the area below. Mark and Hardy were concealed by the overhang, so he wasn't able to pinpoint their position.

"No sign of them," he reported.

Rialto cursed. "They must have slipped out. We'll circle around, see if we can pick up their trail again."

By the time Rialto and Graves settled on their plan of action, Mark and Hardy had already left the rock cluster at different ends and melted into the forest.

Chapter 4

August 14th 1814, 8:00 PM, Washington D.C.

Mark reached the White House first. At least, it looked kind of like the White House. It was in the right place, but something was off about it.

Maybe it was the long series of columns extending from either side. *Were those there in modern times?* They didn't look right. Maybe they were covered by trees in the future and just couldn't be seen. There did seem to be a scarcity of trees here on the southern side, though there were plenty facing the north.

Hardy walked up, a tuft of foliage sticking out of his collar. "How long you been waiting?" he asked.

"'Bout an hour. You've got something on your shoulder." Mark pointed to the small branch as if it were a piece of food stuck in his teeth.

Hardy stopped short of extending his hand to Mark. This was the first time they'd faced each other in a peaceful setting since the fight in Mark's office months before.

"Are we good, Mark?"

"You did just save my life."

"That doesn't matter, and you know it. You've saved mine plenty of times."

Staring at his shoes, Mark didn't look up or say anything.

"Mark, Laura didn't cheat on you with me. She did try once...well...never mind. I made it clear I wouldn't have anything to do with her as long as she was with you."

"So, you told her to break up with me," Mark growled.

"No..." Hardy grimaced. "I wouldn't give her the time of day till I knew you two were finished. Man, look. What's done is done. The only question now is, are we going to move on from here or not?"

Mark extended his hand. "Forget it," he muttered.

Hardy took it, grateful for its significance, though he knew things wouldn't be the same for a while. Maybe never.

"What now?" Hardy asked.

"Rialto and his pal are out there somewhere, and they've got some kind of device that'll detect us if we shift. We're flying under the radar for the moment, but if we shift, we could alert them to our presence."

"So, how long do we wait or how far do we have to go before we shift out of here?"

"I don't know. We need to think this through before we do *anything*. These guys aren't playing around."

"Let's get a beer."

"Sounds good." Mark smiled for the first time. "There are probably some bars down near the wharf by the Potomac."

"I bet they're called taverns in 1814."

"Let's go find a tavern then and get some ale."

***

The tavern was darkly lit by a scattering of lanterns and candles. It was a rough looking place that likely only the toughest of sailors would call home. Whoever the owner was, he apparently subscribed to the Just-Give-'Em-a-Stool-and-Take-their-Money school of philosophy. The man that wanted more was in the wrong place.

The barkeep was unkempt and hadn't shaved in over a week. He eyed them warily.

"What'll it be, boys?"

"Couple of ales."

Mark scanned the tavern. There were a few other patrons in the dump. At one side, three burly sailors sat in a booth discussing something of import in hushed tones.

"I figured we'd find some place a little more lively than

this," Mark muttered under his breath.

"Yeah. Let's down these beers and get out of here," Hardy agreed.

"Hey, Barkeep!" Mark called.

The unhappy man brought their beers in a couple of dirty looking steins. "Yeah, what?"

"Where is everybody? Seems kind of dead to me."

"It's the war, got ev'ry body in town spooked, 'fraid to come out."

"War?" Mark queried. *What war?*

"Boy, I shoulda known ya were teched in the head, wot with them queer looking duds an' all. The war with the British, who else?!"

Mark took Hardy aside for a quick conference.

"What war is he talking about?" Mark covertly checked his shifter, keeping it from prying eyes in the bar. "My watch says 1814, how about yours?"

"Yeah. Mine too."

"So, it ain't the Revolutionary War."

"What other war was there with Britain?"

"It's gotta be the War of 1812."

"Wasn't that just in 1812? Did it last all the way through 1814?"

"Savannah would know."

"So helpful. In case you hadn't noticed, *she isn't here.*"

"Maybe it just started in 1812."

"What do we know about this war?"

"I'm trying to think…there was a big battle in New Orleans — I remember that much. My teachers didn't exactly spend a lot of time on it in school."

"Didn't Washington DC get burned by the British?"

"Sounds right. Now that you mention it, isn't that when Francis Scott Key wrote the Star Spangled Banner."

"Yeah...but that was over in Maryland, I think."

"That battle would be something to see. Maybe we could join in, lend a helping hand."

"Are you boys gonna pay for them drinks?" interrupted the barkeep.

"Oh, sure." Mark flipped him a gold piece, hoping the man wouldn't notice the date stamped on it. Neither one of them had come prepared for this decade. They'd both outfitted themselves with clothes and currency from the 1860's.

The barkeep seemed satisfied. He puttered off, stopping by the booth with the sailors and saying something to them before he disappeared into the living quarters behind the tavern.

Mark and Hardy sipped on their ales. Mark commented on how much he'd like a place to go lie down for a while.

"That can be arranged," said a voice from behind.

The speaker was a tall, burly sailor, the largest of the three who'd been sitting in the booth. His dingy, blonde hair was long, falling way past his shoulders.

They'd turned to face this sailor when he spoke, and Hardy realized too late that one of the shorter sailors had snuck up behind the bar and was swinging a bottle toward the back of Mark's neck. *Where was the third guy?*

The blow hit home, hard. Mark's legs gave out from under him and his body sank to the floor. In an instant, Hardy's hand was moving, reaching to activate his shifter, but his finger was still a few inches away when something struck the back of his neck and then his whole world went black. His last thought was that he guessed he knew where the third sailor had gone.

Chapter 5

Last night I nearly died,
But I woke up just in time.

~ Duke Special

A gentle rolling motion lulled Mark into a wakeful state. Wherever he was, the light was very dim. He couldn't make much out except for the faint image of a short wooden ladder illuminated by the only light visible, which emanated from a hole directly above it. The putrid stenches of human filth and sweat mingled to assault his senses.

He felt confined. His first instinct was to reach for his shifter.

A hand grabbed his wrist.

"Don't shift," Hardy whispered.

"Why not?"

"I think we're on a ship."

Made sense. The rolling sensation, which could only be waves. The stench of the lower decks. If Mark hadn't been so groggy from being knocked on the head, he would have caught on sooner himself.

"I think you're right."

"If we shift out of here, we're gonna find ourselves treading water. Probably in the middle of the ocean for all we know."

"Those sailors...*man!*" Mark rubbed the back of his head and neck.

"Yeah, we need to pay them back for this."

"First, we need to get above deck and figure this out. Are you tied up?"

"No. I think we've been shanghaied."

"Shanghaied? I read about that somewhere. Didn't think it was such common practice."

"They don't need us tied up once they get out to sea. Where are we gonna go?"

"Pretty miserable business if you ask me. All right, let's get our bearings. Is that ladder the only way out of here?"

"Think so."

They crept over to the ladder as silently as possible in the almost pitch blackness of the hold. They couldn't evade detection forever, but the longer they could observe others without being seen themselves, the better.

Sticking his head up through the hole, Mark looked around. They were definitely on a ship of some sorts. The space above their hold looked to be a food storage area. Barrels filled with unknown contents and bags of dry goods stacked five high lined the walls with gaps only for entering and exiting the room. A lone table stood in the center of the small room, and on it a candle burned. There were two chairs at the table, and one of them was occupied by a young man dressed in the uniform of the British Royal Navy. He was writing in a ledger.

As Mark lifted himself further from the hold below, the boy suddenly became aware of his presence. He rushed out, screaming "Cap'n, Cap'n!" and disappeared through a doorway.

"There goes the element of surprise," Hardy remarked.

"What did you want me to do, sit there and stare at him? Come on."

Hardy followed Mark up out of the hold.

"Let's see what we can find out before the 'Cap'n' gets us."

They emerged into salty, ocean air and bright sunlight, which momentarily blinded them, their squinted eyes having become accustomed to the darkened holds below. It was hard to believe they were actually on a real-life sailing vessel of old, but here they were. Just like the movies, except real...much more real.

Men were busy all over the ship, adjusting and tying off riggings, moving stores, scrubbing the deck. Several of the men glanced their way as they came up the ladder, but didn't stop what they were doing.

The 'Cap'n' stood in a doorway at the back of the ship, which probably led to his quarters. His uniform was that of a British naval officer.

"Shank!" he called.

All work on the ship instantly ceased. The crew wanted to see the show. A balding, sweaty beast of a man appeared at the captain's side. Apparently, this was Shank. The captain gave the man some orders, the details of which Mark and Hardy couldn't hear from their distance.

"Sparrow, Taylor!" Shank barked.

Two surly men came to life and moved toward Mark and Hardy.

"What do you think, Hardy?"

"I think we can take 'em."

"There's a lot of them, and we're in the middle of the ocean."

Hardy grinned. "Certainly you're not going to let a little thing like horrendous odds stop us."

Mark grinned back.

Sparrow and Taylor moved in closer, never guessing these two shanghaied men who'd just regained consciousness would be capable of putting up a fight of any sort.

Hardy's left arm shot out, his fist slamming into Sparrow's throat. Sparrow sputtered, hands to his Adam's apple, choking and gasping for breath as he sank to his knees. Hardy hadn't hit him hard enough to kill, but the guy would be out of commission for a while.

Taylor readied himself, seeing what Hardy had done, but it was too little, too late. Mark feigned a move backward, but came around with a solid roundhouse to the temple. Taylor fell to the deck, out cold.

Instantly, ten to twelve more men leapt into action, but the confining space only allowed four or five to attack at once, and these men weren't trained in hand to hand combat. Most of them probably brawled aplenty whenever they went ashore, but it was a far cry from the training Mark and Hardy had received in Special Forces.

They were experts in this kind of fighting. The odds were a little rough, but the fight resembled more of a dance moving to graceful music than a brawl. Their movements complemented each other, flowing like finely-tuned choreography. Men fell, and rose, and then fell again.

They were having fun.

Abruptly, Mark froze, which caused him to take a fistful to the temple. The pain was ferocious, but he didn't move. He was staring into the muzzle of a flintlock pistol. He cleared his throat, letting Hardy know the gig was up.

The captain was calmly pointing the large-barreled pistol at Mark's head, a bored expression on his face. Shank held another gun on Hardy. They were close enough they wouldn't miss, but far enough away Mark and Hardy would have no chance of disarming them before they fired.

"Quite impressive, lads, but not good enough, I'm afraid. Welcome to the *HMS Huntingdon*. This here's *my* ship. You've got exactly three seconds to decide if you want to submit to my authority and that of the British Navy, or we'll put a round through each of yer heads and dump you overboard for the sharks. Makes no difference to me, so decide."

Mark looked into the man's eyes and saw true apathy. Relenting, he nodded once.

"And you?" He waved his pistol Hardy's way.

Hardy also capitulated. They were out of options. They couldn't shift until they got close to land, and no matter how good they were, there were just too many men on the ship to overcome, especially if guns were involved. It was less risky to give in until they were in a better position to shift away.

"Good. You two will man one of the cannon below during battle. The rest of the time, you'll scour the decks. Shank will instruct you once you've come to."

Shank moved behind Mark. He lifted him in a massive

bear hug and squeezed, turning Mark's world a painful black.

When he awoke, he was below deck again, together with Hardy. Shank was immediately aware of their return to consciousness and yanked them up to their feet. Sweat rolled down the man's meaty arms as he stabbed a finger at one of the cannon and spat out incoherent orders regarding the finer points of its operation.

They soon learned their cannon was a 32 pound carronade. It took five men to operate it well during combat, though three or four could manage if needed. Shank declared Mark to be the "rammer" and Hardy the "loader." These were the most dangerous, and thus least desired, of the gunner jobs since they required you to stand directly in front of the business end of the barrel a good bit of the time. If the cannon went off prematurely, both rammer and loader were likely to be decimated.

Mark's job involved inserting a rod with a damp sponge on the end of it down into the cannon's barrel to clean it out and quench any remaining sparks from the previous charge fired. Hardy would then load a bag of gunpowder, which was called the charge. Using the other end of his ramrod, Mark then had to ram the charge down the barrel. Throughout this, another man, the "ventsman" would cover the firing hole with his thumb to keep air from getting in and fanning any sparks. His was the critical job that could mean an early end for Mark or Hardy. This ventsman then pricked the charge and filled the hole with powder. There was another man in charge of aiming the gun and a fifth would actually light it.

It was dangerous work. Mark hoped they'd find a way to get off the ship before they had to actually fight. He didn't relish the idea of putting their necks at risk for no good reason.

The days passed uneventfully. The skin of Mark's hands blistered and cracked from scrubbing the decks endlessly. The captain was exacting revenge for the damage they'd done to some of his crew members. Outside of what it was doing to his palms, Mark didn't mind the hard work, except for the very bottom hold.

The stench of rotting food and human refuse down there was overwhelming.

"Ho!"

They heard the cry clearly, even through two decks. The swab manning the crow's nest had spotted something.

After several minutes, crew members began flooding the lower holds, slinging open shutters and shoving cannon into position.

Shank's massive form darkened the open hatch leading to the deck above. His steps were deliberate and as solid as those of a rhino. The man had to weigh more than three hundred pounds, and it wasn't all fat.

"You two!" He motioned threateningly at Mark and Hardy. "Man, that cannon. We're gonna teach those Americans a thing or two today!"

He moved on, barking rough orders at scrambling men.

Mark looked to Hardy. "Don't know about you," he whispered, "but I'm not about to fire on fellow Americans."

"Me neither. What are we going to do about it?"

"Look man, it's a flat-out disgrace that two Special Forces' men can't take over a ship full of amateurs."

Hardy chuckled. "Yep. So, what's the plan?"

They swiftly formed one. They needed to secure the captain and as many weapons as they could, but the captain was primary. Through him they could control the troops. The ventsman manning their cannon caught Mark's attention. He was barechested, but his pants looked like the ragged remnants of an American-issued uniform.

Mark hissed at him, "Hey, you American?"

"Yeah."

"We're going to make a play. You in or out?"

"I'm in. They grabbed me six months ago. I've had it. If you can do it, there's probably at least seven other men on board who've been impressed and will join you."

Mark remembered that one of the primary reasons for the War of 1812 had been Britain's illegal and ruthless impressment of Americans into the British Navy.

On this ship, they were short on men to man all the cannon, and most stations were operating with a crew of three or four instead of the optimal five. Their senior gunner who would aim the cannon would also act as the "firer," lighting the powder, but he was still distracted helping Shank organize some of the other crews.

"All right. After you prime the hole, get behind us, and do it quick. Hardy, grab that ax and cut that wooden block out from the side of that rail."

Just two chops of the ax, and the cannon was freed from a wooden rail that limited the angle at which the cannon could be fired.

They loaded the cannon's barrel and bade their time. Then, their senior gunner finally made his way back toward them. Mark thought he was going to have to take the guy out, but at the last minute he tossed his slowmatch to Mark. He had to go help another crew above deck. It would be just the three of them on this gun which would make the plan even easier.

Shank barked orders up and down the line. The American ship must have drawn within range, because a couple of the British cannon roared, igniting the battle in earnest. An explosion ripped the air as something smashed through the upper deck.

Shank yelled at Mark and Hardy to get into the action. Seeing no response, he advanced and began bellowing at them, face purple with rage at their apparent inactivity. He drew his pistol.

They did their best to look repentant, pretending to be hastily aiming the cannon. Mark counted to three and then yelled, "Now!"

The other American had hustled to a position behind them. At Mark's command, Hardy pulled hard on the tow rope on the front of the cannon, and Mark pushed on the opposite side. They swung it around swiftly and halted it just as its barrel centered on Shank's large figure.

Even in the low light, Mark could see the blood drain

from his face. He turned to run, pistol still in hand, but he had no time. Mark touched the slowmatch to the firing hole and the giant gun belched. The cannonball hurling through the air did what Mark's fists had not been able to. Shank was no more, and a large hole now gaped in the planks in the back of the ship behind where he'd stood.

The rest of the sailors who'd happened to be standing between their cannon and the back of the ship were too stunned by the concussion to react. There was a big difference between being behind a cannon and in front of it when fired in an enclosed space.

Mark grabbed the American's upper arm. "What's your name?"

"Swanson."

"Are there any other Americans down here?"

"Just one."

"Grab him, we're going up."

Hardy waded through the stunned bodies, grabbing the only other officer below deck. Two blows and the man was out cold. Hardy relieved him of his gun and his sword and shoved the barrel of the antique pistol down his own waistband.

"Let's go!"

They bounded up the stairs, followed by Swanson and another dark-haired fellow. The rest of the men were beginning to recover and a few tried to come up after them.

They reached the next deck just in time and slammed the hatch closed over the lower hold. They pushed a few barrels on top of it, locking the majority of the crew down there.

"They're going to keep firing on the American ship," Hardy remarked.

"No help for it. We've got to secure the captain." Mark threw open the door to a cabinet where he'd seen a couple of other guns. He gave one to Swanson.

"Hardy, secure the rest of the weapons. I'm going after the captain. Swanson, find the other Americans. Once Hardy's got some more guns, distribute them to the others. After that, take over the helm and get this ship turned. We need to get out of range of that American ship and fast."

"Our modern pistols are somewhere on board," Hardy reminded him.

"I'll find them."

Mark was up the ladder first, the others following.

The upper deck was in chaos. Men manned even larger cannons, struggled with rigging, and ran back and forth delivering orders. The captain was at the helm, commanding his men. That there was order to the madness was clear, but their leader clearly had room to improve.

Above deck, a lot more men were in British uniforms than had been below. One officer hurried their way, apparently having been sent by the captain to check on why the cannons below had ceased firing. No one had spotted Mark's mutinous assault team yet.

Mark motioned toward the officer. Hardy acknowledged and moved to intercept, taking the unsuspecting officer out with a single blow. Mark separated from the two of them and ran swiftly toward the captain, who was still focused on the opposing ship and hadn't yet noticed the altercation.

Mark rushed up behind him on the balls of his feet. He grabbed him, pressed his forearm into the man's throat and a pistol muzzle into his temple. Another officer manning the rudder wheel saw what Mark was doing and made a move.

"Don't," Mark threatened.

The man froze, unwilling to jeopardize his commander's life.

"Turn that wheel sharp now. Get us out of here or he dies."

He hesitated.

"Don't do it," the captain growled, "don't give up the ship."

Turning the gun around, Mark slammed its butt into the base of the captain's skull, knocking him unconscious. The only thing which kept his limp body from collapsing to the deck in a useless heap was the strength of Mark's forearm under his chin.

"I don't want to have to get nasty," Mark said flatly, turning the gun on the other officer.

The underling turned back to the wheel and whipped it around clockwise. Slowly, the ship began to turn, coming in line with the wind. The increase in speed was felt immediately. Their ship was now going to shoot past the stern of the American vessel. In a few minutes, they'd be behind the Americans and out of reach of their cannon. By the time the Americans got turned around, Mark's ship would be sufficiently far enough ahead to get away clean.

The melee was building on the lower deck. Hardy had taken out four officers and was working on a fifth. Swanson had gathered a group of five men and armed them. They were successfully disarming the rest of the British sailors.

Their stern passed uncomfortably close to that of the American ship.

The American cannons ceased firing. Perhaps they'd seen the mutiny in progress.

Out of the corner of Mark's eye, he spied movement. The British officer who'd been manning the rudder wheel was making a run for Mark.

Before Mark could fully turn to face the attack, the loud crack of a pistol shot cut through the air. The British officer dropped to the deck in a bloody heap.

Looking up, Mark saw the movement of the ships had brought their helms to within forty feet of each other. The American officers stood at the helm of their own ship, hands at their sides. Their captain held a smoking flintlock in his hand and a slight smile on his lips.

Snapping to attention, Mark saluted. The captain loosely saluted back, and then the ships pulled apart, leaving the American ship in their wake.

Chapter 6

Hardy closed the door to the captain's quarters and turned to see Mark fingering a knife.

"Where'd you get that?" he asked.

"One of the Brits, just before I tied him up."

"So, why didn't we give ourselves up to the good guys, buddy?"

After all was said and done, Swanson had found more sympathetic souls than just the seven Americans. They had a total of twenty-one sailors on their side, none of whom were British navy regulars, and they'd subdued the ship without a single man lost.

"'Cause I've got a plan forming. And don't call me buddy. I haven't fully forgiven you yet."

"Okay...you just let me know when I'm back in your good graces then," Hardy chuckled.

Mark cracked a smile.

"All right, let's assume Rialto's got a tracker like we think," Mark said.

"I'd say that's a pretty safe bet. Don't know how else he could find us so easy."

"Theoretically, what would be the range of such a tracking device? And how would it track us?"

"Not sure. Maybe it detects some kind of signal emitted from the watch. Hadn't you ever considered hiring some scientists to study these things."

"To be honest, no I hadn't."

"It might be a smart investment when we get back."

Mark harrumphed, rubbing his brow heavily with his forefingers. "There's really no way to know the range of their trackers, is there?" he asked.

"No."

"If it's very far, we're in trouble." Mark put away the knife.

"That's an understatement."

"Do you think they could detect us from Britain?"

"What do you have in mind?" Hardy asked.

"I'm feeling a bit patriotic." Mark stood. "We could do our little part in this here war, maybe take out a few British ships on our way to England."

"You're crazy."

"C'mon, it'll be fun."

"That's what you said about going to the tavern." Mark laughed.

***

Mark, Hardy, and the other Americans all donned British uniforms and regularly inhabited the upper deck. The actual British officers, at least the higher ranking ones, were in the brig. The captain, when a potential victim was available, spewed profanities and curses like a machine gunner, so they had to either keep knocking him unconscious or gagged just to get a little peace and quiet. The lower ranking British sailors, once stripped of their uniforms, were chained to the cannons below deck in pairs. If they got into a battle, it would be in their best interest to fire those cannon as quickly and accurately as they could or they'd find themselves blown to smithereens by a cannonball from the other ship, and it really wouldn't matter if that cannonball was British or American as far as they were concerned.

Mark gave the order to hoist the British flag when in sight of another British ship. If they spotted an American ship, they would all strip off their uniforms, hoist no flag, and hope for the best.

It was a thrill fighting in a war long gone by. In spite of the fact they were two hundred years removed from these men,

Mark and Hardy felt a strong kinship with the fellow Americans of 1814. They were brothers and ancestors.

They sank three British ships on their way to Her Majesty's Realm. Each time, they pulled right up alongside the unsuspecting blokes and fired all their cannon from virtually point blank range right at the waterline. No ship of the age could resist such a barrage. Each vessel, however, sank slowly enough that there was more than enough time to rescue most of the enemy sailors. The number of prisoners they'd taken on board was approaching the capacity limit of the ship.

Mark had been forced to move the powder magazine up a deck so he could turn the lower hold into a massive brig. Of course, the Americans they liberated swelled their numbers as well, boosting their fighting ability. Still, if they'd run into a fourth vessel, they might have had to set a bunch of the survivors adrift in long boats.

The plan was to berth in Plymouth, England and restock their supplies. Mark worried about Swanson and the other Americans getting back safely. Their British uniforms would only get them so far in hostile territory.

They delayed their arrival until nightfall and then docked. They would restock as quickly as possible and send the ship back to America in Swanson's charge. Mark and Hardy would stay behind in England.

It wasn't easy to convince the new American crew to take their ship into the heart of enemy territory, so they'd had to make up a story about being on an espionage mission.

To get the necessary supplies, they were going to need the help of one of the real British officers. Mark had the captain dragged up from the lower hold as they pulled into port.

"Who's your purser?"

The captain glared at the floor. You had to admire the guy. Stripped of his uniform and imprisoned in a dark, dank hold for weeks on end, he still had spirit.

"Look, we can do this the easy way or the hard way. Which will it be?"

The captain spat at Mark's feet. "Cook. Randall Cook."

"All right. Take him back down and bring Cook up here."

They dragged the captain to his feet and ushered him out of his former quarters and back to his prison. A few minutes later, Swanson and Hardy returned with the stinking form of a large sailor with long, dingy blonde hair. Mark recognized him as one of the sailors who'd shanghaied them back in Washington DC.

"You!"

The man smiled evilly, a hole where one of his teeth should have been.

Mark wanted to throttle him senseless for that insolent smile, but he restrained himself. "Cook, if you were going to restock this ship in Plymouth in the middle of the night, where would you go to do it?"

"Wouldn't you like to know?" He laughed.

"Hardy...if you don't mind."

Hardy slammed the butt of a long rifle into Cook's stomach. The man doubled over in pain, grunting and heaving to catch his breath.

"Now, how about you answer my question?"

"Aw'right...aw'right. Sam's Tavern and Inn. He's got a storehouse around back that's always full."

"Is he going to be suspicious, us restocking in a hurry at night?"

"He might think it queer, but sometimes ships do that. Depends on the story I tell him."

"You think you're coming along with us?"

"If I don't, he'll know something's up. He's a friend of mine."

"Then, you better think up a whopper. I'll be right behind you and I've got a pistol ball with your name on it if he doesn't believe you."

***

They waited in the dark until the noise from inside the tavern died down, the patrons having either gone home or bedded down for the night. The low glow of a lantern moved from window to window of the lower floor. Somebody was locking up.

Mark, Hardy, and Cook were there with fourteen other American sailors in British uniform to help with the loading. Swanson had stayed back to oversee things on the ship.

Cook rapped lightly on the door. After a minute, it swung open decisively.

Sam was a portly fellow with curly brown hair standing out in tufts on the sides of his balding head. His irritated frown turned upward when he saw Cook's darkened visage.

"Randy, my boy! How's it been fer ye? Ah' thought ye were out to sea."

"So I was. So I was. We've ported tonight though, an' the cap's after me to restock in a hurry. Wants to pull back out 'fore sunlight."

"What's the blasted hurry? I was set to bed down fer the night, I was."

"Got me. You know the navy, Sam. Who knows what crazy ideas an officer's gonna get stuck in his skull?"

Sam laughed heartily. "By gosh, yer right about that. What do you need?"

Cook rattled off the list Swanson had recited to him.

"And payment?"

"Don't worry, Sam. The crown'll pay, you know that."

For the next three hours, the men took turns loading wagons and driving them back to the ship, where more men unloaded. When they were done, Swanson, who was playing the role of captain, sent payment to Sam from the ship's treasury. They could have robbed him blind, but failure to pay might have raised the alarm prematurely. The further they could get away before being found out, the better.

They brought Cook back on board when it was time to say good-bye. He and all the other British sailors would soon be prisoners of war back in the good old USA.

Mark shook hands with Swanson and the other Americans.

"Good-bye gentlemen, and good luck."

"Good-bye to you, Mark. Our hearts are with you both. May God bless your mission."

A loud splash sounded to their left. Whirling, Mark knew immediately what had happened. Cook had dived over the side in a mad break for freedom. In the dark, they weren't likely to be able to recover him before he blew their cover.

"You guys need to get out of here *now*."

Swanson wasn't waiting for instructions.

"Weigh anchors!" he shouted.

Mark and Hardy ran down the gangplank and began helping crew members hastily undo the tie ropes. Shortly, the ship was out of its berth and moving. Mark waved his hat at Swanson before they retreated to the darkness of the town.

"All right. We're in England. Now what?" Hardy asked.

"We shift."

"Back to the present?"

"Yeah, but let's do it in the water."

"Why?"

"Just in case they are capable of detecting us this far away. We'll duck under the water before we shift, and then swim in opposite directions as far as we can under water before surfacing. That way, even if they detect us, they won't be able to see our exact position until we're well away from it."

They were about to dive when Mark was tackled from behind. Randall Cook had been lurking in the dark, waiting for them, and now he was on top of Mark brandishing a wicked looking knife.

"Shift now!" Hardy called.

Mark's answer was a flash of static and then both he and Cook disappeared. Hardy followed.

The thuggish storesmaster was distracted by the sudden appearance of sunlight, though it was muted by dull grey clouds shrouding the sky. A chilling drizzle of rain quickly coated their exposed skin.

Hardy slammed his palm into the back of Cook's neck, knocking him unconscious. He rolled off Mark and fell helplessly onto the wet asphalt. Mark leapt to his feet.

"Guess we don't have to worry about Cook raising the alarm for Swanson and his men now," Mark commented.

"Yeah. Good luck to the jerk, coping with the 21st century on his own."

"You don't want to shift him back to his own time?"

"Why should we? He shanghaied us. We just returned the favor. Not to mention he just tried to *kill* you. Plus, the more we shift, the bigger the chance Rialto will detect us."

"Good point."

They walked down the dampened street, Cook's prostrate form a blot on the pavement behind them.

"We need to get out of here and figure out how to deal with Rialto and his cronies." Hardy muttered.

"First things first. We need to get to London and take a plane back to Boston."

"What about Ty?"

Mark eyed him. "That's my number one priority."

Chapter 7

September 18th 2013, London, England

The atmosphere was jovial in this London pub as they sipped on a couple of beers. Whoever owned this bar must have loved the Middle Ages, because suits of armor and medieval weaponry were on display throughout the premises.

Beige wall treatments and honey-colored wood accents created a warm sanctuary in the middle of an otherwise drizzly day.

"Don't you think Rialto will be watching every plane coming from London?" Hardy asked, head down, fingers playing with his shifter.

"Only if he knew we came to England, and when we came here. How could he?"

"He detected our shifts before."

"We haven't seen hide nor hair of him since arriving here."

"Still..."

"Look, the guy's not all-powerful. And if he's not with the government, there's going to be a severe limit to what he can do."

Hardy said nothing as he continued to play with his buttons.

"Hey, Mark, maybe our shifters have some kind of detector on them too. Maybe we just haven't figured out that feature yet."

"Not bloody likely."

Hardy looked up, laughing. "A Brit already, eh?"

"It's the atmosphere. Look, don't worry about it. We'll fly from here to Paris, and then fly to Boston from there. Even if he somehow knew we came to England, he wouldn't know to look for planes coming from Paris."

"Why not call Savannah and have her send the corporate jet?"

"'Cause if Rialto's watching anything, it'll be Savannah and our headquarters. We have to get home incognito."

Hardy held his shifter out for Mark to see, his expression mischievous.

"How about we shift there?"

Hardy's shifter read:

120000P-08031100

"1100 AD? You wanna shift back to the Middle Ages?" Mark asked incredulously.

"Why not? We're in England. Let's go see some real life knights while we're here."

"Man, we don't have time to play around. Maybe we'll come back after we find Ty."

"What do you mean we don't have time? We can return to the very second we leave."

"I know, but..." Mark rubbed his hand along his jaw. "It just seems like we shouldn't have fun on the mind until we find Ty."

"I guess I know what you mean. Sorry." He looked dejected.

"Hardy?"

"Yeah."

"Don't turn, but I just saw the usher from Ford's Theater pass in front of that bay window behind you."

"You mean the usher who kidnapped you after the Lincoln assassination?"

"Yeah, and we need to move *now*. He works for Rialto. "

Abandoning their beers, Mark hastily scribbled his

signature on the credit card slip. They moved to the back of the pub, looking for another way out. Their best bet seemed to be a side door that would let them into a side alley. They slipped out...

...and immediately regretted the move.

Usher stood at the head of the alley, blocking their exit to the street. Rialto himself guarded the alley's rear. A third man with a grey patch in his hair appeared in the doorway they'd just used. They didn't know him, but he was obviously part of the Rialto gang. All three men raised their weapons.

"Shift!" Hardy grabbed Mark's shoulder. They both reacted instantly, reaching for their shifters at the same time, but Hardy's finger was a fraction of a second faster.

***

Gunshots shattered the silence of the alley as all three men fired their weapons. Cries rose up inside the pub.

"Call the bobbies!" A voice yelled faintly.

"You idiot, you almost shot me!" Rialto scolded Graves.

"If they hadn't shifted out, I would have been dead on," Graves grumbled.

"Where'd they go, Torino?"

Torino looked at the detector in his hand. "Uh..."

"Spit it out, man! We've got to move," Rialto hissed.

"Are you sure this thing is working right?"

"Why wouldn't it be?"

"It says they went back to 1100."

"As in 1100 AD? Why would they go to the Middle Ages?"

They looked at each other, surprised by the turn of events.

"No matter," Rialto decided, "If they want to die 900 years ago, let 'em. We'll finish them off one way or the other. Let's go."

***

August 3rd 1100, London, England

As they shifted in, Hardy saw the alley had transformed into a very rustic looking horse stable. It was a huge stable actually, with hundreds of stalls, separated into rows and divided by walls made of roughly-hewn, wooden planks. The stall Hardy now found himself in was thankfully devoid of horses, or any other animal life for that matter, but the distinct odor of manure indicated there had been one here not too long ago.

The static hisses of shifters crackled beyond the walls of his stall on all sides. He couldn't see them yet, but multiple shifters could only mean Rialto and his crew. He was getting sick of Rialto's tracking devices…and *fast*.

When Hardy had gripped Mark's shoulder, it had been out of reflex. As they arrived, he let go, dropping to the floor in readiness. He hadn't intended to bring them both back to 1100 AD, but that had been the last setting on his watch.

To Hardy's dismay, Mark faded in and out with a delay of only one second. His finger had already been in motion to press his own button. If Hardy hadn't grabbed him, they would have shifted to separate times, but Hardy must have hit his first, dragging Mark back with him to 1100 before Mark's shifter activated.

So, where had Mark gone? Probably 1814. That would have been the last setting on Mark's watch. Hardy went to change his own settings to 1814, but stayed his hand in mid-motion.

The display glowed red. It was inoperable.

The only thing separating him from Rialto's men were thin wooden planks, and he now had no escape. These horse stalls weren't very large, and while those walls would conceal Hardy's position within the stable for the moment, they would hear him if he weren't careful.

From the orientation of the static he'd heard, he guessed Rialto and crew were on different aisles from him, but they would know roughly were he'd been, so as stealthily as possible, he scurried down his own row to a stall about ten doors away, buried himself under some hay, and waited.

***

They'd come armed to the teeth. Each had an Uzi, several smaller firearms, and a few hand grenades. Graves had even brought along some nasty looking knives. Rialto had outfitted Torino with a duffel bag filled with other goodies, including several sniper rifles and an RPG launcher.

In addition to their handheld detectors, Stanley Irvine, their in-house physicist, had designed a satellite-based detection system for Rialto. From space, this system could detect a shift signature on the ground accurate to within one hundred feet, provided the shift occurred outdoors and was not shielded by metal.

Once the system was complete, Rialto had transported it back to 1987. Irvine had determined that was the first year satellite technology would be sufficiently advanced to support their package. Paying NASA to send a satellite up for him wasn't a problem.

What was a problem were the results once it was operational. First, he was limited to covering the eastern United States. He'd have to put up more satellites if he wanted to cover more territory. The worst part, however, were the results themselves.

Tens of thousands of 'shifts' were detected by his satellite between 1987 and 2013. There was simply no way to know if a shift signature detected by the satellite was caused by him, his men, Carpen, Carpen's crew, or even somebody he himself might 'hire' in the future. Though the satellite had recorded shifts which occurred in past years, those shifts might still be something he himself would do in his future. The only way to know who had caused a shift signature was to travel to the actual location and time of that shift. However, the very act of shifting in and out of a time in order to investigate would cause a shift signature detected by the same satellite, which might have been what it was detecting in the first place.

He chalked the satellite idea up as a temporary failure. It might prove useful in the future, under the right circumstances, but for now it was useless.

In the end, he tracked Carpen down in London the old fashioned way. He'd tapped one of his contacts at the IRS (whom he paid handsomely) to constantly monitor the electronic activity on Carpen's bank accounts. The moment Carpen used his debit card to purchase a couple of beers at that pub, Rialto had him.

It was the simple things that always tripped a criminal up, he laughed to himself.

The horse stalls annoyed Rialto the moment he saw them. It was the first inconvenience in this leg of the chase. They'd positioned themselves to have Carpen and Phillips surrounded when they shifted in, but the walls were blocking their line of sight. Not to mention the hay dust, the stench of manure, and other unpleasantries which accompanied a site like this.

Carefully, Rialto made his way down a row of stalls until he found a break. He met Torino two rows over, and Graves joined them shortly after. There was no sign of Phillips or Carpen anywhere.

"They're gone, Rialto."

"How do you know?"

"There was another shift signature almost immediately after we got here. Looks like they shifted forward to 1814."

Rialto sighed. "All right. Let's go."

"Uh...boss."

"What?"

"My shifter's not working. It's all red."

Rialto and Graves hastily checked theirs and saw they were in the same boat.

"What's that mean?" Graves asked suspiciously.

"Not sure. We haven't shifted six times yet, but it's acting like we have."

"You think they did this?"

"Like a trap?"

"Yeah, maybe they know something we don't."

"Or maybe they remotely disabled our shifters somehow."

Rialto reclaimed control of the conversation. His men were obviously disconcerted — and with good reason.

"Look, I don't know why the watches shut down, but they've never shut down for more than 24 hours before. Let's go get some beer and relax. We'll get another chance at 'em."

"We're in the Middle Ages. You think they've invented beer yet? "

"Man, there's always been beer."

Chapter 8

September 17th 1814, London, England

Mark was back in the alley again, but now it was dark and damp. There were no electric lights in 1814, and it was raining again. Heavy droplets quickly soaked his hair, running rivulets down his face.

He was alone.

At first, he thought Hardy hadn't shifted with him at all, but then he understood. Hardy was still in 1100 AD.

Mark needed to shift back immediately. Hardy was surrounded by three armed men intent on killing him. His concern turned to alarm when he saw the face of his shifter burned red. It was inoperable.

What's the matter with it? He hadn't used it six times yet. Was it running out of juice? Was the trip back to the Middles Ages too much? A panicked thought trampled the normal calm he maintained. *What if it were dead for good?*

Regardless, he needed to get out of the alley. If Rialto followed him, he'd know where Mark's last position had been.

The business adjoining the alley in 1814 was still a pub, just like it would be in 2013. The establishment was closed at the moment, the hour being a little past three in the morning.

Mark left the alley.

The street in front of the pub was deserted. Ducking under an overhang, Mark hugged the building as tight as he could to ward off the bone-chilling rain. If anyone came after him here, he would be able to see them before they saw him. Unless they set up a sniper post in one of the windows across the street.

Best not to think about possibilities like that. But that was all he could do at the moment...think. He didn't want to stray too far from Hardy's position in case his shifter reset. He had nowhere else to go.

He shivered in the wet cold as he dwelt on Hardy and whether or not he'd survived Rialto's attack. He wondered about Ty, where he might be. About Laura and their brief, but fiery, relationship...and about Savannah and how much they could have used her on this crazy venture, though this mission would have been far too dangerous for her.

In spite of the small awnings covering his head, the rain's icy fingers still managed to find their way under his heavy woolen clothing. The feeling was thoroughly miserable.

After what seemed an eternity, joy finally burst through the gates of his doubt when he saw his watch had actually reset. It was back to normal.

Breathing a sigh of relief, he checked the hour. How much time had passed since he arrived? Four or five minutes? It seemed so much longer than that. He'd never had the shifter reset itself so quickly...but then again, he'd never had it malfunction after only one shift either.

It didn't matter. It was time to help Hardy.

***

Mark hastened down the row of hay-filled stalls hunched over to avoid being seen. His shifter had gone red again, but he'd just have to worry about that later.

He stopped in front of a stall about ten doors down from where he started.

"Dude, if you're trying to hide, at least do a good job of it," Mark whispered when he saw the toe of Hardy's boot sticking out from the hay.

Red-faced, Hardy stood, brushing straw off his shirt and pants.

"Man, you stink too!"

"Comes free with the hiding place," Hardy replied grimly.

"Did you see any of Rialto's crew."

"Nope. You?"

"No, but I heard them. They were in the aisle behind me, and then they moved off. I thought you were them at first."

"Is your shifter functional?"

"No. Yours?"

"Mine's dead too. I shifted forward to 1814, and it died on me for about 5 minutes then reset. It was really weird."

"Well, maybe mine will come back online after five minutes too then. I heard Rialto and his boys complaining about theirs not working either."

"Well, that's a relief. There must be something unusual about this time which shut all our shifters down. You think they're still here?"

"Unless theirs reset faster than mine, they're out there somewhere." He pointed at the main exit.

"Then let's avoid making ourselves a target and find another way out of here."

There was a smaller door on the back side of the building, so they used it. Outside, on the opposite side of the road, was a large medieval festival attended by at least several hundred people. Yet, he realized that what he and Hardy considered medieval, these people would consider modern.

Twelfth century London was quite a sight to take in. Like it or not, Hardy had gotten his wish.

It was like being at the Renaissance Fair. Everywhere he looked were rows of single story wooden houses and buildings. Every roof was made of thatch. Even here in London, stone was not yet a common building material.

One building in the skyline stood out, the only building he could see, in fact, that was made of stone besides a couple of larger churches. It was a large, multi-storied squarish, castle-like fortification, its stones white in color. Mark recognized it as the White Tower, which in modern times was the central portion of the Tower of London.

The streets were not teeming with people, but there was

plenty of activity. Men, women, and children were dressed in rough, woolen clothing for the most part. For all the care that had been put into their making, their attire might as well have been made of sackcloth.

Children were helplessly dirty. The stench of the unwashed was everywhere as people passed by on the street. Mark and Hardy remained in the recessed side street, still hidden from the sight of most, which was good because their attire did not match the era.

A couple of more nicely dressed gentlemen were engrossed in a conversation on a corner up the hill about two hundred feet away. One of them was vested very colorfully in what appeared to be silk.

Across the street at the festival was an open forum and small stage. About a hundred men, and a few women, were gathered in front of it. The stage was occupied by several men dressed just as humbly as the crowd. The "bard" on the stage was telling some story which had the crowd fascinated. They alternately laughed, then yelled along with the thread of the tale.

Wooden steins, undoubtedly filled with grog, filled the fists of all these merry men, golden liquid sloshing and spilling as they made jokes and carried on. They were celebrating something.

Mark and Hardy were beginning to receive more and more prolonged glances from the people passing by. A young child spied them and panicked, running off down the street yelling for somebody.

"We need to get some local clothes, fast."

Hardy nodded in agreement. They backed further into their side street away from the people.

"How do you want to do it?"

"We may have to grab a few passers-by and knock 'em out."

Their reflexes weren't fast enough to react to the all-too-familiar shriek of an RPG plowing through the air before the house next to them exploded in a cloud of fire and splintered timbers.

The joyful London peasants were suddenly scrambling for cover, abandoning the streets. Mark and Hardy did the same, pistols drawn, withdrawing, seeking cover. Rialto had seen them before they'd seen him.

They raced for the other end of their street, only to see "Grey Patch" block their exit wielding an Uzi.

"This way!" Hardy yelled, throwing himself through the thin wooden slats which made up the wall of a house to their left. They burst through wall after wall, randomly changing directions, gaining access to new buildings and unpredictable pathways, shocking not just a few unsuspecting medieval serfs. Mark's shoulder burned from the impacts with these walls. Though they were thin, they still resisted brute force. Thankfully, adrenaline numbed most of the pain.

The benefit of this tactic was that Rialto and crew would not be able to guess accurately where they were, in spite of the racket they were making. They were creating an urban warfare maze.

Still, they were the rats in the maze and they needed to get out.

Random machine gun fire tore through the air and wooden homes at random. Rialto didn't know where his prey was exactly, but that didn't stop them from firing indiscriminately, caring not at all who might get hurt in the crossfire. One stream of bullets hit too close to home, striking planks a few feet from Hardy's head.

"Go!" Mark ordered, pointing in the direction of the main street.

Hardy followed him as they plowed new entranceways to their objective. If they could cross unseen, they might conceivably take up sniper positions, though they had no rifles. Thankfully, no one was in sight when they made their move.

The main thoroughfare was completely abandoned. Mark and Hardy rushed across it and through the front door of a house on the opposite side, hoping Rialto would not expect them to have crossed. To their dismay, the home was not empty. A lone woman began to scream bloody murder, terrified by their unexpected appearance in her living room. Well…it was actually her *only* room.

Hardy put his finger to his lips and made a threatening gesture with his pistol to shut her up, but she only screamed louder.

"Knock her out," Mark said.

"Mark…" Hardy hesitated.

"Knock her out!"

Hardy obliged. They could only hope she hadn't given them away.

The cracks between the slats in the walls were large enough to sight and fire their pistols if a target presented itself. A moment later, Mark was rewarded with the sight of Rialto himself searching for them. The screams of the woman had drawn him out.

Mark depressed his trigger. A pistol was never as accurate as a rifle, and thus never a good choice for sniping, but here the distance was close enough he wouldn't miss. Just as he fired, though, the woman jumped on his back and began flailing at his head, causing his shot to go wild.

Either she had recovered very quickly, or Hardy hadn't hit her very hard. Either way, she was now in crazy mode, attacking him without regard for her own safety.

"Hardy!"

"Sorry, Mark." He conked her good this time and she fell limp.

Mark's shot hadn't completely missed. A trail of blood showed where Rialto had dragged himself into a darkened recess.

"Cover's blown, Mark. We've gotta get out of here."

Their enemy was armed with Uzis, RPGs, and who knew what else, while Mark and Hardy only had a couple of handguns. The wood which made up the walls of these buildings would shred like paper under a barrage of heavy fire.

"Bring her along," Mark commanded.

"She'll slow us down."

"They're going to strafe this house. She'll die for sure if we leave her."

Hardy hoisted her onto his shoulder and they ran out into the street again.

"Lay her down over there. She'll be all right there."

Hardy did so hastily, and Mark signaled they would head back to the stables again. There were lots of stalls and they'd have more hiding places.

A shout went up from behind. They'd been spotted. Machine gun fire splintered the stable's door frame as they dove through it.

Once inside, Mark pointed to the rafters above. It was a risky move, but probably their only real option. People never thought to look up. If they did, however, Mark and Hardy would be sitting ducks.

They scrambled up as high as they could and laid themselves in position, each with his own rafter below him. Thankfully, the rafters were fairly massive and concealed a good portion of their bodies.

Rialto, Usher and Grey Patch entered warily, Uzis at the ready. Rialto limped in, a cloth tied around his thigh. Blood heavily stained his pant leg.

All three of the men held what looked like hand grenades. Pulling the pins, they launched all three of the mini-bombs toward the far end of the building. Timber, hay, and horse blood filled the air as they detonated. One of the grenades must have fallen near a support post, because the far side of the building suddenly collapsed, closing off the only other door of escape. As the roof at the opposite end dropped closer to the ground, Mark and Hardy were almost shaken from their posts, but they held on with grips of death. To fall off would mean annihilation.

Usher and Grey Patch unleashed a hail of devastating machine gun fire through all parts of the stable, while Rialto lobbed a few more grenades into the far end. The Uzis strafed through every board in the place. They did not aim high, but low.

If Mark and Hardy had tried to hide themselves under the hay anywhere in the stable, they would have been decimated by the continuing fusillade.

After the men had exhausted several clips, their weapons fell silent. They advanced into the havoc they'd wrought, looking for bodies.

As fortune would have it, their advance gave Mark and Hardy the perfect opportunity to turn the tables. For just a moment, one perfect moment, Usher stood directly below Mark, and Grey Patch was lined up under Hardy.

Mark raised a hand. Hardy acknowledged. He wiggled silently into a little better position.

Rialto saw them and yelled, but it was too late. Mark and Hardy fired their weapons as they dropped, both their bullets and feet slamming home. Rialto snapped off a hasty shot, but missed.

It was doubtful their bullets had killed Usher and Grey Patch, but they were definitely out for the count. Rialto high-tailed it out the door he'd come in.

"Get him! He's behind all this."

They raced after Rialto, but he was long gone by the time they got to the alley. They took stock of the situation. Rialto had disappeared again. If they tried, they could probably flush him out. Still, he had an Uzi and they had pistols.

"Hey, Mark."

"What?"

"My shifter's working again. Yours?"

"Yeah, mine too."

"You wanna just get out of here?"

"Rialto's still got a detector. If we shift out now, they'll have time to regroup, heal, and come after us again, right at the moment we shift into 2013."

"Then what *do* we do, Kemosabe?"

"We go back in, make sure Usher and Grey Patch are finished, then get away from London and shift forward to 2013 from a different place."

Suddenly, the wall next to them disintegrated under a

barrage of more machine gun fire. Rialto was back, and he looked half-crazed.

"Forget it! To the river!"

The Thames River was and always has been the main artery of London. Large enough to handle large boats, it made London a port city. It was also swift enough to carry them away.

They plunged into the dark grey water with a splash. It was surprisingly refreshing, even if it did stink a bit from the waste dumped in from the city. There was no sign of Rialto following. Mark finally permitted himself to relax a little as they floated out of London.

Chapter 9

They floated several miles downriver until they were far enough in the country to escape unwanted attention. Then, they walked another ten.

They had reached a large, rustic barn when they saw a wagon approaching on the road from the opposite direction. They took cover behind some brush, waiting to see which way the wagon would go.

The barn couldn't be described as anything resembling a modern red barn, though there were some similarities. This barn was two stories high, but it was more triangular in shape than polygonal. It had an enormous thatched roof supported by thick, roughly hewn, unpainted wood posts. The spaces between these posts were covered by the same thin wooden slats they'd seen in London.

Behind the wagon followed three large, healthy stallions, and astride them were three finely dressed riders. A fourth man drove the wagon. He looked like death itself, wrapped in a dark cloak, hood pulled down so far it covered his face.

In the back of the wagon lay a prone figure, a sack covering his head and face. When they reached the front of the barn, the small caravan stopped. The riders prodded and pushed the hooded man from the back of the wagon while the driver sat motionless, staring straight ahead. Once on the ground, it became obvious the hooded man's hands were tied behind his back.

"Let's check it out," Mark whispered.

Hardy wanted to keep going. Just get far enough away they could shift safely and then go home.

But Mark was different. Mark couldn't stand by and let someone be victimized. If an innocent person were in danger,

Mark would find some way to insert himself into the middle of it.

This fact Hardy knew all too well, so he just sighed and followed his friend as he scurried over to get closer to the action.

Near the barn, all they could make out were muffled voices. They circled around to the back and found a door ajar. Through it, they could not only hear the discussion more clearly, but also observe the drama as it unfolded.

"Thes ær bith the cild?"

"Yi, thes the vilein bith!"

"The murtherour af Rufus, eh smæl cild?"

"Anhenghim bi the nekke."

Not that they understood what was being said though. Their ears distinguished the syllables, but it sounded like a foreign language of some kind.

"What are they speaking?" Mark asked.

"Not sure. Don't recognize it."

"Sounds kind of like English — but not quite. Know what I mean?"

Hardy snapped his fingers, understanding having dawned.

"Dude, they're speaking *Middle* English."

"Middle English?"

"Yeah, English hasn't always sounded like it does today."

"It changed enough that we wouldn't understand it?"

"Yes."

"How do you know that?"

"Back in high school, they had us read an old version of Robin Hood one time. It was written in Middle English, and it *was* weird. Impossible to understand in places, at least for me."

Inside the barn, one of the men held a noose. Another yanked the sack off the hostage.

"He's just a boy. Can't be more than twelve years old," Mark said.

"You're right."

"We've got to do something."

"Look, we don't know who else is involved. For all we know, there might be an army coming up the road as we speak.

We don't know if our shifters are going to shut down again. We don't know what this boy did. We don't know anything."

"We can't just leave him."

"I know what you're feeling. I do." Hardy wasn't budging.

"You don't know what I'm feeling," Mark growled.

But he did. Mark was thinking about his kids and how he hadn't been able to save them. "We've got to save Ty first, Mark. If something happens to us, he's lost."

"We can't just let them hang this boy."

"He'll always be here, in this time, in this moment, ready to be hung, waiting for you to come back and save him. Let's go save Ty while our shifters are still working. If they're still working after that, you can come back and save him."

A long moment passed.

Finally, Mark nodded.

Chapter 10

May 17th 1863, Madison, GA

The weather-beaten, outhouse door creaked on its rusty hinges as Hugh Plageanet opened it to relieve himself. Stepping inside, he never saw the dark figure waiting in the corner. Nor did he have time to, for a shadowy arm shot out, gripping his wrist with an iron grasp as soon as his foot had crossed the threshold.

His shock was exacerbated by the sudden disorientation he felt. The darkness around him brightened to daylight, and the hand released its grip as suddenly as it had taken his arm. Stumbling, he fell to his knees in the grass.

Grass! There wasn't any grass in the outhouse. How was the sun shining on him through the walls? Who had grabbed him?

Turning, he saw him. An olive-skinned man in odd cloth-ing with a fat, silver bracelet on his wrist. The man held a gun on him. A gun like no other he'd seen before.

The outhouse...was gone. So was the house. Nothing but grass and trees all around. *What was happening? Where was he?*

"Who are you?"

"Name's Alexander Rialto, and I just saved your life."

***

September 17th 2013, Plymouth, England

Grabbing a handful of dirty blonde hair, Rialto yanked the waterlogged man up off the pavement, and threw him into the back seat of his waiting sedan. He and Torino entered the back seat next, flanking the man on either side. Graves took the driver's seat and whipped the car into motion.

Their captive was still semi-conscious and groggy from his recent encounter with Mark Carpen. He shook his head several times to regain his bearings. As the fog in his head cleared, puzzlement clouded his eyes, along with a growing panic.

"Wot kind of carriage be this? War be the horses?"

Torino and Graves sat like silent sentinels, allowing Rialto to handle the exchange. Rialto ignored his questions, responding instead with one of his own.

"What's your name?"

"Randall."

"Randall what?"

"Cook, Randall Cook."

The man was becoming increasingly agitated by his strange, modern surroundings. He glanced nervously back and forth between his captors and the odd sights passing by the vehicle's windows.

"Profession?"

"Able seaman, warrant officer. Purser 'board the HMS Huntingdon. Who are you?"

"You good with that thing?"

"Huh?"

Cook wasn't sure what Rialto meant until his saw his knife lying in Torino's lap, covered by the man's left hand. Torino didn't look like he would be willing to give it back to him any time soon.

"Had mah share o' fights."

"Good. There's a lot we need to explain, Mr. Cook."

***

April 30th 2013, Boston, MA

The light breeze wafting through her linen curtains felt like delicate, ghostly fingers brushing across her skin. Her toffee-colored, silk sheets slid over her legs as she pulled them closer to her chest.

It was the middle of the night, and she couldn't sleep. She couldn't blame her insomnia on being uncomfortable, because she wasn't. She lived in the lap of luxury. The autumn night air was refreshingly cool as it permeated her bed chambers through the open french doors of her balcony.

She referred to all these things as hers, though Hardy had paid for them all. They were really hers though.

Hardy hadn't come home tonight. This concerned her for more reasons than Hardy would have suspected, though she reckoned he was probably shrewder than she gave him credit for.

Time was not an obstacle for Hardy Phillips, just as it was not for Mark or Ty, so when Hardy didn't show up as expected, it lent strongly to the possibility that something might have happened to him.

This worried her tremendously, but not because she cared that much about his welfare. She *did* have an affection for him, though her feelings for Mark actually ran much stronger. No, it wasn't that.

If Hardy disappeared, his shifter disappeared with him, and with it, her access to wealth and the things she loved — the things she needed. She might be able to enjoy this penthouse apartment for a while without him, but that wouldn't last forever. Bills would come due, and she would have no way to pay.

Once upon a time, Mark had talked about giving her some millions of her own, but they'd broken up before he'd gotten around to it. That had been a miscalculation on her part.

In spite of her feelings for Mark, she couldn't bear the way he wouldn't bend to her will. She didn't just want a man who *could* give her everything, she wanted a man who *would* give her everything, a man who would do whatever she said. Mark just wasn't the type you could push around.

She'd guessed Hardy would be easier to manipulate than Mark, and she'd been right, though she'd had to wait a few weeks between men. Hardy wouldn't have anything to do with her while she was still seeing Mark.

Once she'd hooked him, Hardy melted before her material desires like butter on a hot plate. He was more doting than Mark, less prideful, and easier to control in the smaller things. Still, he wasn't dumb. He hadn't even mentioned setting up a bank account in her name like Mark had. She guessed he knew, even if only subconsciously so, that money was the only hold he had on her.

Now, Hardy was gone. Well...at least, he was *not here*. And he should have been. That was why she couldn't sleep.

A tiny whisper broke through her growing anxiety. The sound of a foot brushing against concrete as it stepped across her balcony. Startled, she bolted upright, sheets cascading down her beautifully tanned body in shiny ribbons, revealing a silken nightgown beneath.

The dark outline of a man stood in the balcony opening.
"Hardy?"
"Hello, Laura," the man rasped.
It wasn't Hardy.
Her hand shot out for the lamp by her bedside. At her touch, light flooded the ample bedroom.

The man standing before her was olive skinned, looked to be of Italian descent and had a very prominent nose. He dressed well and her first impression was that he didn't look like a criminal. He held himself more like a policeman...still, his eyes...

His eyes *were* criminal.

That was okay. She knew how to deal with that type. They could be easier to handle than the clean-cut ones. She'd seen it all, dealt with it all, and survived it all.

"Who are you?"
"I could be the best thing that ever happened to you...or I could be your worst nightmare. It's really up to you."

This guy was certainly full of himself.

"Okay, what's your name, big boy?"

He laughed lightly, and a bit derisively.

"Rialto. Alexander Rialto"

"What do you want, Mr. Rialto?"

"You can call me, Alex."

"Okay, Alex. What do you want? You did just break into my apartment, remember?"

"Funny, I thought this was Hardy Phillips' apartment." He saw that comment had pricked her pride. "Are you happy with this set-up, Laura? Are you happy just waiting for Hardy to dole out goodies to you, always dependent on him for your survival?"

She said nothing, waiting.

"I've got an opportunity for you, sweetheart. How would you like to be the master...er the mistress, I should say, of your own destiny?"

Rialto extracted a silver shifter from his coat pocket and held it aloft for her to see. Her eyes riveted to it. She'd never thought she'd see one that wasn't eternally clamped around someone else's wrist, one that was *available*. Her mouth began to water.

"Did you take that from Hardy?" she asked coldly.

"Would you hate me if I did?"

She could care less where he'd gotten it. Her mind was fully occupied with scheming of ways to make sure that watch ended up on her wrist.

"Relax, I didn't get it from Hardy. You never guessed there were more out there, did you?"

Her breathing had involuntarily deepened, her chest heaving in anticipation.

Rialto's eyes narrowed like a serpent's. "Do you want it, Laura?'

"Why wouldn't you take it for yourself?"

He held up his wrist, letting his shirt sleeve slip down, revealing a shifter already in place.

"What's the catch?"

"No catch. Let's just say I like to make people happy."

Her mind raced, calculating every possible trick Rialto could have up his sleeve. She knew his type. She could see it deep within his eyes. He wouldn't offer his grandmother a brownie without wanting something in return, much less the world to a former stripper he didn't know from Eve.

"Throw it on the bed."

He did.

She picked it up, examining every side of it, comparing it with what she remembered of Hardy's. There weren't any apparent differences and her overwhelming desire slipped it over her wrist before she even realized what she was doing. The band instantly began to whir and contract until it was snug against her skin. It felt *good.*

She looked up at Rialto, his wide grin disarming her.

"Now, Laura, dear. Let's talk about why you're going to do exactly what I say from here on out."

Chapter 11

September 19th 2013, Somewhere over the Atlantic Ocean

"Mark, I've been thinking." Hardy took a sip from the glass of wine the flight attendant had brought them.

"That can't be good," Mark laughed, grateful for the distraction from the in-flight movie. It was some Mike Myers flick. Hardy though the guy was funny, but Mark couldn't stand him.

"Seriously, how did Rialto find us in London?"

"He must have detected our shift again."

"But we hadn't shifted out yet, we had only shifted *in* to 2013."

"Maybe they can detect us shifting in just like they can when we shift out?"

"Then, why didn't they come after us in Plymouth instead of London. If they detected us shifting in, they would have come to where they knew we'd be. And we know there wasn't anybody on our trail to London."

"What are you thinking?"

"What was the last thing you did before you spotted them?"

"I got us the beers."

"And you paid for them with a card, right?"

The truth dawned on Mark. "Of course! And before that I withdrew a bunch of cash from an ATM outside the pub. They must have had surveillance on my bank activity."

"The question, then, is how do we deal with it?"

"We've got several options, but the easiest is probably to stick with cash until we get to the U.S."

"We could set up an ambush for them at an ATM. One of

us withdraws money while the other lays out in a sniper position for cover."

"That could work, but I'm really tired. We've been on the run for months. Let's just get back home, rest, and regroup. We've got a lot of planning to do."

"Fine." Mark was right after all. There would be plenty of time to deal with these goons now that they knew their game.

Hardy turned back to the Mike Myers movie and laughed loudly as one of his favorite scenes played out. Mark groaned, leaned his head back, and closed his eyes. With luck, maybe he'd get some sleep. Man, he hated Mike Myers.

***

The woman was in trouble.

She was running, stumbling down the dirt path, away from the village she must have called safe until just now. Smoke rose from one of the thatched roofs behind her. The panicked screams of a few women mingled chaotically with the savage cries of unseen attackers. Somewhere, a baby cried.

The woman turned, searching for the baby, her face a picture of frantic anguish. She'd taken no more than two steps when her back arched suddenly, the sharp point of an arrow rudely protruding from her chest.

One more step and she fell, crumpled in the dirt, her lifeblood leaking into the dust.

Mark jerked awake, heart racing, as a bit of turbulence rocked the plane. The hair on the back of his head was wet with sweat. He reached up and twisted the tiny, round vent until it was fully open to get some cooler air.

"You okay?" Hardy saw the pallid color of his face.

"Yeah, I'm fine. Just a bad dream."

This was the second time he'd had that dream. *Who was that woman? Where and when was she from?* He thought about her, and crying babies, and somehow the smell of burning wood lingered while they cruised at thirty-thousand feet.

***

September 23rd 2013, Boston, MA

Bobby Prescott was a graduate of M.I.T in Boston, which was the best technical school in the country. He held a PhD in Physics and was commonly regarded as one of the most promising, up and coming physicists in the United States.

The main reason Mark sought Prescott out was because he needed to know why their shifters had experienced such long periods of inoperability during their trip to the Middle Ages. Mark worried the shifters were running out of juice. If that were true, they needed to know it before they went after Ty.

He hadn't chosen Prescott haphazardly, of course, and had sought out not only the best of the best, but someone who could be trusted. Mark hoped that Prescott would not only be able to help them with their research, but also become part of the team and keep his mouth shut.

After having Prescott sign a confidentiality agreement, Mark had explained the nature of the watch on his wrist. Prescott listened, first in open-mouthed amazement, then with intense curiosity. As Mark predicted, Prescott was ecstatic about joining their team and studying the shifter.

"So, what's the problem you're having?"

Mark twisted his wrist so Prescott could observe the watch's display. "The shifter will only work 6 times in fairly quick succession before shutting down for 24 hours. We think it's some kind of energy consumption protection, though you get violently nauseous by the sixth time, so it could also be a user protection.

"When the watch shuts down, the display turns a reddish color, and while you can manipulate the numbers, the "shift" button stops working. Every time we shift, the watch always shuts down like that, but usually only for a second or so. I think it's some kind of recharge mechanism.

"Anyway, it's never been a problem before, since a second passes so quickly, but Hardy and I just shifted back to the Middle Ages, and both our shifters shut down for much longer."

"What was it like?"

"What was what like?"

"The Middle Ages."

"Oh...exciting. Different. Dirtier than I expected."

"This is so incredible. Unbelievable."

"Look, some day I'll take you to meet Henry VIII in person if you want, but can we get back to the shifter problem?"

"Sure, sure. Sorry. How long was it inoperable?"

"We were a bit...distracted, you might say, so we're not exactly sure. Seemed like somewhere between 20 to 30 minutes? I'm afraid it may be running out of juice. When I shifted back to present day, it shut down for the same length of time."

"Have you ever gone back that far in time before?"

"No, the furthest we'd been before then was 1814."

"Unbelievable. You're talking about time travel nonchalantly, as if it were common place."

"I guess we're used to it by now."

"So, the most you'd traveled back before this was about 200 years. Okay." Prescott was scribbling notes furiously.

"There's something else. I don't know if this is related or not, but we can't seem to go into the future past the year 2029. When we try, we get this strange bouncing sensation. It's like the shifter tries to work, but then stops. You feel like you've dropped a foot, but you haven't moved and there's this strange sound like a low boom out of a sub-woofer or something, but it's only audible to the person trying to shift."

Prescott was still writing.

"You think they're related?" Mark asked.

"No idea yet. You wanna do some experiments?" Prescott was grinning from ear to ear. He was obviously thrilled by the opportunity to play with the space-time continuum.

"Sure."

Mark advised him that they needed to go to a place which wouldn't be likely to change much over the centuries, so they traveled to some remote country acreage in northern Massachusetts.

Bobby brought all kinds of equipment along, which he set up around Mark before he shifted, presumably to measure whatever fluctuations might occur at the moment of the shift. He had Mark hold a stop watch as he shifted which could measure to the hundredths of a second. First, Mark went back to the year 1900, starting the stop watch at the same moment he pressed the shift button, and stopping it the moment he finished shifting. Next, he went to 1850, and then 1800.

Since they had to wait 24 hours for the shifter to recharge, they rented some rooms at a local motel. Over the next couple of days, Mark got to know Bobby Prescott as a person and firmly decided he'd made a good hire. Prescott was a pretty neat guy, a good addition to their team. Oddly enough, time travel itself didn't interest the man nearly as much as *the possibility* of time travel did. He wanted to study the mechanics of the device more than he wanted to go back and meet Abraham Lincoln.

Bobby had Mark shift to a variety of years between the present and the year 1600. During their experiments, Mark learned something else he hadn't known. Not only did the length of time the watch shut down increase with the number of years he crossed, but it seemed that the further back he went in time, the fewer times he could shift within 24 hours.

He learned this the hard way, for on his fifth shift one day, he found himself stuck in 1650 for a full 24 hours. He had to spend a miserable, rainy night in the wild frontier of the 17th century Massachusetts woods completely unprepared and shivering to his very core. By the time he was finally able to shift back to the present, he'd learned a valuable lesson and had caught the beginnings of a cold.

Prescott had laughed at the suddenly soaked, dripping Mark Carpen that reappeared before him. For Prescott, only a couple of seconds had passed.

After a week of experimenting like this, Prescott announced he had enough data to analyze.

"So, what's the verdict?" Mark asked.

"It's all very interesting. I won't bother you with the details of my calculations, but to sum it up, you don't have to worry, you shifter is not running out of juice. Though I can't fathom how such a tiny device is conjuring the kind of power needed to perform such physical miracles."

"Then, what is it?"

"There's an exponential relationship between the power of your shifter and the number of years you can transverse. In short, the amount of time your watch will shut down will increase exponentially the further back you go. At this point, I have enough data I can predict accurately exactly how long you'll be shut down depending on your target year."

"Really?"

"Yep. It turns out, you don't actually shift as instantly as it feels. It takes you almost a full second to complete your shift. Interestingly enough, it doesn't seem to matter how far back you go, the actual shifting process only takes one second."

"After that, your shut down period will be 1.0078 seconds to an exponential power equaling the number of years you are traversing. That's why you didn't notice a change in the shut down period at first. From here back to about 1800, your shut down time will only range from between 1 to 4.7 seconds. 4 seconds is such a short time, you wouldn't have noticed a difference."

"However, exponential growth has a way of accelerating quickly. So, while there is only a 4 second variation for the first 200 years, when you went back to the year 1100 AD, your delay would have been 18 minutes 9 seconds. That's near the range you gave me."

"Seemed closer to 30 minutes to me."

"Like you said, you were distracted."

"Okay, that makes sense."

"If my formula is correct, and I've got no reason to think otherwise, I can predict that if you were to go back 1,000 years, you'd be stuck there for almost 40 minutes. If you went back 2,000 years, it would take a little over 2 months for your shifter to work again."

"That's a huge difference!" Mark exclaimed.

"Yes, you're lucky you didn't go back 3,000 years on a lark. If you had, you'd have been shut down for 420 years. You would have died, stuck in the year 1000 BC."

Mark let out a low whistle. Good thing Hardy hadn't wanted to go visit the Roman Empire instead of the Middle Ages.

"Are you sure about this?"

"Yes, it's a pretty straightforward calculation."

"All right, change of subject. Do you think it would be possible to create some kind of detection device that could tell you what time a person had shifted to?"

Prescott rubbed his chin in thought while he considered the possibility.

"Yeah...it might be possible. I'd need to do a lot more experimenting. The electro-magnetic fluctuations your shifter is putting out seem to be unique each time. Detecting those fluctuations is easy, the hard part is interpreting them into a day, hour, and minute."

"What would the range be for such a detector?"

Prescott turned to his desk, rifling through his notes.

"Based on the strength of the field being put out at the moment you shift, I'd say somewhere between 50 to 100 feet, if the device is unamplified."

"That's a big range. What do you mean 'unamplified'?"

"I mean a passive device running off a battery, like a radar detector for your car. Amplified means you add a significant power source, like a larger battery or plug it into the wall, in order to amplify the signal to be read."

"What if we amplify the signal?"

"Well, such a device would be a lot heavier, but your range could increase dramatically, maybe even up to several thousand feet. However, at that great a distance, you'd have to have the detector pointed directly at the person shifting, or the surrounding noise would drown out the signal you'd be trying to detect."

"So, if I wanted a detector I could easily carry around with me, its range wouldn't be more than 100 feet?"

"Not with today's technology and the strength of the field you want to detect being so weak."

"Why don't you go ahead and design a few of those devices for me, amplified and unamplified. How long would it take you to finish?"

"If funding's not an issue..."

"It's not."

"A couple of weeks, if I work on it by myself."

"Get started, then. I'll shift ahead to a couple of weeks from now and pick them up."

Bobby shook his head incredulously.

Chapter 12

A time to kill, and a time to heal;
a time to break down, and a time to build up

- Ecclesiastes 3: 3

May 1st 2013, 2:00 AM, Boston, MA

They'd been afraid to return to headquarters right away, at least until they knew what to expect. Mark feared Rialto would be watching the street outside the building, and Mark was not eager to start the chase again. Hiring Bobby Prescott to develop detectors similar to Rialto's was their first act of defense.

Mark and Hardy then adapted these detectors into a state of the art security system. The four-story building in Boston which housed their headquarters had been built in the early 1900's. They traveled back to the year it was constructed and installed the new shift detection system throughout. Sensors were hidden out of sight in the attic, basement, and walls.

Prescott had also designed special, tiny signal emitters which Mark and Hardy attached to the underside of their shifters. These emitters operated on a completely different frequency from the waves given off by a shifter, so Rialto would never detect this secondary signal.

Their security system would automatically detect anybody shifting within 100 feet of its walls. If it simultaneously detected the secondary signals coming from friendly watches like Mark and Hardy's, it would do nothing. However, if a shift unaccompanied by the friendly emitters was detected, a silent alarm would be set off and could only be reset manually by someone with an access code. With this system in place, they could never be taken by surprise within the safety of their own building. It was a safe zone.

Mark also installed special bullet-proof windows throughout the building. These special windows were also designed to insulate against the small vibrations caused by human conversation, preventing anyone from eavesdropping in on their meetings with a laser listening device.

Their security system also monitored the electrical, telephone, and networking systems in the building. Any discontinuities or irregularities in service were noted as possible attempts to bug the building. Any wireless signals broadcast by hostile electronic listening bugs would also be detected.

Mark paid crews to install steel plating underneath the plaster in the walls throughout the building. He put in steel doors with tamper-proof locking mechanisms. From the outside, the building appeared perfectly normal, even back in 1910. However, if a person got past the foyer and front office, they'd be confronted with an impenetrable steel door and an impossible-to-crack security lock.

They also shut off all other possible access points, such as roof vents, with perforated steel plating.

In short, they created a camouflaged fortress in the middle of Boston. It was the only place in the world they could feel safe from any type of infiltration by Rialto or someone like him.

The only Achilles' heel to the whole setup was that Rialto could monitor the streets outside the building and snipe one of them before they ever got inside.

The solution was to create an underground access entrance in the sewers. Back in 1910, Mark had the sewers enlarged directly underneath the building to accommodate his plan. They added another steel vault door down there. Once past the door, stairs or an elevator would take you up to the headquarters.

Shift detectors were installed down in the sewers along with infrared motion detectors. If anyone tried to ambush them down there, they would have ample warning ahead of time from the security system.

Savannah came to work every day entering through the

front door. She would be the only person seen coming in and out of the building each day. Mark, Hardy and Ty (if they could rescue him), would always come in through the sewer, never being seen. This was especially practical because the sewer could be entered from virtually any point in the city.

To facilitate the sewer tactic, Mark used several un-traceable, dummy corporations to purchase other buildings at various locations within several blocks of the headquarters. He built access ways from these building to the sewers, again with coded entry locks on steel doors covering their entrances. They would randomly use these different locations to enter the sewer each time they traveled to headquarters, which would make it impossible for anyone to effectively plan an ambush.

They hoped they would only have to keep all of this up until Rialto could be taken out.

Mark and Hardy had been on the go for months now, first running from Rialto, then doing research with Prescott and turning their headquarters into a fortress. To say they were tired would be an understatement.

Satisfied with the defensive actions they'd taken, they shifted back to the night of the same day Hardy had originally left to rescue Mark from the Lincoln plot. They would pick up with their lives where they'd left off. Now that they had a safe house, the first order of business was to rescue Ty. After that, they'd begin an offensive plan against Rialto. Nobody ever won a war playing defense.

They decided to take the rest of the night off to recuperate before going after Ty. Mark crashed on his bed at headquarters. Hardy wanted to go back and see Laura.

He crouched in the dark shadows of the street below his apartment building for a long time. He peered through the dark-ness for anything or anybody who didn't belong. Rialto was just as likely to watch their residences as he was the office. Just being seen could mean death for any of them.

He waited for hours, but nothing seemed out of place. An occasional vehicle passed, mostly taxis bearing drunken revelers to their homes. He used high-powered binoculars to scrutinize the roof line of every building in view, including his own. The doorman visible in the yellow light spilling from the lobby was the same man he'd seen every day since he'd moved in.

He was going to have to duplicate the security system at headquarters for his and Laura's apartment. He couldn't go through all this trouble every time he wanted to come home. It would not be easy convincing her to move, especially to an older building. He certainly couldn't take her back to headquarters. Flaunting their relationship under Mark's own roof day in and day out didn't seem like a good idea.

Stealthily, Hardy crept to the rear fire escape, hugging the shadows all the way. He silently climbed the rungs up to the penthouse, one floor at a time. As he stepped onto his balcony, he sensed something was wrong.

The doors leading into their bedroom were flung wide open, cotton curtains slowly billowing in the breeze.

That by itself was normal. She liked to do that.

No, something else was up. He sensed it like a cat senses water without seeing it.

Sliding his pistol from its holster, Hardy advanced to the opening. He found the bedroom empty, a single lamp lit by their bed. The bed sheets were strewn as if Laura had been sleeping but had gotten up. Alarmed, he checked the bathroom. Nothing.

He made his way through the rest of the apartment, but every room was empty. His pulse raced. Her silk nightgown lay in a puddle in the floor of their closet. Her clothes had been rifled through. A number of empty hangers hung like silent witnesses to the truth, hangers that had been covered in blouses, dresses, and skirts this morning. He wasn't sure, but it looked like a suitcase was missing too.

The note in the kitchen clinched it, confirming a worse truth than the kidnapping he'd feared.

"Bye, Hardy," It read, scribbled in big red letters, like she'd written it with lipstick.

She was gone.

***

The worst part of her leaving was that he would have to face Mark and tell him what had happened. He hoped Mark wouldn't humiliate him. He might even get angry all over again. At a minimum, he'd probably act smug, feeling just deserts had been delivered. Mark didn't really believe Hardy hadn't stolen her from him.

Still, Hardy had no desire to spend the night in the empty, luxurious apartment. Wasn't his style. He'd really only bought it for her.

He was mildly surprised to see how little he was broken up over her leaving. He'd thought he cared for her, at least a little bit. Maybe the novelty of her had just worn off, like gold paint wears off a piece of fake jewelry. Sure, she was a looker, but he'd find someone else. No big deal.

He really should have broken up with her when Mark had flown off the handle. Their friendship was more valuable than some shallow romance. Funny how crystal clear hindsight can be.

His main concern was what Mark would say. He didn't care if Mark rubbed his nose in it, he just didn't want to hurt the guy again.

Headquarters was enshrouded with night when he got back, all of its lamps extinguished. He went up through the elevator. Light flooded the dark hall outside its doors as they slid open on the second floor.

"Hardy?"

"Yeah."

"Good. Guess the new security system works. It said you were a friendly."

Hardy smiled and walked in. Mark looked to have been sleeping.

"Man, I was out for the night. Thought you went home to be with Laura."

"Yeah, about that...she flew the coop."

"What?"

"I mean, she's gone. Took off. Hightailed it."

"Why? Where'd she go?"

"How should I know? Left a note. It said 'Bye, Hardy.'"

Mark's brow creased in concern. "Are you sure she wasn't kidnapped? I wouldn't put something like that past Rialto..."

"No, Mark. It was just a matter of time. The only reason she was with me was 'cause I could buy her things. I knew that."

"She wasn't like that."

"Yes, yes she was. You just couldn't see it."

"Then, why did she leave *me*? I've got more money than you do." Even in the dark of the room, Hardy could see Mark's face darken.

"Who knows. Same reason she left me? Whatever that reason is, only she knows it."

Mark stared at him for a full minute, both men silent. "So, are you done with her then? Even if she came back, are you done with her?"

"Yeah. You?"

"Yeah, I'm done," he sighed, having finally resigned himself to the truth about a woman that had infatuated his heart. "Let's get some sleep. Tomorrow we're gonna find Ty."

Chapter 13

Surreal was the only way to describe it. The scene unfolding before them was so eerily familiar, one which had played over and over again on television sets throughout their lives. They'd seen the black and white photographs. They'd seen the pale, grainy color video of Jackie Kennedy in her pink dress crawling toward the trunk of her vehicle, having just witnessed the violent death of her husband. Mark had even been to the Book Depository Museum once.

But this...

This was real life. Full vivid color, up close and personal.

The President's motorcade was coming around the corner. Mark and Hardy watched its progress from the other side of the street opposite the book depository. They kept away as far as they could without handicapping their ability to operate. Knowing Rialto could recognize them, Mark and Hardy resorted to disguises. Not your average handlebar mustache disguises either, but professionally done latex masks which altered the shapes of their faces.

They spotted Ty. He stood at the front of the crowd, about a hundred feet away. Mark and Hardy would not approach him until they were sure where Rialto's men were. Otherwise, they might walk into a trap.

Hardy's job was to keep an eye on Ty, observing who took him and where they went. Meanwhile, Mark scanned the scene for Rialto, Usher, or Grey Tuft.

Bringing more than a concealed handgun to a presidential assassination was liable to get them arrested or worse, so they resolved to just follow Ty and his captors to wherever they were going to hold him. Then, they would return for weapons.

Mark studied the faces in the crowd as well as he could

from that distance. He couldn't resist glancing up at the famous window on the sixth floor of the Book Depository from where Oswald would take his shots. Mark was about to witness first hand whether or not there had really been a conspiracy or just a single shooter.

He had no doubt there was a shooter up there. Mark could see the shadow of a man just beyond the window's opening. A rifle snaked out as Kennedy drew closer.

To his astonishment, Mark saw that it was obviously not Lee Harvey Oswald up in that window. Oswald was clearly wearing an orangish shirt and standing down on the sidewalk in front of the depository, watching the motorcade pass by.

Mark shook his head to clear it. If that was not him, then Oswald had a twin. It certainly was the spitting image of the accused assassin.

On the grassy knoll, two men dressed in suits stood together just behind a picket fence at the top of the small hill. One of those men looked strikingly like Rialto. *Now, that is interesting,* Mark thought.

Inconspicuously, the two men behind the fence raised rifles to bear on the string of official cars. They fired their weapons, one very quickly after the other, followed shortly by a third shot from the shooter up in the depository. After that, the man behind the fence who didn't look like Rialto fired a fourth shot.

Mark could see the panic etched across Jackie Kennedy's face as she madly scrambled to get away from the horror that had just invaded her life. The motorcade accelerated. People screamed. Cops ran, darting to and fro, barking orders, adrenaline rushing.

Mark calmly made his way over to Hardy. The scene they'd witnessed had not been unexpected. Mark didn't believe it was preventable either. The mysterious force that held his children in eternity would never allow such a monumental event to be changed. There *had* been a few unpredicted twists however.

"So, what happened?" Mark asked.

"Grey Tuft and a couple of thugs grabbed Ty and dragged him behind that building over there. You figure out who really killed Kennedy?"

"Yeah, and you won't believe who might have been involved."

***

Mark followed the men holding Ty as discreetly as possible to an abandoned warehouse on the outskirts of Dallas. Hardy hung back, providing security for Mark. If Mark were ambushed by a time shifter, Hardy would be far enough away to see it and shift back in time to prevent the ambush on Mark.

Mark observed the warehouse and then fell back to give Hardy a report.

"Where is he?" Hardy squinted in the sunlight.

"Not where they want us to think he is," Mark replied. "They took him inside that door over there, but my new detector registered a shift signature from inside that building. Someone shifted to later tonight. Something tells me that if we were to go in that building right now, there might be some happy gunmen waiting for us, but no Ty."

"You think they shifted him out?" Hardy asked.

"I'd bet on it."

"Rialto doesn't know we have detectors yet. He thinks we're blind to any shifts he does out of sight."

"You got it. Let's jump ahead to tonight. See what we see."

"How about we take turns? If we hang on to each other, you can shift me in, and then, I'll shift you. That way we'd have up to 12 shifts before we get shut down instead of 6. That could give us an edge."

"Good idea. Let's do it."

Hardy gripped Mark's shoulder, hit his shifter, and the sky melded into a deep, dark blue. A few stars were beginning to twinkle in its wide expanse. They were now a few moments away from full twilight.

They watched as the warehouse door swung open warily. The kidnapers reemerged, dragging Ty with them. They hauled him to a warehouse on the opposite side of the run-down, industrial complex.

They were not only disguising Ty's location in time, they were moving him physically. Without the time detectors Prescott had designed, they would have been lost.

Mark and Hardy followed and staked out a new observation post, waiting patiently to assess the situation. After ten minutes, they detected another shift signature.

"You think they shifted out again to confuse us further?"

"Doubt it. They don't know we can detect them. Plus, that signature was for somebody shifting in, not out."

"Then, who was it?"

"Grey Tuft was the only guy there with a shifter before, so that was probably Rialto or Usher coming in for a visit."

"Or someone else we don't know about yet."

"Or someone else," Hardy nodded.

After another ten minutes, that someone shifted back out.

"Should we scout it out and make sure Ty's still there?"

"Let's wait till it's fully dark first."

Once the blackness was complete enough to cover an assault, Mark pulled a pair of infrared vision goggles from his backpack. They'd outfitted themselves with all the weaponry they could possibly need to complete this mission. They would take no chances — not when dealing with Rialto and their friend's safety.

Four warm bodies glowed inside the building. Two of the figures were in a front room, and they looked to be sitting. The other two were in a large, back room. One was prostrate on the floor. The other stood over him. Most likely, Ty was the guy lying down. Apparently, there was only one guard in the room with him.

After about thirty minutes, the thug guarding Ty moved to the front of the building with his comrades. Hardy marked the time. Now would be the best opportunity to attack.

Most good plans were simple ones, but the nature of their adversaries made simplicity impossible in this case. The rescue would begin simply enough, but with shifters on everybody's wrists, it was certain to descend very quickly into unmanageable complexity.

They would shift into that back room, cut Ty free and shift him out. Rialto and crew would inevitably use their detectors to follow. They had to find a way to evade those detectors, and they had to assume Ty would most likely be unconscious throughout the ordeal.

Hardy's idea for chain shifting would not work because neither of them knew for sure if a shifter would transport three people at one time like it could two.

Still, Mark planned to use a variation of the idea. Each of them made a list of six sequential times to which they would shift and gave a copy of the list to the other. Once they had Ty, each would begin a long series of rapid shifts with Rialto and his men in close pursuit. They'd have less than a second to change their target time, so after each shift they'd change only one digit in the time, date or year. The list would allow them to meet back up if they got separated in the melee.

"I'm not sure this plan will work, Mark."

"Why not?"

"Rialto's going to have us right where he wants us. He'll have all three of us in one place at one time."

"I know. But Ty's gonna be out of it, and neither of us is going to be able to hold them off by himself."

"Agreed, but this won't work. Even if we manage to get twelve shifts in before we shut down, they can still outshift us."

Mark saw he was right. "One of us could break off from the other at some point, without shifting, escape, wait twenty-four hours and jump back in the fight. Theoretically, we'd have unlimited shifts that way."

"They can do the same thing. It'd be a never ending chase through time."

"What if we don't shift at all, just fight it out like we were trained."

"They'd shift in right on top of us. We'd be surrounded before we knew it. Both sides have detectors and shifters. This is *not* going to be easy. We're going to have to use our heads."

"Got a better plan?" Mark asked skeptically.

Hardy wracked his brain for a several minutes, brow furrowed, searching the scene below for an answer. "How about this? You shift in and retrieve Ty by yourself. I'll keep post up here with the infrared goggles and a sniper rifle. As soon as somebody shifts in to take you out, I'll snipe 'em from behind."

"How do we keep somebody from shifting in behind you and taking you out once they've determined your position?"

"Before I man this post here, I'll shift back and establish another sniper post 100 yards further away. If I see anybody make a move on my own position here, I will preemptively take them out. I'll basically cover myself. That ought to frustrate them pretty good. And if they try to take me out at the secondary position, I'll be able to provide cover for myself again from my primary position on this roof. If that proves to be insufficient, I can always triangulate and create a third position."

"You're going to provide cover fire for yourself? I swear, doing battle this way is really weird."

"Tell me about it. Look, either side has the capability to keep this fight going indefinitely. As long as we stay separate, you and I can keep undoing the history that's just been made. If one of us is killed, the other can undo it. It's going to come down to which side gets tired first. If they catch us together, they can end it. We've got to defeat them psychologically, wear them out till they retreat."

"That *is* a better plan, but you didn't explain what to do with Ty."

Hardy nodded knowingly.

That stupid, silly grin of his was so annoying.

Chapter 14

Still sortin' out life, but I'm doing alright
Yeah, it's good to see you too

"These Days"

~ Rascal Flatts

Mark went after Ty alone. He found his friend sitting on the hard concrete, his body listing to the side. His wrists were cuffed to two steel rails embedded in the wall, and his face was a bloody mess. Seeing what had been done to him, Mark muttered angry epithets as he moved closer.

The abusers were grouped in the front of the building. In a conventional setting, Mark would have stormed the front and taken them out before they had time to let their midnight snacks fall to the floor in panic.

However, these enemies could pop in right behind you at any moment with no warning, and if you were good enough to take that guy out, his friend would appear behind you a second later, or even a second before and stop you. You had to careful. Very careful and very smart or you'd wind up deader than a rabbit crossing the interstate regardless of how well you could hop.

Mark extracted a pair of bolt cutters from his backpack and sheared the metal links holding Ty to the wall. He'd come equipped with everything they would possibly need. Ty groaned and Mark caught him as he slipped toward the floor. He laid the big man down gently. Ty wasn't going to be contributing much to this fight.

A small closet at the back of the room housed a water heater. Mark dragged Ty into that closet and shut him inside. Then, he began to set the larger room up for the coming battle. As quietly as possible, he rolled steel drums and other heavy equipment into rows, creating barricades they could use for cover when then bullets began to fly. Rialto's men wouldn't think to move them at first.

Retreating into the small closet-like room where he'd left Ty, Mark closed the door and grabbed Ty's arm. He shifted them both to the next night, same time. Hardy was staked out on the roof of a nearby building with infrared goggles, and they were depending on him to keep any attackers at bay.

Mark flung the door back open and ran to the cover of the drums, dragging Ty behind him. Two thugs were down on the ground at the other end of the room. Blood pooled around their dead bodies. Hardy had already sniped them successfully through the walls using a .50 caliber M107. Taking a peek around a steel drum, Mark was disappointed to see the guys weren't time shifters, just your common goons.

He took comfort in the fact that Rialto and his men could only know into which time they'd shifted, but not *where* in the room exactly they would show up. That's why Mark had hidden in the closet while shifting.

The static hiss of a shift sizzled somewhere near the fallen thugs. Breaking glass and a shrill scream immediately followed. Hardy was on top of things all right.

Somebody had just received a rude awakening and shifted right back out.

Mark wasn't taking the bait. No bad guys were visible at the moment, but they could appear anywhere at any second. Straying from their prearranged plan was the only real danger. He hoped.

Grasping Ty's wrist, Mark shifted again, to a night three months in the future. As he'd expected, the enemy had removed all the steel drums thinking Mark would use them for cover. He and Ty were in the open now, sitting ducks.

Rialto and Usher stood confidently before them, feet spread wide, weapons leveled, ready to kill. Mark also held his weapon ready.

The question of who would get off the first shot was never

answered, for Hardy interrupted with one of his own. They'd expected Rialto to be looking for a sniper this time, so instead Hardy had shifted into the front of the room, a split second before Mark. This set him directly behind Rialto and Usher.

His first bullet caught Usher low in the side. The man's legs buckled and he spilt to one knee. Hardy's aim had been compromised by the way he'd fired right as he materialized, or he would have killed him for sure.

Usher fumbled to regain control of his weapon. It went off and a stray bullet struck the floor, ricocheting wildly. Rialto started to whip around to face Hardy, but immediately reconsidered, remembering the threat Mark represented. Abruptly, he switched plans, using his own shifter to flee from the ambush.

In fact, Mark's bullet would have taken Rialto right in the chest, but the villain was already fading before the bullet crossed the space he'd just occupied.

Usher groaned on the floor. Blood leaked from a bad-looking wound. His gun had been flung too far for him to reach. He moved to shift out too. As his form faded, Grey Tuft shifted in, spraying bullets without aim. One bullet struck Ty in the calf, which elicited a low moan from his unconscious form.

Mark ran to Ty as Hardy turned his sights on Grey Tuft. Hurriedly grabbing his wrist, Mark shifted Ty to a night exactly one year after the Kennedy assassination. As if on cue, Hardy did the same.

This was it, the moment they would turn the tables.

If this didn't work, Mark and Hardy would be forced to split up and make an escape, leaving Ty behind until they could try again.

It was the same room, just more marked up now by multiple bullet scars that pocked the walls. It was also empty except for the three of them. No thugs, no Rialto, no other time shifters.

They'd guessed this would be Rialto's strategy. He knew all three of them were in here together. His best plan of attack would be to mount a full assault with a mini-army of paid mercenaries on all the windows and doors of the facility at the same time, hoping to kill or take them prisoner in one fell swoop.

Until this moment, Mark and Hardy had given Rialto the impression they were randomly shifting from time to time in a desperate attempt to escape. This had been the thrust of Hardy's plan, to lull them into a false sense of confidence.

It had not, however, been a series of unplanned shifts. They'd planned every move they were going to make down to the last detail, and tonight, this warehouse was wired with more booby-traps than you could shake a stick at. Booby-traps Rialto wouldn't know about.

The loud concussion of several distinct explosions confirmed their plan had worked. Two different windows and a door exploded violently, killing those who'd tried to open them.
Mark heaved Ty's body up and shoved him through one of the windows that had just blown, covering the expanse beyond with his pistol. Hardy dove out the other.

Mark drug Ty behind a dumpster nearby. Three bodies lay underneath the window they'd just used as an exit, but their faces were unfamiliar. More common thugs.

Rialto stood with Grey Tuft several hundred feet away. Usher was running away from the booby-trapped building. There was no sign of his previous injury, but the way he was dragging one of his feet indicated he'd been hurt again in this latest assault.

Rialto waved at Usher disgustedly to get his attention, and then all three men shifted out. They were too far away for Mark's detector to pick up Rialto's signal, so he should be safe to exit with Ty too. Gently holding his friend's injured leg, he shifted them to the last prearranged time he and Hardy had chosen.

Chapter 15

May 6th 2013, Boston, MA

They were home, back at headquarters in Boston. Savannah had brewed a pot of freshly ground coffee, and the smell of it flooded the office gloriously.

"I like the new table." Ty leaned back in a leather recliner, one leg propped up in bandages. The bullet hadn't done much damage, but he was going to have to wear compresses for several weeks.

Hardy and Mark sat in hard-backed chairs around a large, round table in the center of their lounge. It was a new purchase. The old table had been long and rectangular, like a conference room. This was more like the Knights of the Round Table. It was also good for poker.

They were playing 5 Card Draw at the moment. Mark peeked at each of his cards as Hardy dealt it to him.

"Thanks."

"What's it supposed to be? Like King Arthur or something?" Ty asked.

"Something like that," Mark grinned.

Ty picked up his cards when Hardy had finished dealing. "Anything wild?"

"That's for kids, man."

"Sorrrrreee," Ty laughed. They hadn't spoken about the rescue much since they'd gotten back, but Ty knew they'd risked their lives greatly coming after him. He was deeply grateful for their friendship and even happier to see Hardy and Mark getting along again.

"What are we going to do about Rialto?" Hardy asked. From the sliver of a grin on his face, he obviously had a good hand. He never disguised it very well.

They'd filled Ty in on everything they'd learned since he'd been taken captive. Ty had learned Vincent Torino's name, who they'd been internally referring to as Grey Tuft.

"I had an investigator look into Rialto and Torino," Mark informed them. "Just got finished meeting with him."

"What did he say?"

"Alexander Rialto used to be a top investigator with the IRS. Now, I understand how he knows me. A while back, there was an investigator named Rialto making inquiries about the antique coins I made."

"Why would he care about that?"

"When I set up our historical armory, I contracted with an antique coin expert named Angelo Lombardi to fabricate about a thousand historically accurate coin molds. I used the molds to produce enough coins to fully fund us in any era we needed. Somehow, Rialto got wind of it. He thought we were trying to do some kind of con job and began investigating me.

"He kept poking his nose around, so I called in some favors to shut the investigation down. I didn't know it at the time, but he got fired because of it."

"I guess a guy could get mad enough to kill you over that. Still seems over the top though."

"You never know with people. Could be he's just trying to eliminate competition. One thing's for sure, he did not have a shifter back then. A person who can jump through time at the drop of a hat does not keep working for the IRS. Nobody loves taxes that much. He had to have acquired a shifter *after* I got mine."

"Maybe not," Hardy interrupted, "in linear time that might be the case, but we well know how these shifters can change the apparent order of events."

Mark nodded. "That's true, but that time when I cornered

him in the bank, his shifter disappeared off his wrist precisely *because* he burned my Wal-mart shares. In other words, he only has his shifter because I became wealthy and started this company. Something I've done...or will do...gave him the opportunity to get a shifter."

"Can't be something you will do," Hardy piped in, "You haven't done it yet. That means all your future decisions are still up in the air. It had to be something you've already done."

"That's not true," Ty countered. "Everything we've ever done or will do is predetermined, we just don't know what that is yet. We can't choose differently than what we're supposed to choose. Mark may be destined to find another shifter at some point, and Rialto steals it before we can put it to use."

"Here we go with that crap again," Hardy replied disgustedly. "What about us saving you? Let me tell you something, we had to be pretty darn creative to get your butt out of there and still we took a chance on figuring wrong. That was no piece of cake."

Mark stared silently at his cards as they debated the ancient argument of fate versus free will.

"Predestined," Ty answered curtly.

"Thanks, man. I feel *reeeeal* appreciated."

"Come on, I appreciate what you did. Both of you. You had no way of knowing how it was going to turn out. Neither did I. You're both giants as far as I'm concerned. Look, it's like this. The future is predetermined, that is *reality*, but it always *appears* open to be changed by us because we don't know what's going to happen. In other words, to God, it's all set, a done deal. To us, it's all up for grabs. Anything could happen."

Hardy grimaced, "Man, I'm not sure I buy into this whole God thing regardless, but what you're saying means we're not responsible for anything we do."

"I never said that."

"Yes, you did. You said it's all predetermined."

"Just because we can't change the future doesn't mean we're not going to be held responsible for it."

"That's crazy."

"It may sound crazy *to you*, but we've all seen for ourselves there are certain events which can't be changed, not even with the shifters. That's because those events are predestined."

"No, those are just things that would create paradoxes if we changed them, so we aren't able to."

"Why not?

"What do you mean 'why not'?"

"What stops us from creating a paradox?"

"The universe."

"Does the universe think? Does it have a mind that monitors all time travelers to make sure we don't violate some law against paradoxes we don't understand?'

"I don't know."

"What's the difference between a universe that thinks and an intelligent God anyway?"

"I don't care."

"Yes you do. By the way, it doesn't really matter if you buy into the whole God thing or not. He's there. You believing or not doesn't change the fact of His existence."

"Guys," Mark interrupted, "Let's get back to the original question. What are we going to do about Rialto?"

They both fell silent, lost in thought.

Finally, Ty broke the silence. "What do you think we should do, Mark?"

Mark laid his cards down, face up. He had two pair, ace high.

"I say we call a truce."

***

May 14th 2013, Boston, MA

Mark faced Alex Rialto across the concrete picnic table, each man's eyes locked on the other's like a radar targeting system.

They appeared to be alone in the city park Mark had named for their meeting site, but the reality was they were not. Hardy and Ty kept a close watch on the situation from afar. Rialto's men would be doing the same.

It was a little past midnight and only a thin sliver of the white moon remained, barely providing enough light to see each other. The nearest street lamp was several hundred yards away. The cool night air was pleasant with only a bit of a chill to it. No breeze, no mosquitos to molest them, just stillness.

Mark had called the meeting by sending a simple note to Rialto's residence once they'd figured out where that was.

"What's this all about?' The former IRS investigator asked.

"Let's call a truce, Rialto"

The man's eyes were cold, cunning, like a snake's. A shadow of doubt floated through Mark's mind. *Was he doing the right thing?*

"Why?" Rialto asked flatly.

"Frankly, I'm not really sure why we're fighting the first place, but I figure it must have something to do with me getting you fired."

Something dark flashed behind Rialto's eyes.

Mark continued, "Anyway, I don't know if you've noticed, but we seem to be at a draw."

Rialto nodded grimly. "I thought we had the advantage," he growled, "but I'm willing to concede it may not be that straightforward."

"You mean your detectors? Yes, that was a definite advantage, but we're ex-military. That more than compensated for the deficiency." Mark wasn't about to tip his hand that they had detectors too.

"I'm no fool, Carpen, You guys must have them by now as well. *You'd* be fools if you didn't. No, our chance to catch you off guard with *that* little surprise was back in those Virginia woods."

Zack Mason

"Rialto, I don't know how you or your men got your shifters and I really don't care. Do you know what we're doing with ours? We're helping people. We're saving people, keeping them from getting killed or hurt."

"Very noble," he sneered.

"We don't care what you do with yours. Use them to make yourselves a massive fortune. I don't care. As long as you're not hurting people, we don't care what you do. Let us alone and we'll leave you alone."

"And if we *do* hurt people?"

Mark's face darkened. "*Then*, we would have to do something about it."

Rialto threw his head back, chortling. "My, my, you are the little elitist, aren't you? Who elected you judge? Regardless, your idea has some merit. We're just spinning our wheels when our teams fight each other. These battles could go on forever. What good would that do?"

"Glad you see my point."

"Don't get me wrong, Carpen. I do hate you. I hate you with every fiber of my being, but it doesn't seem like I can do much about it, does it?"

"You shouldn't hate me. You know why I had to stop your investigation. You'd have done the same."

Rialto stood. Mark did as well.

"All right. It's a deal. We'll leave you alone if you leave us alone. That suit you?"

Mark nodded in assent.

Rialto turned, then stopped and spat one last comment over his shoulder. "I'd shake on it...but I wouldn't want to get your hand dirty."

Chapter 16

January 22nd 1674, Swansea, MA

The smell of fresh bread warmed the otherwise dreary morning. Normally, she would have been the one up early to bake it, but on the Sabbath day, Father always let her sleep in a little late and cooked her breakfast. The sweet butter melted into liquid yellow as Abigail Cooper spread it on a thick, fluffy slice of bread.

Father had also stoked the morning fire and put more wood on, banishing some of the day's cold from their small cottage. The crackles of the superheated wood popping was a familiar and homey sound. The faint scent of smoke lingered in spite of the strong aromas from the Sunday morning meal he'd prepared for them both.

Their family had emigrated from England to Massachusetts fifteen years ago on a leaky ship held together with a little more tar than nails. Some families could afford better, but not theirs. Her father had been a poor cooper back in England, as had been his father before him, and thus their surname.

Her dear mother, may God bless her soul, had perished that first winter after their arrival of the coughing sickness, along with her older brother, Edward. The sickness that year had not devastated their village as much as it had the Separatists further east in Plymouth nigh fifty years before, but it had taken a number of good souls to be sure.

Since then, their small family had consisted of just her and her father. He'd grieved hard for the loss of his beloved wife, and though there were a number of available widows in the village, he had chosen not to remarry. Instead, he'd raised her alone, pouring all the love that remained in his heart upon her. Bittersweet was their meager existence, tragic in their loss, yet joyful in their trust in God's providence and their love for one another.

"Dah, I don't want to marry that boy."

"Abbie, dear, you cannot stay a maid forever, takin' care of me an' this hovel. Yer nigh on nineteen years now. Clemency's a good man."

"But he is not for me," she said.

"How do you know that?"

"I know. I do not believe God wants me to marry."

"That be wicked talk, Abbie. What else would you do?"

"Tis not wicked, Dah. The scriptures teach the Lord does not intend matrimony for all."

Her father didn't bother dwelling on that. They'd had this conversation a hundred times already. She knew he loved her and just wanted her to be happy. He thought marriage and children would do that, but she felt something else burning in her heart. Something unusual, something odd. Something she didn't comprehend even herself yet, but she was sure it was from God.

"My fair child, I know what you say to be true, but tis hard to trust unconvention when convention be the way of things. Still, my heart be yours, as it always has. Do what ye will."

She threw her arms around his neck and hugged him tight. He turned red in the face as he always did when she was so enthusiastic with her affection.

"Girl, the Lord knows I've done me best to raise you in the fear o' Him. You've got a mind an' a heart of your own though, to be sure," he grumbled.

"No fear, Dah. I shall embarrass neither you nor Him." She bussed him on the cheek. A reluctant smile peeked through his forced, stern demeanor. He could never resist when she wanted something so badly.

Abigail leaned back in her chair, enjoying the taste of the creamy, buttered bread on her tongue, feeling the warmth of the fire on her skin. The chill of the world outside was held at bay by the walls of their snug home.

Yet, a sliver of doubt entered her thoughts, like a draft through a small crack in the boards. Was she doing the right thing? What if her father was right after all? What if she couldn't make it on her own?

She stoked the fire deep within her heart, hoping it would be sufficient to keep out the cold fingers of doubt.

***

The crackling of thatched roofs burning singed his ears and the pungent odor of their smoke filled his nostrils, heating the lining of his throat intolerably with each breath.

The screams of several women from the village mingled with the heart-wrenching wails of children. It was complete chaos.

The villagers looked like pictures of Pilgrims he'd seen in history books. They were under attack by painted, bare-chested warriors whooping savagely as they wreaked havoc upon the innocent with hatchet and knife. Scarlet blood stained and ran across the earth in tiny rivers as it poured from the wounds of the fallen.

There she was...again. Her face, which normally must have been angelic, was tight with the concentrated stress of the moment. She ran. Her long auburn hair had been pinned up, but now bounced rhythmically as she fled. Her clothing was different from most of the other villagers, a deep forest green tunic being the most noticeable variation.

Then came the horrifying scene his repeated nightmares inexplicably forced him to watch over and over again.

The cry of a baby.

The woman stopped, changing direction to find the baby.

It was a move which would bring sudden death. This time, Mark saw the arrow as it flew before striking her graceful back. This time, he saw the killer, watched his face as he loosed his deadly missile from the doorframe of a burning cottage.

This time, the dream did not end as this beautiful woman fell, destroyed in an instant. It continued, and he was powerless to stop it. It continued and the baby cried. It continued as the baby abruptly ceased crying. It continued as Mark helplessly remained conscious to the horror.

Then, mercifully, and finally, it stopped.

"Man, what happened to you?" Ty handed Mark a cup of joe.

"What do you mean?"

"Your eyes are bloodshot. Looks like you didn't sleep a wink."

"Had a rough night."

Hardy was shooting billiards. "Bad dreams?"

"You could say that." That evoked quizzical looks from both his friends. Mark leaned out the door and called down the hall, "Savannah? Would you come here for a minute?"

Hardy put down his pool cue and took a chair. Mark sat in another, rubbing his forehead with his fingers as if he were either trying to rub away a bad hangover or come up with the answer to a difficult problem. Savannah waltzed in wearing a simple white cotton blouse, blue jeans and sporting a pony tail.

"Savannah, I think I may need your expertise."

Ty was growing impatient, "Spill it, Mark. What's up?"

"I have this horrible, recurring dream. Seven times now I've dreamt the same thing, and it seems so *real*...I just don't know. It's taking a toll on me."

"What's it about?"

"There's this village, and a lot of people...and these Indians are attacking. All the people are dressed kind of like the Pilgrims, and there's this girl. It's always the same girl. Maybe she's a woman, I don't know. I just see her for a moment before she's killed by the Indians. I keep seeing her die over and over again, night after night, and I don't know why. Maybe she's calling to me, or maybe the dream is calling to me, like I'm supposed to find her or something."

"That's ridiculous," Hardy chuckled.

Mark didn't hear him. He was lost in thought.

"Do you think this is something that actually happened?" Savannah asked.

"I do," Mark replied, "I think I'm supposed to go find these people."

Hardy shook his head, scoffing. "You think the universe is calling you, Mark? C'mon."

"Ain't the universe, my friend," Ty interjected. "Things can't think."

Hardy scowled.

"I don't know what it is," Mark mumbled, "but something's telling me I'm supposed to go."

"What about that boy back in England?" Hardy asked. "Did you forget about him?"

"What boy?" Savannah queried.

"Back in the Middle Ages, Mark and I ran across this boy they were going to hang."

"I haven't forgotten," Mark asserted.

"Oh, I see. Can you describe the village to me in more detail, Mark?" Savannah gently prodded. She'd took a pen and began scribbling notes on a pad.

Mark described everything as best he could and answered her questions about the buildings, the villagers, their clothing, things they said, what the Indians looked like.

"Well, I doubt they were Pilgrims, Mark. It sounds more like a Puritan village."

"Isn't that the same thing?"

"No, not really. The Pilgrims were Separatists while the Puritans believed in reforming the Church of England from within...anyway, no, they're not the same thing. They did share a number of similar customs and beliefs, but the Pilgrims had a distinct form of dress, usually more colorful than the Puritans. Plus, there weren't that many Separatists, their settlements were usually on the coastline. Puritans migrated much further inland and had settlements throughout Massachusetts."

"So, how do we find out where this village is?"

"Not sure. There was an Indian uprising in the late 1600's and a number of Puritan settlements were attacked. I can't remember many of the details though. I'll have to do some research."

"Could you please?"

Savannah nodded.

"You guys want to come along?"

"Sorry, Mark, I've got a couple of things I'm working on," Ty said.

"That's fine. Hardy?"

"Yeah, I'll go later if you need me."

"All right. Savannah, when will you know something?"

"Couple of days, maybe?"

"Good, I'll shift ahead and meet you then."

Chapter 17

The mourners had left. She was alone now. Alone in the humble home where she'd grown up under the caring hand of her father, and she felt scared. She had never known life without him.

Unlike her mother, it had not been sickness that took him, but a bullet. He had gone to check his rabbit traps and not come home. She'd found her dah on the trail the next morning, dried blood encrusting the large wound on his cold body.

How lifeless he'd looked.

Yet, how at peace.

He'd had no known enemies. The general consensus in the village was it had been a lone Wampanoag armed with a rifle traded to him by settlers.

She could feel the anger and bitterness encroaching deep within, trying to possess her heart. It would be so easy to give in to it.

But that would not please her Dah. He had raised a decent daughter, a daughter devoted to forgiveness and the gentle ways of his Savior. He was happy now, at peace by his Lord's side. Surely, he now enjoyed the company of her mother once more. He had missed her dearly over the years.

How easily the hatred came to her surprised her. Hatred for the savagery that had so violently ripped him from her life, hatred for the savage who'd borne the gun. She could hate the savagery, but she must not allow herself to hate the man possessed by it. Were not all men savages at heart? Did not all men stand guilty before their Creator?

A gentle knock broke through her thoughts. She did not

want another sympathetic ear today. She wanted to sleep. She went to the door and opened it.

It was Clemency Bradford, a fine young man to be sure. He was the same man her father, till recently, had wanted her to marry, and who she particularly did not want to see at this moment.

She tried her best to appear ladylike and patient. "Yes, Clem?"

He held his hat in hand. "Abbie, I uh..."

"Spit it out, Clem." She could probably do better with the patience part.

"Abbie, it's not safe for you to be living at the edge of the village like this...especially after what's happened."

"This is my home, Clem. Where would I go?"

"Father and mother have said you can live with us for a time."

"And then?"

"Well...I thought we could be married. I'd build us a house of our own."

"Clem...no. It's a nice offer, but I'm sorry, no."

"Wait, Abbie. I know you're grieving, but tis really what's best."

"I've said what I have to say."

"But...the ladies of the village will start to talk if you live out here by yourself..."

"Let them!" She slammed the door in his face.

Aaarrgh! He had another thing coming if he thought she'd marry him out of necessity. He was a nice boy, but too naive. That was for sure. She had no idea what she *would* do, but marrying Clemency Bradford would certainly not be one of her choices.

May 23rd 1674, Swansea, MA

Now that she'd packed, the house looked emptier, though she wasn't really taking that much with her. Perhaps the emptiness she sensed was more from the absence of her father than the few essentials she'd removed.

Much of the larger furniture she was forced to leave behind. There was no way she could transport that stuff to where she was going. She'd have to rebuild it along with a new house.

Clem had been right about one thing, it wasn't long before tongues started wagging.

They were good people. They just couldn't conceive of a young lady of her age being anything but married. A girl who refused to follow convention was to be suspected. The gossip and rumors grew like festering weeds. She'd decided it was time to leave.

Her father had taught her how to hunt and trap. In the wild Massachusetts woods, she could get along on her own as well as any village boy. The tunic she'd chosen was dark green. She'd sown it herself and could make whatever else she needed. All the other changes of clothes in her knapsack had dark greens and browns woven into them. Those colorings would help her blend into the forest as she hunted.

A bow and a quiver full of arrows graced her shoulder and hung low across her small back. In addition to the clothing items, she'd packed a knife and a few other basic necessities in the knapsack. She threw it over her other shoulder.

Setting the fire was hard. This was all she'd known.

In this cottage were a thousand warm memories of her father and the simple life they'd led, memories that would never again be triggered by the sight of this home. A lump tightened in her throat as flames licked up the side of a wall.

She turned without a word and went out the door for the last time, melting into the woods.

Chapter 18

The boy was young and innocent.

John Wilshire's youngest child had no idea he was being followed. He'd been gathering kindling in the forest, no doubt to take home to his mother. He'd strayed a little farther than he'd needed to because he was also checking his father's traps, hoping to find a rabbit.

The stalker intent on destroying the boy was a powerful male of the Wampanoag tribe. Lightly tanned buckskin leggings were laced around his thighs and calves with rawhide strings and looked very similar to a pair of pants. Those together with a breechcloth and a fringed buckskin shirt with no sleeves completed his attire. Each item was adorned with small seashells dangling from the ends of braided leather strips.

His skin was bronze, his stature muscular. He'd covered his skin with a mixture made of animal fat and a reddish pigment, a practice common to the Wampanoag which added a maroon hue to their golden skin.

This warrior had also applied bright scarlet paint to his forehead and cheeks and shaved the sides of his head, leaving a long, raven-black mohawk down the center. This hair was braided in the back.

A tattoo of a wolf was visible on his right cheek and another round design had been tattooed onto his right breast. The more unusual designs created from yellow and black paint that adorned the length of his torso indicated he was on the warpath.

Stealthily, the warrior had tracked the boy, having come across his sign about five hundred feet back. Once he'd spied the tracks, he had changed course to pursue.

She guessed his intent was slaughter, but it could be kidnapping.

Abbie didn't refer to the Wampanoag as savages like many of the others, but she did condemn a number of their practices that way. They were a people still enslaved to sin, as evidenced by their bloodlust which surfaced at times like these.

As the boy was blissfully ignorant of his would-be assassin, the Wampanoag warrior was also unaware of her. She'd found his sign several miles ago and had moved ahead to intercept. This had been her fear, that his mission was not a peaceful one. He was far from his own village, and the war paint didn't bode well.

She was perched overhead in the limbs of a tall tree. Her clothing was designed to blend with the colors of the early autumn foliage surrounding her. She would not be detected by either party before they collided, and that looked like it would happen almost directly below her.

The Wampanoag drew closer, hunkering low behind brush as he advanced. His moccasined feet stepped lightly and silently as he swept through the forest toward his prey.

The child stooped to examine an insect, distracted by a type he'd never seen before.

Her hand was taught on her bowstring. She would wait until she was sure. She did not desire spilt blood, much less innocent blood. If it could be helped, she preferred to take no life.

The Wampanoag had almost reached the boy's position now. So far, he'd made no motion to attack with either bow or hatchet. Maybe his purpose was kidnapping after all.

Suddenly, he rose up, arm extended, a knife in his fist glimmering wickedly in the afternoon light. She could not allow a kidnapping any more than she could a murder. The penalty in Scripture for either was the same.

Her fingers released the bowstring, a soft twang the only sound accompanying the launch of her arrow which soon found it's appointed place in the attacker's spine. The Wampanoag shrieked abruptly, then collapsed onto the path and fell silent, broken branches of a bush pushing up pointedly at his naked belly.

Startled, the boy screamed at the sight of an armed, dying Indian falling toward him and ran off down the path back toward his home. He would be all right now. There weren't any other Indians around, nor wildcats for that matter.

She would retrieve her arrow and lay out the dead man in a more respectful pose. The villagers would find and bury him before the day was over.

***

April 20th 1675, Swansea, MA

"Her? She's a witch."

The boy looked alarmed to be asked about the woman. She was one nobody liked to talk about, and when they did it was in hushed whispers outside the ears of children.

"A Witch? You're kidding, right?"

"She be one, I swear it. Everyone knows it." The boy waved his hand around the village to indicate who he meant by everyone and ran off to some destination out of sight.

Mark turned to a shoe cobbler who'd emerged from his tiny shop to sweep his front stoop.

"What do you say about her, sir?"

The cobbler paused, "I've not seen ye before, have I, sir?"

"Tis true, I am a stranger to this town." Savannah had given Mark a brief dialect lesson before he'd left so he could make his speech sound more familiar to Puritan ears.

"May I inquire as to the nature of yer interest in the lady?"

"Nothing nefarious, I assure you, kind sir. She seems such a gentle soul, yet all I've been told so far smells of slander."

She was oblivious to their conversation, being a good hundred feet away and fully engaged in a discussion with a man further down the row. She appeared to be trading some rabbit meat for a basket filled with a variety of vegetables.

"Her name is Abigail Cooper."

"Do you also say she's a witch?"

"Ye will not hear me say that. No, sir. She's a godly woman. Kind-hearted, like her father and mother before her."

"And they?"

"The good Lord saw fit to take her mother when she was young, her father just last year. She's got no other family here in Massachusetts. Perhaps there be some back in England, I do not know."

"Why do people call her a witch?"

"'Cause she refused to marry Clem Bradford and lives by herself out in the woods. Truth be told, she refuses to marry at all. Folk just don't understand that kind of thinking. Keeps to herself. People attack what they don't understand. It's the sinful nature."

"Tis a shame."

"More so when ye know what she really does out in those woods."

"What's that?"

"She protects us. Watches for savages, wild animals, and other threats to the village. Tis not just a few villagers who've been miraculously saved from certain death on the trails since she took to a solitary life. We've not lost a soul since. She saved my sister's son. He narrowly escaped being murdered at the hand of a Wampanoag.

"Tis not all either. She comes and trades, like ye see there, an' she always takes the worst end of the deal. I guarantee Mr. Tanner over there will come out ahead on the trade he's striking with her now. People don't see that though. They cannot stand it that she won't take the yoke they want to lay on her."

"That's too bad."

"People are odd. Some villages would have no problem with her choice. This one needs more teaching from the Scripture."

"The Scripture? I would think teaching from the Scripture was the problem."

"Blasphemy, man! Hold your tongue. I pray ye hold no base opinion regarding the Word of God!" The man shook his head.

"No, sorry. That's not what I meant."

"Then, ye be as ignorant as the rest. If this village were taught the Scripture well, they'd know God does not intend for all to marry."

"I'm glad to see someone thinks well of her."

"I try to judge correctly, nothing more. I shun gossip. Tis an evil that harms all involved."

Mark extended his hand to the man. "Thank you, Mr..."

"Fuller. William Fuller." They shook.

"Thank you, Mr. Fuller. You've been very helpful." Mark studied Abbie's quick smile and bright eyes as she conversed, his eyes lingering longer than necessary. She'd finished her business and would probably head home shortly, which he now knew was not in the village.

There was no doubt about it, she was the beautiful woman from his nightmare. Somehow, he needed to turn that nightmare into a dream.

Chapter 19

April 20th 1675, Massachusetts Woodlands

Mark could remain hidden for hours, for days really, if he needed to. He was in his element again, blending in with the vegetation, stalking prey.

His prey this time was Abigail Cooper. He wasn't really stalking her though, just waiting for the right moment to approach.

She squatted by a rabbit trap just off the trail, freeing her latest catch, which would probably be her dinner.

Her attire was simple and rustic, yet it graced her form delicately. He marveled at the extraordinary mental strength she must have to survive as she did in the wild by herself. She obviously did well at it. She not only fed herself, but caught enough meat to trade with the villagers too. The fact she served as their unseen protector impressed him even more.

Her lifestyle showed obvious strength of character and a tremendous amount of grit, yet she'd taken time to smooth her skirts beneath her when she'd knelt by the trap, a distinctly feminine gesture. Her nimble fingers worked delicately to free the rabbit.

Stepping lightly from the woods, Mark called her name. "Abigail?"

He'd feared she might startle, appearing so suddenly, but she didn't even blink. Just continued working on the trap.

"I hope I didn't scare you."

"Ye did not scare me," she said, not even looking up, "If ye had not emerged soon I would have come in after ye."

"You knew I was there?" Mark was incredulous.

"Ye first watched me back in the village. On the trail, ye were quite inconspicuous, I'll give ye that. Still, I always knew where ye were. Now, what do ye want? I pray ye art a gentleman. It oft portends evil when a man pursues a woman through the woods."

"You weren't scared?"

"I care for myself."

"So I've heard. I mean you no harm, I swear it."

"No need to swear, sir. A man's word should not require it. I've asked ye before, and I'll ask once more, what be yer business?"

He hesitated. He'd prepared an elaborate speech for just this moment, but her forthrightness threw him off.

"Ms. Cooper," Her propriety automatically evoked an unnatural formality in him as well, "I am here to warn you. There is a dream...a dream that I've had, not once, but many times. I've seen you in that dream over and over again."

She blushed a deep shade of red. "Forwardness is *not* a virtue, sir."

"It was not that kind of a dream. It was a nightmare, of the worst sort. It plagues my sleep, and in it, I see you die every time. Until today, I'd never met you before in my life, but there's no doubt you're the one I see. I had to find you, to warn you."

His words, of course, were completely unexpected. Her eyes dropped, her expression pensive, contemplating.

"This is no joke, Abigail. I would not tease you in such a way."

"I've no doubt of yer sincerity, sir, tis clear in your eyes."

"My name is Mark."

"Well...Mark. If what ye say is true, what good does this omen do? Do you not believe in the sovereignty of our Lord? If he wishes to take me, should I doubt His judgment?"

"If my dream is from Him, might not His intent be one of forewarning?"

"Might be at that," she acceded.

"In a few months, Indians will attack a village near here.

You'll be killed trying to save a baby. You must either stay away from that attack or we must find a way to save you."

"There be a third choice, to die in the noble act of saving a life."

Mark bowed his head, shaking it. "You don't save the baby. That's the worst part of the dream."

She was visibly shaken. "Tell me, sir. Do you ever see the face of my killer in your dream?"

Mark nodded, eyes glued to the ground.

"Can ye not find a way to kill him before he kills me?"

"I can try," he muttered half-heartedly.

"There is something ye have yet to reveal. The Spirit has graced me with the gift of discernment, an' I sense you hide something still."

"Spirit? Gift?"

"From the Colony, ye are not. Am I correct, sir? Yer clothes are right, but your speech be off. An' any man raised in New England would know of the gifts of the blessed Holy Spirit."

He blushed, caught dead to rights, yet still not wanting to tell all.

"Mark, how do ye ask me to trust yer words when ye are not fully truthful?"

"Fine. There is something I haven't said, but you'll never believe me."

"Ye cannot know if ye do not try."

"I will have to show you. Understand, what I am about to do is not magic, it's science."

"Science?"

"Yes...uh...science...it's...well, does your village have any tools now that did not exist when your parents were young? Or have any of the common tools in use been improved upon since you can remember?"

"Of course. I know what science is. It means 'knowledge'. I do not understand what ye mean when ye say ye will 'do science'.

Mark moved toward her and held out his hand. "I'm going

to put my hand on your shoulder."

She recoiled. "Ye shall not, sir! A chaste woman am I, an' shall remain so till I be wed."

"Okay, relax." He withdrew his hand. "Look, I mean you no disrespect, but there's no way for me to show you without physical contact. How about you lay your hand on my shoulder? Would that be acceptable?"

She pondered, then nodded, hesitantly lifting her hand to his shoulder.

Once she had done so, Mark lifted his sleeve, revealing the shifter. Her eyes widened at the sight of the strange material and the glowing display. Before she could react further, he pressed the red button shifting them eight months into the future and at night.

Suddenly, they were enshrouded in the darkness, the only light being the blue glow of the full moon overhead. Biting, cold air stung their exposed skin and white snow blanketed the forest all around.

She reacted violently, throwing herself back and away from him. "Tis magic, to be sure!" She screamed. "What have you done?" The shock of the moment reverted her back to informal speech. He realized that he had forgotten to be using the more formal "ye" throughout their conversation.

"I told you. It's not magic. It's science, a tool that has been invented."

"A tool that gives you power over the sun and weather! Change it back! How many people must be freezing right now, caught outdoors, unprepared!"

"I cannot control the weather, Abigail. It's not that. We have moved eight months into the future. It's winter now."

"What?"

"This device can move a person through time, just as we move through physical space with our feet. It is a device that God has provided."

That might actually be true, he ruminated. Though his cynical agnosticism would not allow him to believe such a thing wholeheartedly, he saw the need to present things in her language.

Falling silent, she stared at him, then glanced around. Reaching down, she plucked some snow up and rubbed it between her fingers until it melted. She pinched herself lightly, then harder and harder until she'd obviously hurt herself.

"Abigail, it's real."

"What day is it?"

"December 16th 1675."

"Can you take me back?"

"Put your hand on my shoulder again." She did and he shifted them back to April.

 Clearly, she was flabbergasted, and not used to being so.

"How does that...thing work?" she asked.

"I'm not sure."

"What do you mean 'you're not sure'?"

"I mean...I don't know how it works."

"You cannot explain how it works yet you wish me to believe it's not magic?"

"Uh..." She had him there.

"Follow me."

"Where are we going?"

"To my cottage."

"Is it close?"

"No. I was leading you away from it."

Chapter 20

"You claim Metacomet is going to begin an all out war on the Christian settlements in Massachusetts colony within the next few months?"

"Well, yes. Everybody from my time calls him 'King Philip'. They call the war 'King Philip's War'."

The warmth of the fire she'd made in her small hearth to make some tea created a cozy ambience in the cottage in spite of the hot spring weather outside. Her cottage was small and quaint, yet surprisingly well-made considering she'd built it herself. Being on her own, she hadn't been able to lift some of the heavy logs necessary for normal cabin construction. To compensate, she'd made the exterior walls out of two thinner, parallel walls built with medium-sized logs. She'd then filled the gap between them with earth, stones, and other insulating material, which made the cabin even warmer in winter than traditional construction would have. Since she could not lift heavy beams up to the roof line, she'd had to make do with smaller logs once again, using rope and vine to support the roof's weight by tying the narrow roof supports to large tree branches above. It was a very interesting and creative construction technique.

Why *had* she left her village? Why did she insist on living out here by herself? It couldn't be an easy life.

"Yes, there are some who call him that."

She'd forced Mark to shift with her again into the future so she could see a burned-out town as evidence for what he was saying. It was hard for her to accept, but she couldn't deny her own eyes. She struggled with the concept of time travel itself more than the idea Indians would attack a settlement. She hadn't grown up on Sci-Fi movies like he had. Time travel was a novelty not generally conceived of by the 17th century populace.

"Philip will start the war. It will take almost two years before he's finally killed. In that time, there's going to be a lot of killing, Christians and Indians both. Many villages will be looted and destroyed."

"And I am killed in one of those attacks."

"Yes."

"Which one?"

"The first one. Swansea. I recognized the town from my dream. When I saw it, I hung around. I was hoping to spot you, and I did."

"Swansea? That's my village. At least, since we left Rehoboth."

Tears welled in her eyes. He'd just given her the grievous news that many people she knew and loved might be killed. She still cared about them in spite of the way they gossiped about her.

"I cannot abandon my people, Mark. God has charged me with their protection. Can we not stop this war?"

Mark was silent. He shook his head.

"Why not?"

"There are some things in history that just can't be changed, Abbie."

"How do you know that?"

He looked directly into her tear-filled eyes, his own becoming watery. "I just do."

She saw his pain and tactfully probed no further. "How do you know this war is one of those things that can't be changed?'

"I don't, I guess. Not for sure. It's just that experience has shown me major historical events usually can't be avoided."

"I take it you're a Calvinist?"

"A what?"

"A Calvinist. You believe in predestination."

"Oh. No, of course not. I'm just a pragmatist. I know what works and what doesn't."

"But you don't *know* about this particular war."

"No, I don't"

"Then, you won't mind if we try."

***

June 14ᵗʰ 1675, Mount Hope, Rhode Island

Mark followed Abbie to Metacomet's village. She wanted to speak with the chief before he started the war to convince him to change his plans.

"If you really want to stop this war, the best way is to shoot Metacomet before he can start anything," Mark said.

"I won't participate in murder," Abbie scowled.

"It's not murder. It's called saving lives. How many Christian settlers is this guy going to kill? How many of his own people is he going to get killed with this bloody war?"

"He hasn't killed anybody yet."

"But he will."

"But he hasn't done it *yet*. I cannot kill a man whose hands remain unstained. He's committed no crime. Not yet."

"You've killed Indians before, Indians who were about to attack settlers, but hadn't *yet*. Didn't you kill them to prevent the taking of innocent life?"

"That's different."

"How is it different?"

"It just is."

They were entering the Wampanoag village now, so they ended their debate abruptly. A muscular warrior rushed them, halting their progress harshly before they'd gotten more than twenty feet inside the village's perimeter. Abbie communicated to him her desire to speak with the chief. This was not the first time she'd been here and the Wampanoag knew her. The warrior disappeared into the maze of wigwams.

Other warriors replaced him, forming a half-circle around them and preventing the foreigners from penetrating further into their village until he returned.

After a short time, the first warrior did return, his expression firm and stern. Shaking his head negatively, he spoke to Abbie softly, but forcibly, in his own language. The chief was not willing to see them.

They left quickly, conferring as soon as they were far enough away not to be heard.

"What's the deal?" Mark asked.

"Chief Metacomet wouldn't see us. Years ago, his brother, Wamsutta, who was chief before him, died suddenly while in Plymouth negotiating a treaty with colony officials. Since then, Metacomet has always been suspicious. He thinks the settlers poisoned him. I think he's decided now is a good time to avenge his brother."

"Any possible truth to the poison allegation?"

"Not likely. The people of Plymouth are very godly. It was an unsavory affair, I'll admit. Josiah Winslow, the governor of the Colony, is not nearly the godly man his father or William Bradford were. He was only elected because he was Edward Winslow's son."

"Wamsutta had started selling land to other colonies, so Governor Winslow sent armed soldiers to force him to come and negotiate the new treaty at gunpoint. It was not the most honorable moment for the Colony. Still, everybody knows Wamsutta simply fell ill while they were treating. Regardless, Metacomet is convinced his brother was murdered and does not want to talk with any whites now, not even me. He's obviously preparing something, as you've said."

"What's next, then? Should we go back in time and speak with Metacomet before his brother dies?"

The twisted expression on Abbie's face revealed her continuing struggle with the concept of time travel. "Would do no good. Metacomet wouldn't be chief yet while Wamsutta is still alive and the tribe wouldn't understand our wanting to treat with someone who wasn't chief. Plus, how would we explain foreknowledge of Wamsutta's death without making them more suspicious."

"So, what do you want to do?" Mark asked.

Her face hardened. "How does this war start?"

***

June 24th 1675, Swazey Corner, MA

"You should know, I don't think you're going to be able to stop this," Mark stated flatly.

"Yes, you've made that abundantly clear," Abbie snipped, a light smirk lightening her tone as she checked and rechecked the loads in her rifles.

King Philip's war had begun with a scattering of Indian attacks on isolated homesteads. A few days later, a farmer by the name of John Salisbury and his son caught some Wampanoag slitting the throats of some of their cattle. Salisbury's son shot one of those Indians.

The next day, Salisbury and six other settlers were ambushed and killed by the Wampanoag in retribution. From there, the war escalated out of control.

Since there could have been hundreds of Indians involved in the original attacks on the isolated settlements, Mark and Abbie decided their best bet to stop the war was by preventing the ambush of the settlers.

They waited in some mulberry bushes a little off the main trail. They'd spied somewhere between ten to fifteen Indians hiding in various places along this section of the path so far. Their goal was to surprise the Indians enough they would lose confidence and flee.

After much waiting, the would-be settler victims finally made an appearance further up the path. They were seven puritan men, dressed for hunting, quietly conversing amongst themselves, unaware of their destiny to become part of history.

Once the settlers had inadvertently surrounded themselves with the unseen ambushers, chaos erupted. Shrill war whoops sparked instantaneous panic among the settler men. Frantically they turned, seeking emergency cover.

Three rifles lay ready at Abbie's feet. Calmly, she raised the first, setting her sights on a savage, and pulled the trigger. Her bullet missed. Mild surprise lit her eyes as she changed the first long gun out for a second. That shot also missed.

Her brow creased in frustration. She was a very good shot and could not for the life of her comprehend why she was missing. By now, one settler was already down. Blood poured from a horrendous head wound. He was probably already dead. A second settler had been wounded in the side, and an Indian sat astride a third man who floundered helplessly on his back, hatchet raised high for the killing blow.

Throwing down the second gun, Abbie snatched up the third and put this Indian in her sights. This time, it misfired. Panicked, Abbie drew it back and checked the powder, but it was dry. The flint was in place. As quickly as she could, she re-packed the powder and wad. By now, the third settler was dead, and that Indian was moving on to other targets. She sighted him again, and again the rifle misfired.

Mark sat calmly beside her throughout the ordeal, his back pressed against a maple tree. When she turned his way, her look was frantic. Almost apathetically, he handed her his rifle which had also been loaded and primed.

She lifted it, took aim, and then threw it to the ground in disgust after it too misfired. Picking up her bow, she loaded it with an arrow from her quiver. When she drew the bow back, its string snapped suddenly with a hollow twang.

She whirled to Mark, tears flowing freely down both her dirty cheeks, leaving trails as they ran. It felt like someone had ripped her heart from her chest, watching her countrymen fall so mercilessly and being powerless to stop it.

Grabbing her arm, Mark shifted them both out of the scene, ignoring her sensitivities to physical touch. A battle was

Zack Mason

no place to be worried about chastity.

Chapter 21

June 14th 1675, Massachusetts Woodlands

Secretly, Mark had felt his heart being drawn to this woman even when she'd been nothing more than a mirage from his dreams. Yet, his heart was as reluctant as it was foolish. Between Kelly and Laura, he'd had enough pain induced by females, or lack thereof, thank you very much. Still, his heart was foolishly giving itself away again, even against his wishes.

Instinctively, he knew Abbie was too good for him. She was *pure*. She was the kind of woman a man was hard pressed to find in the 21st century, and even if he did, he'd wouldn't be the kind of man such a woman would want. She had great depth and dedication. Her religious speech unnerved him, yet it was oddly attractive. Still, if she could ever read his heart of hearts — if she knew the things he'd done — she would want nothing more to do with him. She would reject him, and rejection was a risk he did *not* want to take again.

So, he bolstered his defenses and did his best to harden his heart against the affection he might have otherwise begun to feel. That wall of iron he continued erecting around his heart kept melting away as it was besieged by the repeated mental image of those large tears running down her cheeks.

They were back at her cottage. She'd made some strong, black tea while they talked. She got up to refill his cup and paused before the stove. She stood motionless, her back to him, tea kettle in hand, but then her shoulders began to shake subtly from the sobs she was trying to hide.

"Abbie..."

"It's okay," she managed to choke out. She wiped her

eyes with her sleeve before turning around. She refilled his cup and sat down.

"Did you know any of those men?"

"No, not personally. That's not why I'm crying."

"I know. You're frustrated for being helpless to stop it."

"Yes," she sighed, shoulders sagging as she exhaled deeply.

"You'll get over it."

She flinched as if he'd verbally slapped her. "Are you that cold-hearted, Mark?"

"Sorry," he repented, "I didn't mean it like that. I've just been through this before. That's all."

"I'd assumed as much. What happened to you?"

"I'd rather not talk about it."

"As you wish."

They sat in silence for a while, the blissful, outdoor sounds of the afternoon surrounding them as they took their tea.

"You're sure there is no way to stop this coming war?" she asked.

"Yes."

"Why come to me at all if you can't save me?"

"I didn't say I couldn't save you, just that we can't stop the war."

"What's the difference?"

"I have a friend named Ty who has a time shifter like me. He fought in the Vietnam War which takes place about 300 years from now, 1968 or so. From time to time, he shifts back to save some of his buddies before they're killed in the war. He's saved a lot of them too, but there's no way he could completely stop the Vietnam War from happening at all. It's too big an historical event."

"1968?" She rubbed her temples, contemplating such a date.

"You'll get used to it."

"You said that already. Why would God allow you to save a few but not many?"

"I don't know. Changing an entire war would obviously have a tremendous impact on all of history, but perhaps saving one life doesn't alter things enough to matter. That said, there's been a number of guys Ty wasn't able to save."

"I'm not sure I can accept such Calvinistic teaching."

"The proof's in the pudding. You saw what happened. Do you have any other explanation for how your rifle misfired."

"You must know that Swansea, my village, was founded by Baptists who were unable to fit in with the Congregationalists in Rehoboth. My Dah was Baptist and so am I."

"So?"

"So, Congregationalists believe in predestination. We do not."

"Doesn't really matter what you believe, just what *is*. Plus, I'm not so sure God's involved anyway."

"What?" Her head snapped around. "Are you pagan?"

"A pagan?" He chuckled. "No, I'm not a pagan. Just not sure about this God thing."

"Don't be ridiculous."

"I'm dead serious!"

"How do you explain all that's around you? How did you come to exist?"

"Look, I just have trouble believing in a God that allows so many bad things to happen to good people. That's all."

"What is it you just said?...It doesn't matter what you believe, just what *is*."

He took that in stride, not willing to concede the point.

She set her jaw firmly as she changed subjects, "You say you've friends who have these shifters?"

"Yes."

"I think you should go get them. I have a feeling we may need all the help we can get."

Chapter 22

June 25th 1675, Swansea, MA

    Ty declined. He was heavily involved in the rescue of a squad of soldiers he knew in Vietnam who'd been wiped out.

    Hardy reluctantly agreed to come along, unsure at first why he was needed. But, when Mark described the size of the enemy force involved, his enthusiasm grew.

    The first assault by the Indian forces would be on some settlements outside the town of Swansea. Then, the siege would move to the town itself. In light of the recent attacks and the massacre of the previous day, Governor Winslow sent 70 soldiers to Swansea to help defend the town. The soldiers had stationed themselves at three different garrison houses and most of the town's citizens planned to move to the houses as well during the course of the day for protection.

    Hardy was camouflaged in a sniper's nest on a knoll overlooking the town. They'd brought modern sniper rifles and telescopic sights back with them to fortify their advantage. Still, the enemy would number somewhere between two and three hundred. They had no real hope of stopping the massacre. Their more realistic goal was to save Abbie, the baby Mark had heard crying in his dreams, and as many innocents as possible.

    Mark would wander the village in era-appropriate dress as a stranger. Once the first shots were fired, he would duck into a house for cover. He'd already chosen the house. It was a smallish cottage facing the path Abbie ran up in his dream.

The morning's stillness was suddenly pierced by the shouts of a frantic settler racing toward the village. The war cries of his attackers soon followed. A rifle shot rang out and the body of the screaming villager fell lifeless on the path.

The village erupted and a mad scramble for safety immediately ensued. Throughout the settlement, villagers emerged from their homes in a panic, any attempt for order thrown to the wind. Women hugged babies and toddlers under their arms as they ran, while the men clutched rifles and powder horns. Older children stumbled along carrying any portable possessions they could grab in a moment's notice, all moving towards the three reinforced homes which served as garrisons.

The town had been warned of the coming attack, but even though they knew where to go, they weren't prepared enough to do it quickly.

The yells of the Wampanoag grew louder as they closed in and the first arrows began to rain down. Mark saw one sturdy looking man stop and turn to face the attack on his home. He was trying to give his wife and children time to make it to the nearest garrison house. An arrow struck the dirt harmlessly by his feet, its shaft pointing from the ground to the sky. The man was distracted by the near miss.

An Indian's long gun roared and its ball struck the man in the side, spinning him helplessly. He stumbled, but succeeded in replanting his footing. Determined, he sighted his own gun and fired, downing the Indian who'd shot him. Then, a second Wampanoag was upon him, swinging his hatchet. The settler deflected the blow with the butt of his gun and continued the movement upward, knocking that Indian to the ground with a powerful slam on the jaw. A third Indian ended the man's fight, putting a bullet in his back, but not before the man's wife and children made it to safety.

Mark had to remember this was not his fight. He was here to save Abbie, not the whole town. At the first sign of trouble,

Mark retreated to the house he'd chosen for his stand. He helped the family who owned it mobilize and escape faster. Then, he settled into a crouch behind the door frame, observing the battle from cover as it unfolded.

Since the long guns of this era could only be fired once without being reloaded, the Indians had waited to fire most of their guns until they were at a close enough range to inflict maximum damage. They weren't waiting any more though. Clouds of grey gun smoke floated like a man-made fog throughout the village. The wails of the wounded were beginning their soul-piercing cacophony.

Mark watched the residence across the street. The home where the baby would be. A woman appeared in its doorway, her face a portrait of fear, which twisted to agony as an arrow from an unseen attacker buried itself in her stomach. Grasping the wounding shaft with both hands, she turned and stumbled back inside her home.

Then, he saw her. Abbie was running at full speed up the lane, looking exactly as she had in his dream. Fear was written across her face too, even though she knew what lay in store, or maybe *because* she knew what lay in store.

She was so beautiful. The dimmed daylight from the overcast sky made her creamy white skin appear to glow with angelic purity. Auburn tresses of hair bounced rhythmically upon her shoulders in time with her pace as she ran.

Sweat broke out on Mark's forehead. He knew his efforts to not fall in love with her had significant cracks, like a dike pressed by too much water. The strong emotions evoked from witnessing her death over and over in his dreams had been powerful.

Why did he have so little control over his heart? He knew he wouldn't be able to bear seeing her life bleed away in full color, only yards away from where he stood.

He just prayed this wouldn't turn out like when he tried to save Daniel and Brittany — though he wasn't sure who he was praying to.

Now was his moment, the reason he was here. His rifle was already up. The savage face of killer appeared, peering from the doorway of another home, readying his bow to spill her blood.

At last, Mark would know if the repeated nightmare had been given so he could save Abbie, or if this was just another cruel instance of unchangeable fate.

He sighted the man's nose and squeezed the trigger.

The killer's face evaporated, and Abbie was safe.

In the innermost parts of his being, his heart leapt and rejoiced.

He waited, knowing another Wampanoag would approach shortly, for in his dream a hatchet-bearing savage had silenced the crying baby after Abbie's death.

Abbie entered the cottage and reemerged, carrying a small bundle. The second Indian would have been upon her by now, except Mark had taken him out as soon as he'd spotted him.

Staccato bursts from a different kind of gun punctuated the air now. They were the short claps of a modern weapon, which meant Hardy had entered the fray. The dull thud of a body falling sounded from behind the house Mark was in.

Abbie ran now, racing away from the village toward the woods. She left Mark's immediate line of sight and he was forced to trust Hardy to watch over her for the moment. He left the protection of his hiding spot and took up her back trail, determined to keep any other attackers from taking advantage of her weakness.

By the time they reached the safety of the woods, Mark had eliminated several more threats.

Once they were under the cover of trees, Abbie hastily unwrapped the baby, checking for any injuries. Hardy continued to rain down fire upon the village, saving a settler here and there.

The baby cooed. Abbie breathed a deep sigh of relief and finally allowed an answering smile to peek through.

The battle below was ending now. The settlers had lost. The three of them watched as the Wampanoag closed in on one of the remaining garrison houses, bodies strewn about its perimeter.

A woman emerged from within and descended the steps,

her eyes sweeping across the destroyed forms of her loved ones.

"That's Mary Richardson," Abbie whispered.

A Wampanoag warrior was taking aim at her with his long gun. Hardy sighted down on the warrior and fired an instant before the Indian did. Hardy's bullet slammed into his wrist, deflecting his shot enough it only hit the woman in the side. She stumbled, and Abbie screamed, but it soon became clear that Hardy's shot had saved her from any serious injury.

The Wampanoag chief waved off his warriors, effectively ending the attack. The Indians began gathering up the surviving villagers to carry off as captives, shooting those who were too severely wounded to travel.

"It's just so...hard to believe," Abbie breathed, awestruck.

"Yet, there it is," Mark said.

***

The three of them held vigil over the dreadful scene. All the survivors from the garrison houses had long since fled to the next closest settlement seeking safety, reinforcements, and vengeance. The Wampanoag went south with their captives. The day was drawing to an end.

What remained was a picture of emptiness, a devastation dulled and dampened by a soft afternoon rain which had fallen. Charred skeletal remains of homes raised their blackened, burnt fingers toward the sky, as if pleading. The heavy odor of smoke had been the only sense of vitality remaining after the brutal attack, but the drizzle had now washed it away, leaving nothing but the smell of damp earth.

They'd exhausted themselves trying to bury the bodies, but there were just too many. They'd eventually given up, knowing the villagers would return the next day with help, and they would bury the rest.

Abbie had been strong throughout the ordeal, but Mark saw a tear running down her face now, matching the lump he felt in his own throat. What should have been a beautiful summer afternoon felt empty, wet, cold and dreary.

"What are you going to do now?" Mark queried Abbie.

Hardy sat on a nearby stump, rolling some tobacco into a cigarette. He wasn't a smoker by habit, but he'd found a stash that had survived the burning in a ruined home and was intrigued by how authentic colonial tobacco might taste. He'd remained silent for most of the day, quietly observing Abbie and Mark.

"I don't know. There's nothing for me here now," she said softly.

"You could come back to our time and help us."

She was surprised.

"It wouldn't be easy," he continued, "Our century would be completely foreign to you, but we'd be happy to have you. We could always use another good shot on the team." Mark didn't mention that in spite of his resistance, his heart was losing ground in its battle against falling in love with her. A simple, but strong affection for her was growing within. He wanted more time with her.

She turned her gaze back to the burnt village.

"I'll think about it," she whispered.

Chapter 23

July 8th 2013, Boston, MA

He forewarned her as best he could, but no conceivable warning could have prepared Abbie for the shock she received when he brought her to the 21st century.

He took it as slowly as possible. Before going, he'd described a lot of the gadgets and modern inventions used in the daily life of the future to get her used to the idea of modern technology. When they'd finally shifted, he'd made sure they did it in a place which was still forested in 2013.

He moved her toward civilization slowly. Her eyes grew wide as saucers when she first saw Mark's car. Only the trust she had in Mark allowed her to get in the beastly thing. The myriad of devices inside the vehicle were just as much of a shock, especially the radio.

Once she'd gotten used to the idea of electricity, emotional adjustment came much easier to each new piece of technology she encountered, but the speed and pace of modern life were still a shock. Not to mention the blatant immorality she saw splashed everywhere she looked, from billboards, to handbills stapled on telephone poles, to the clothing choices of women on the sidewalks.

When Mark finally got her to headquarters, he showed her to her room on the third floor. A room Savannah had helped him prepare for her arrival. Abbie collapsed onto her new metal spring mattress and into a deep sleep, mentally exhausted.

***

"How'd it go Ty?"

"Saved a few, but I ran into another one I couldn't do anything about."

That one grieved Ty, clouding the joy he would have felt over the others. He'd just gotten back from Vietnam again. He'd run out of friends to save and had moved on to other marines in his battalion. He was running into more and more instances of men he couldn't save, and that was bothering him.

"Shake it off, man. Be happy for the ones who live now because you intervened. You're doing a great thing."

"I know, but..."

"But, what?"

"There's something that's been gnawing on me. I've got to kill a VC, if not several VC, in order to save one of ours."

"So what?"

"Is that right, morally, I mean?"

"You're a soldier, Ty. We're Americans, and it's war. What's different about you killing VC now and back before you knew about the shifters?"

"Nothing, I guess. Just been thinking is all. Those Vietnamese have families too."

"They're communists, man. After the US pulls out there's widespread massacres all across Southeast Asia. Those guys aren't angels."

Ty tumbled a penny between his large fingers. He was listening, but still looked unconvinced.

"Should I have left you dead back in 1968? Should I have spared those VC who killed you?" Mark pushed.

"No."

"Well?"

"I guess you're right." Ty wanted to change the subject. "So, tell me about this girl you brought home. I hear she's a real beauty."

As if on cue, the door to Mark's dormitory opened. Abbie hesitantly emerged. She wore a white dress shirt and a pair of blue jeans Savannah had pulled from Mark's closet. She looked fabulous. Her skin was the color of pale cream, accentuated by burnished, auburn hair pulled back in a pony tail. Unless she spoke, you couldn't tell her from a 21st century woman.

"Mark..."

"Hey, Abbie. Come on in. I want you to meet a friend. This is Ty. He's a partner in the company."

Abbie curtseyed abruptly as Ty extended his hand. He hastily withdrew it as soon as he realized she was not expecting the gesture.

Then, Hardy entered the conference room, bearing coffee, followed by Savannah who had several boxes of donuts in hand.

They were all going out of their way to make Abbie feel welcome, but the past 24 hours had clearly been a major shock to her system. Modern day technology was inconceivable to the average 17th century mind, and the fact that Abbie was coping at all was a testament to her metal fortitude.

"So, what's got you freaked out the most, Abbie?" Ty grinned.

"Freaked out?"

"Um, what are the hardest things to adjust to?"

"Uh...cars, lights, airplanes, those tel...telo...telephones. Definitely the compu...tation instruments..." She was naming things in the order she'd encountered them.

"Computers?"

"Yes, that's it, computers. Everything to be truthful. I don't understand how any of this is possible unless it's magic of some sort."

"It's electricity," Mark said. "That's what makes all this technology possible."

"I don't really understand electricity."

She looked demure, insecure in her new environment. Until now, Mark had only seen her in states of supreme confidence. This new meekness endeared her to him even more.

Savannah opened one of the boxes of donuts and offered Abbie one. She bit down and her eyes grew wide. She wanted to say something but couldn't bear speaking with her mouth full. She hastily chewed, a funny expression on her face until she finished.

"My goodness, that is sweet," she scrunched her eyes in distaste. "I've never had anything that sweet."

They all laughed.

"I'll explain electricity to you, Abbie, along with a lot of other things you need to know," Savannah offered, ever the considerate one.

"She'll fill you in on all the history since 1675 too," Mark added, "She's our resident expert on that subject. We'd be sunk without her."

Savannah blushed at the compliment. "I'd be glad to," she said.

Abbie smiled at her gratefully. Mark hoped she wasn't having second thoughts. He'd known it would be difficult for her, but the reality of just how difficult, even he hadn't really understood.

Hardy piped up, "I'd have figured the way people dressed would have bothered you."

She nodded. "A little. It's quite odd to see women wearing pants. I mean, I always wore leggings in the woods, but it is unusual to see so many women dressed that way."

"Don't you think the young ladies show too much skin?" Hardy, the cheerful antagonist, asked.

"That didn't shock me as much as pants. I went to London once with father. There were ladies there who dressed like that, though they were usually looking...for clients of a certain sort."

Hardy guffawed and slapped his knee. Mark couldn't tell if he was egging Abbie on to poke fun at her, or if he sincerely thought it was funny. Savannah blushed a deeper shade of red.

Abbie quickly curtseyed again, "Present company excluded of course, Savannah," she corrected, realizing the inadvertent offense. "You are not dressed like that at all." Now, it was Abbie's turn to blush.

"Don't worry about it," Savannah replied.

This clash of cultures would be full of unperceived mines which could go off at any moment. They would have to navigate carefully for a while.

"So, what's the plan, boss?" Ty asked.

Mark leaned forward. "I thought we'd give Abbie a couple of weeks with Savannah to get used to things and settle in. In the meantime, we'll go about our normal business, doing saves as usual wherever we feel led, though I think you should lay off Vietnam for a time, Ty."

Ty nodded.

"Then," Mark continued, "we'll take Abbie back with us to medieval England to rescue that boy. She's an excellent shot with a bow and might be of help culturally too."

They all agreed, and Savannah led Abbie out of the common room into the hall. Ty headed off to the bathroom, but Hardy remained behind.

"Mark, do you really think that's a good idea bringing her with us on a shift?"

"Why not?"

"She doesn't have a watch. We'll always have to be looking out for her. She'll be completely dependent on us if something goes wrong."

"Isn't that what we do anyway — look out for people? She'll be extra help."

"I don't see the sense in it."

"I've got a feeling about it, okay?"

"All right, whatever you say."

***

There was visible fear in Abbie's eyes as she boarded the corporate jet for London. Mark admired her strength, for in spite of the horror she felt at being forced to trust a mechanical bird to transport her safely across the Atlantic Ocean, she bolstered herself and mustered up the courage to get on anyway.

It was hard for her to relax, but after an hour into the flight, her desperate grip on the hand rests lightened. Still, a twinge of anxiety lingered as Mark went over their Middle English study notes.

Remembering how unintelligible most of the speech had been during their last visit to medieval England, Mark had asked Savannah for help. She'd hooked him up with a professor at Harvard who was an expert on Middle English.

Mark wanted the whole team to take lessons from the professor. Ty and Hardy came for the first couple of classes, but then stopped. In their military days, they'd gotten used to deploying and performing tasks in countries where they did not speak the language. This would be not any different in their eyes, and they didn't want to invest a significant amount of time in gaining a skill they might need for only a few moments. The fact that they came at all was out of respect for Mark and he didn't hound them when they stopped showing up.

Abbie came to a lot more of the classes, but she'd had to start late. Initially, most of her time was taken up with modern history and science lessons from Savannah. So, Mark became the most proficient in this forgotten language, at least enough so he felt he could competently interpret simple conversations. Somewhere in his gut, he sensed there might be a lot more to this mission than just saving the boy.

The Harvard professor had been a little surprised by their small group's mysterious interest in understanding spoken Middle English rather than the written form. However, the check Mark wrote him was big enough to quell his curiosity.

The soothing hum of the airplane was usually calming to all but the most claustrophobic of souls, and Abbie's eyes soon began to droop. She was growing sleepy in spite of her uneasiness. Frankly, Mark was tired too.

"Let's take a break," he said, closing the notebook. Leaning his head back against the head rest, he closed his eyes, mentally planning their attack as he drifted off.

Chapter 24

August 3rd 1100, Essex, England

As usual, Mark felt a morbid aversion to the idea of seeing a past version of himself. Just the thought of running into a past self gave him the creeps. So, he insisted they all wait *inside* the medieval barn until the small posse showed up with their young prisoner. Mark would avoid approaching the rear of the barn until he was sure his previous self had shifted out.

The wagon rumbled up the dirt path, surrounded by the same horsemen they'd seen before.

Hardy scrambled up a rustic ladder and hid himself in the loft. He would take out any rider who escaped the initial fusillade. Mark, Ty, and Abbie concealed themselves under the hay piled in the back of the barn. They were each armed with a longbow and quiver, which were styled for the times. Stashed in the hay and in other strategic locations outside the barn were duffle bags filled with modern weapons and explosives. If arrows proved to be insufficient to finish the job, or if the situation escalated out of control, they would have more potent tools at their disposal.

Barring such a case, they wished to leave as minimal a footprint on the past as possible and would choose to use the weapons of that time when feasible. However, if their lives were threatened, anything was game.

The driver's heavy cloak shrouded him in vague folds of dark cloth which made him look like the incarnation of death itself. He halted the wagon directly in front of the barn doors. Circling around, the three horsemen forced the hooded boy in the back out onto the ground.

As before, they herded him into the barn, where one of the men forced him to stand on a stool in the center of the hay-strewn floor. This same man threw a rope up over one of the rafters and tied it off on a post. He then proceeded to knot the other end into a rough noose.

One of lynchers seemed more reluctant than the others. He was the one who asked:

"Thes œr bith the cild?"

At first, the sounds of their odd tongue sounded just as foreign to him as they had before, in spite of the lessons the professor had given him. Yet, after a moment of processing, his brain translated it to: "This here is the child?"

Fascinated, he understood the rest of their conversation.

"Yes, this is the villain," the second watcher replied. He was the leader apparent. The man working the rope into a noose said nothing.

"The murderer of Rufus, a small child?"

"Hang him by the neck," the second said to the rope man, ignoring the question of the reluctant one. Having finished his work, the hangman moved to put the rope around the boy's neck, and the leader reached for the sack that covered his head.

Mark kicked his foot out under the hay, which was the go signal for Ty and Abbie. The three lynch men reacted to the unexpected noise, but it was too little, too late.

In unison, Mark, Ty, and Abbie burst up from the hay, straw cascading down their forms and bows in hand preloaded with deadly missiles that were sailing toward the chests of their targets before the movement was even finished. The twangs of three bowstrings echoed through the rustic barn. Three solid thuds and the victimizers fell to the dirt, one by one. The trembling boy screamed, unsure of what was happening. He stumbled off the stool and landed on his knees.

Mark's arrow had missed his target's heart, for that man began a mad and bloody crawl toward the door, gurgling and yelling to the driver of the wagon. Mark swiftly loaded another bolt and finished him off. He'd been the rope man. Mark felt no sympathy for the would-be executioner of a mere boy.

The deathly driver raised himself up from his seat and swept the hood from his pale, white pockmarked head so he could see what was happening inside the barn. Completely devoid of hair, he looked like a fragile skeleton with a thin layer of skin stretched over his skull.

Hardy stood in the loft, bow in hand, ready in case the man moved to join the fight. Instead, the bony figure sat back down in his seat hard and whipped the horses into a frenzy as he made a mad rush to escape. The wagon was well down the trail, lost in a cloud of dust before Hardy descended the ladder to join his friends.

"Why didn't you take out the driver?" Mark asked testily.

"Why didn't *you*?" Hardy replied, sarcasm dripping.

"That was your job."

"He took off, man. He wasn't a threat."

"He'll tell others now and this boy will be in danger again."

Hardy glared at the ground, knowing Mark was probably right, but another part of him resisted. Sometimes, you just grew weary of killing, even when justified.

"If that happens, I can always shift back and take him out further down the road," he answered.

"'Tis a great virtue, mercy," Abbie affirmed, looking at no one in particular. She had regained some of her old confidence, especially now that she was back in a world without electricity.

The boy was still hooded as the lynchmen hadn't had the chance to take it off before their demise. Ty slipped the sack from the youngster's head and sliced his rope bonds in two with a quick swipe of his Bowie knife. He tossed the noose disgustedly into a corner. "I hate nooses," he muttered.

The boy shivered, rubbing his wrists, eyes darting furtively between them. He seemed to understand they were helping him. He relaxed more visibly when he saw Abbie. Surely, the presence of a woman was a sign of mercy.

Gently, Ty lifted him to his feet by the elbows and set him

lightly on the ground.

Let's see how good that prof is, Mark thought.

"What is your name?" he tried. That was a simple phrase in any language.

"Robyn," the boy replied. His fear was dissipating. "You killed them," he stammered, looking at the bodies of the three men who'd come very close to taking his life.

"Dead as a doornail," Ty snickered. His modern English words were senseless sounds to the young man. He looked at Ty quizzically.

"Why were these men trying to kill you?" Mark asked in the best Middle English he could muster.

"Because of my father."

Thankfully, Mark ears continued to decipher the strange syllables of this medieval tongue. There were so many similarities with modern English, it wasn't that difficult once you got used to picking out the sounds.

"Who is your father?"

"Robert Smith. He's a blacksmith. Our family lives nearby."

"Why did they want to kill you because of your father?"

"Because he's a freedman. Lord Geoff wants our lands for his own. He says we're his serfs, but it's a lie! Father paid his freedom several years ago."

"Who is Rufus?"

"William Rufus. The king! Are you daft?"

"Sorry, we're strangers to these parts."

"You must be from very far because Rufus is the king of England. Was, I mean. Someone killed him. Good riddance, I say."

"They said you killed him."

"All lies! We'd no use for him, 'tis true. Nobody did. How could I kill him? I'm just a boy."

"Why did they say that then?"

"They want our land. I already told you that." He motioned to the body of the man who'd ordered the hanging. "That was

Edgar. He worked for Lord Geoff. The other two were knights visiting from Lord Roger de Clare. Edgar *had* to tell them I'd killed the king or they wouldn't have been willing to hang me, but I heard Lord Geoff tell Edgar to kill me to punish my father. Father won't pledge fealty to Geoff and he won't submit our lands to him, so Edgar was to hang me as a lesson. Said he would hang my brothers and sisters one by one until father gives in."

Mark peered into the boy's eyes, measuring every word of what he said. He hoped they hadn't just killed three knights in an effort to rescue some juvenile delinquent who'd killed the king.

"Who did kill the king, then?"

"How should I know?"

"How did he die?"

"Somebody shot him with an arrow while he was hunting."

Mark didn't sense deception in the young lad. He seemed sincere, scared, and just angry enough to be believable.

"What's he saying?" Hardy asked.

Mark explained the whole story.

"What do we do now, Mark?" Everyone looked at him expectantly, even the boy.

Mark grinned, feeling good again for the first time in a while. "I guess we pay this boy's parents a visit."

Chapter 25

One Day Prior — August 2nd 1100, New Forest, England

William Rufus, King of England, held his hand up to his brow to block the bright afternoon sun which was directly in front of them. His brother, Henry, had suggested this hunting party, and he'd jumped at the idea. The worries of the crown were too much sometimes. If it wasn't the people complaining and whining, it was the church. And if it wasn't the church, it was his noblemen.

Nobody wanted to pay their due taxes. How did they expect him to pay for things? He had expenses. Many expenses. It cost a lot of money to plan for the future defense of a country, defense against land-thirsty kings and imposters like his older brother, Robert Curthose. And, he had certain tastes...tastes which were also quite expensive.

Not that they needed to understand those things. He was their king. They existed for his service as he saw fit. That was all *he* needed to understand.

He intentionally broke this all too familiar thought pattern of his and let his temper cool off. It had become too easy to work himself into a maddened frenzy over these frustrations. He'd been engaged in one of his famous, murderous rages yesterday when Henry had suggested this trip. The idea had calmed him instantly. He loved hunting. His rages were becoming all too frequent. He would work on that. It just bred further distrust among his subjects.

He felt an affection for Henry, though that didn't mean he trusted his younger brother any further than he could spit. He'd sent Henry, together with the Clare brothers, off to another section of the forest for that very reason. Henry, hunting, and the natural ambition to make a grasp for the crown which could easily strike any younger brother of an heirless, older sibling, were not a wise mixture. And the Clare brothers — there was something treacherous about the pack of them too.

Tyrell had gone off with them, leaving his servant, Raoul, behind. Rufus was happy for that. Raoul was an excellent shot and this part of the woods had a high concentration of deer. Anything Raoul downed, the king would be able to take credit for. That was another reason he'd sent Henry and the Clares off.

He loved this forest. His father, William the Conqueror, had created it years ago by forcing entire towns off their property in order to return the expansive acreage to a state of virginity. Only the king, and noblemen who had his permission, could hunt in the king's forest. This appropriation of resources did not bother William Rufus, the son, in the least. A king needed his diversion.

As sunlight danced through the late summer leaves, its rays were like constantly changing shafts shining from heaven, illuminating a hundred shades of green, from the strong leaves of the oaks on all sides, to the dark mosses and the vibrant grass which carpeted the forest floor. It was a beautiful afternoon. God seemed to approve of the hunt.

A rustling sounded from the bushes to his right. He slowed his horse and stayed it. Raoul stopped too, a number of yards behind him. He, the king, would have the best shot between the two of them, and he intended to take it. The rustling of the unsuspecting animal grew louder and Rufus drew his bow, notching an arrow with the natural movement of a practiced woodsman.

The stag suddenly showed itself and Rufus' arrow sailed toward its heart. It struck deep, but the aim had not been quite true. The arrow had not hit the heart. The deer stumbled, fell, and leapt up again. It disappeared into the brush on the other side of the path, trailing blood as it went. The wound was mortal, but it would not die quickly. They would have to track it.

Unexpectedly, another stag burst forth from the brush and crossed the king's path directly in front of him. He didn't have time to react, to draw another arrow. This one would get away, he realized regretfully.

A sudden pressure in his chest, a choking pressure, invaded his consciousness, piercing his reverie. He looked down. The shaft of an arrow protruded rudely from his breast. Numbness gave way to a strong, sharp pain surrounding it.

The faces of the many men he'd ordered killed in this very forest in this very way came to mind. One trusting face in particular flashed before him, a man he'd dispatched personally and with relish.

His trembling fingers grasped the arrow's head, while his other hand held the shaft firmly at the point it exited. He snapped the front of the arrow off, and it fell to the ground.

Then, he was falling. Agony spiked as the impact with the ground thrust the arrow further through him. Blackness enshrouded him in its cold grip.

The riders cantered their horses over to his body.

Rufus was definitely dead.

In silence, the noblemen viewed their fallen king. Nervously, they glanced at one another. The king was dead and with him, the law of the land.

One by one, each rider spurred his horse sharply, racing back to his castle in order to secure their lands against potential anarchy or unbridled avarice in the face of the sudden lack of leadership. Prince Henry sped directly to the Treasury to secure funds to support his claim to the throne.

The body of King William Rufus lay where it fell, in the dust, until later that day when a poor charcoal-burner by the name of Purkis finally hoisted the stiffening form onto his cart to take to Winchester Cathedral for a proper burial.

August 3rd 1100, Essex, England

The boy's house was a smallish three room cottage with a thatched roof. A main room took up most of the center of the dwelling, with two smaller bedrooms on each side, one for the parents and one for the children. Robyn was a middle child of five. He had two older brothers who were 16 and 14 and two younger sisters, 8 and 5.

Robert Smith, Robyn's father, was of medium build. He was not as burly as Mark would have expected of a blacksmith, yet a certain sinewy strength could been seen in the slender, taught muscles of his forearms, a strength born of many years of hard work.

Robert had been wary of these strangers accompanying his son until Robyn finished recounting to his father all that had transpired. Once the boy was done with his tale, Robert flung his arms wide and engulfed each of them in a massive bear hug, tears welling his eyes. They'd saved his son. That was all he needed to know.

Elisa Smith, Robyn's mother, was quite a petite woman. Her eyes were aqua blue which reflected a gentleness of soul, an uncommon deep compassion, and a steeliness of spirit which appeared to surpass even that of her strong husband. She did not hug them, but was equally, if not more, grateful for having her precious baby home again unharmed. She immediately set about preparing them a veritable feast of a breakfast.

Country ham, eggs, cubed potatoes, and buttered bread rolls. It seemed the food would never end and Mark knew this poor family was using a significant amount of its resources to feed them. There was something about eating breakfast amid the aroma of a wood fire that made it even more enjoyable.

Robert broke down in tears once during the meal, but hurriedly regained his composure. He had to be strong for his family. Almost losing his son had been an unexpected turn. No land was worth that. Mark knew that even better than this man.

"What will you do next, sir?" Mark asked.

"We shall submit, I suppose." Smith's spirit was broken. "Ne'er expected Lord Geoff to do something like this. Thought he would honor the law, I did. Should have known better. He's a harsh one, to be sure."

Slowly pivoting a wooden cup on the table with one finger, Mark pondered the situation.

"Why does Lord Geoff want your land so badly, Robert?"

"Greed. He's done the same to others. Last year, he threatened three freemen to the east of here. They protested, but in the end they were too fearful. Signed their lands over to him. Now they're serfs like everyone else. I should have done the same."

"Robyn told me you became a freedman several years ago."

"Yes, an uncle of mine passed, left me a good inheritance. He was a knight, had no heirs. Once his debts were paid, I'd enough left to purchase my freedom."

"Who did you purchase it from?"

"From Lord Geoff."

"Lord Geoff? The same Lord Geoff?"

"Yes, I paid him in front of several witnesses and the Sheriff, but the Sheriff's in his pocket, of course."

"I see."

Mark did see and he was getting steamed. Turning, he translated the conversation for his friends. Without hesitation, Ty gave Mark the thumbs up. Abbie looked angry too, but a touch of admiration for Mark's willingness to step in shone in her face. Hardy was more reluctant, but seeing Abbie's clear approval, he nodded. Mark slammed the wooden cup on the table, startling the family.

"Robert, what if I told you we would help you fight for your freedom?"

A flicker of hope flashed across the man's eyes. Yet, it was only a flicker and passed quickly, extinguished by doubts and emotional defeat.

"What? Would you take on the Lord himself?"

"Don't call him *the lord*, he's not God."

"Lord Geoff then."

"If need be."

"You believe me then?"

"Why shouldn't we?"

"Not many a man will take the word of a peasant over that of a lord."

"The actions of Geoff's men speak louder than any words he could utter."

"He had the ear of the king, you know, and now, he will have the ear of his son. To fight Geoffrey de Mandeville could be seen as treason by the crown itself."

"We have methods of fighting which will be unexpected and swift."

"I do not wish to become a murderer. I'd be branded an outlaw for life, an' my children too."

"We will limit our actions to defending your family and property."

The man thought hard. To fight, refusing to acquiesce to Geoff's will, would be suicide if Mark couldn't deliver. Trusting in their ability to defend him was a difficult thing. He was not only risking his life, but the lives of his wife and children too.

Elisa came to his side. Her husband's head was bowed in concentration. She laid her hand gently on his shoulder and he looked up into her eyes. This was the woman he loved, the woman whose life he'd be risking.

In her eyes, Robert Smith saw an iron sharpness which decided the matter for him. Elisa nodded slightly and he in turn nodded to Mark. "My wife is Scottish," he said — as if that explained everything.

"Lord Geoff will exact a terrible revenge regardless, now that we've killed some of his men," he continued, "We've no choice but to fight or flee, an' I shall not flee."

Elisa's strength had emboldened and buoyed his own.

"Then, we wait for him to make the first move, " Mark

smiled. He loved knowing he was serving the cause of justice. That gave purpose to his life like nothing else.

They didn't exactly wait around though. The rest of the day was spent planning their defense, and they'd brought plenty of equipment for a battle such as this.

Chapter 26

Sir Randolph and his men rode at a fair clip. *What a pleasant afternoon*, he mused to himself. Not cold, nor dreary, as many days were in England, yet still cool enough, probably due to the nice breeze coming out of the south. A few grey clouds did dampen the sky's otherwise vivid blue hues, but they were inconsequential. Birds chirped in earnest, heralding the approaching sunset.

Yes, he thought, *It's the perfect afternoon for a fight.*

He was one of Lord Geoff's most favored knights, a warrior with skills unrivaled in all of eastern England. The only man closer to Lord Geoff than he was Geoff's own right hand man, Clyde of Dorchester. Though Clyde had never been knight-ed, Sir Randolph still feared the man's prowess. The lack of the title 'sir' had not affected in the least the man's confidence, nor his meanness. In fact, it was precisely that cruelty in the man from Dorchester which had delayed his knighthood several times now.

The latest setback for the man had occurred last year. Clyde had been exceptionally close to receiving the ceremony then. Everyone knew Geoffrey was planning to bestow the title upon Dorchester within a matter of weeks. Then, one day, Clyde, out of boredom, had taken a litter of kittens from young Beatrix's favorite cat and punted them into the river for fun. Beatrix, Geof-frey's teenage daughter, had bawled for weeks over it. Clyde's reason: He'd had nothing better to do that day.

A less important man to Geoff's plans would have been executed for the affront. Clyde, however, was too valuable, so he survived, but was still not a 'sir' as Randolph was.

The main reason Clyde was Geoff's right hand man was

because of the man's cunning. Some of the men called him the 'Earl of Dorchester' behind his back, but never to his face.

Today, Clyde led this pack of knights and men-at-arms to the completion of the mission Lord Geoff had given them. A squatter named Robert Smith had openly rebelled against his authority. Geoff had sent three knights to force some sense into the man, but a small pack of bandits had killed them, and Geoff was frothing at the mouth over it. Blood spilt — no, make that blood poured onto the ground in rivers — was all that could acquit the Smith family of their insolence now.

A lone rider appeared on top of the ridge ahead of them. Tugging back on their reins, each man pulled his steed up short, wary of an ambush. The mysterious figure grew in stature as he approached steadily along the road. His mount was a fine specimen. Strangely, he wore no mail, but that he was a warrior, there was no doubt. In his eyes, Randolph saw not the feebleness of a bandit, but the strength of a man of war.

Mark Carpen stopped his horse ten feet in front of the group. He took his time examining each man in turn.

"I am Clyde of Dorchester. How might we be of service?" Clyde asked, false courtesy dripping from his lips.

"I speak on behalf of Robert Smith, freedman," Mark declared.

A few chuckles rippled through the group. "Freedman, he be not. Speak your peace all the same."

"He is a freedman indeed, having made payment for that same freedom to Lord Geoff himself, who now blatantly violates the laws of England."

Clyde sat up straighter in his saddle. "Guard your tongue, man. It may land you in some trouble yet."

Mark ignored the threat. "I am here for no other reason than that of courtesy, to warn you. If you persist in your illegal persecution of this man and his family, we shall cut down every single one of you, save one. That man we'll leave alive to scurry back to Geoff with a message."

The medieval swords for hire hastily scrambled to extract

their blades, assuming they were already surrounded. Frantically, they scanned the brush and hills for some sign of the enemy.

Mark held up a hand to calm their sudden agitation. The fight would not begin here.

"You have been warned." With a kick, Mark whipped his horse around and drove it off the path toward some nearby brush.

Clyde ordered a couple of men to pursue him, but they would find nothing for Mark had already shifted out.

***

Shortly thereafter, the twenty mercenaries arrived at the Smith home riding in single file. They swiftly fanned their ranks out until they'd formed a neat semi-circle about fifty feet away from the front of the house, three archers hanging back from the rest of the group, protected by the forward line. What should have been a simple, yet chaotic raid, was quickly turning into something else entirely.

Mark, Robert, and Ty emerged from the house. Side by side, they confronted the attackers. Clyde of Dorchester spurred his horse a few steps closer to begin the parley. As the steed trotted forward, Mark raised his right hand high in the air, then let it fall. This was a pre-planned signal. Hardy was staked out a few hundred yards away in a copse of trees with a sniper rifle.

One by one, the three bowmen jerked unnaturally in their saddles and then slid off into silent heaps on the muddy soil. The faint reports of a rifle echoed in the background.

Mark liked to try and limit how much modernity they brought back to any historical setting, but not if such limitations would put their lives at risk. Sniper rifles and other such things were sometimes necessary insurance that their plan would succeed, or at least not lend itself to complication. Plus, sometimes it was just fun to know the advantage was all yours.

The rest of the men stirred, twisting in their saddles to see what had happened behind them. Clyde's mount cantered nervously to one side, and he saw that his archers were fallen. Not understanding how, but unwilling to allow the enemy any further success, he snapped his mouth shut, cutting off whatever great words of wisdom he'd been about to preach to the homeowner, and waved another attacker forward. This man bore a flaming torch.

The torchbearer spurred his horse hard and made a mad dash for the dwelling. He meant to fire the whole house, regardless of who was inside, but he hadn't gone ten feet before his body also spasmed.

He slid from his horse, a great new hole in the side of his head testifying as to why. Hardy's telescopic sights seemed to be working just fine.

Next, Mark signaled to Ty.

Suddenly, the scene erupted violently in four separate explosions of dirt. Thick clouds of it spewed high and rained back down in unison on the assaulters.

Mark and his team had strategically planted sticks of C-4 in a number of locations and covered them with a thin layer of soil. Earlier, Ty had shifted forward to see where the men would stop their mounts and returned to bury the explosives exactly where the mercenaries would be.

Horses screamed and men wailed. Mark hated it for the horses. Innocent creatures shouldn't have to suffer. Yet, there was no other easy way to insure they kept the advantage against such numbers.

The taught twang of a bowstring began its song to Mark's left. Abbie was posted in a window of the home, poaching any men who seemed to be recovering from the blasts. The explosions themselves had immediately killed around seven or eight of them. Abbie took out another five with her bow by the time Mark and Ty, who had both armed themselves with broadswords, reached those struggling to their feet.

Mark had never fought with a sword before. It was a new sensation, but one he thought he could take a liking to. Three men had survived the blasts, the sniping, and Abbie's assault. Clyde of Dorchester, the leader of the pack, had perished almost instantly in the explosions.

Two men-at-arms were close to Mark and Ty, and they dispatched them both quickly.

The remaining man was uncommonly tall, strong, and confident as well. Confident in spite of the shocking manner in which his comrades had just been cut down.

Mark did not hesitate. He swept into the man aggressively, feigning with his sword and then popping the hilt of it into the man's chest, pushing with it forcefully. He'd snuck his right foot behind the big man's ankle before doing this, so the man fell hard onto his back. He was still stunned from the explosions, so it was easy for Mark to kick the sword out of his hand.

Mark brought the point of his blade to bear on the throat of the prostrate man, threatening to end his life with a flick.

"What is your name?" Mark growled.

"Randolph. Sir Randolph DeCleary," the man choked out.

"You are a knight?"

"Yes."

"In the employ of Lord Geoff?"

"Yes."

Mark spat on the ground beside the knight's head. "Tell your *lord* that he shall leave Robert Smith and his family alone from this day forward, and he shall make a public declaration of his status as a freedman, or I will visit my wrath on him personally. There won't be any warning next time."

Mark whipped his sword from the man's neck and sheathed it, a dot of blood marking the skin where it had touched. Ty and Robert Smith stripped Randolph of his mail and smaller weapons. He would ride back to his master humiliated.

"Oh," Mark turned back momentarily, "Tell him he's got two days to make the declaration. No more."

Randolph DeCleary gulped hard, struggling to his feet. His humiliation in being stripped of armor and weaponry was the least of the worries on his mind at the moment.

Chapter 27

"How many men did you say there were, *soldier?* "

Lord Geoff, Earl of Essex, was livid. Angry shades of purple pulsed through his face and neck as he paced the Great Hall.

"You...uh...had to be there, sir. It is hard to explain," Randolph pled.

"I bet it *is* hard to explain. Explaining how three men and a *woman* overcame twenty trained soldiers in a matter of seconds must be very difficult!"

"It's not that...they had..." Randolph stammered.

"Oh, yes! I forgot. They had magic! Their leader just waved his hand and men and horses fell over dead or flew into the air as if hit by a catapult."

Randolph realized he would be wiser to hold his tongue, so he did.

"I cannot believe this incompetence. Do you *hear* me? I cannot believe it!" Spittle sprayed from the noble's mouth.

Randolph nodded.

"Get me fifty men and do it now! We're going to show Smith and his bandit friends a thing or two, and we're going to do it tonight."

"Uh..."

"Do you object?" Geoff snarled.

"No, sir. It's not that. I don't mean to be disagreeable, sir, but I don't think I can get fifty men together on such short notice."

"Fine. Get a hundred for tomorrow night."

"Yes, sir. What about their leader's warning?"

Though Randolph deCleary was a head taller than the earl, Lord Geoff was practiced in the art of intimidation. He wrapped his fingers around Randolph's throat and squeezed hard.

Through gritted teeth, he sneered, "You will get me those men and we will wipe this puny man from the province."

All Randolph could do was nod.

August 4th 1100, Essex, England

Randolph DeCleary had been knighted by King William himself and he was a man whose pride was accustomed to being nurtured, not pricked. Between this bandit and Lord Geoff, his ego had suffered two vicious blows now, and no mere prick either time.

He rode, chest puffed forward, leading his men toward the darkened forest. He could not, would not, allow such humiliation to happen again. He could not reasonably resist or insult the earl, so naturally his wrath was directed forcefully at the man who'd held him on the ground with a sword tip biting into his Adam's apple. The next time they met, Randolph would not be recovering from some magic explosion. He would not be cowed by the bandit again.

More than a hundred and twenty men followed him. A significant portion of these were archers. More than thirty bore well-oiled torches so they could fire the house with impunity, and another forty were well-trained men-at-arms. Those were all mounted. The rest were helpless serfs who had no choice but to serve when their lord called.

They arrived at the Smith property. He burned with desire to exact revenge and see that house destroyed. Still, the prowess of the bandits had to be respected. They *had* killed nineteen armed men in mere moments.

Recognizing this undeniable but regrettable truth, Randolph halted his men a safe distance from the residence before approaching. He sent a group of fifteen serfs toward the miserable hut, flaming torches in hand. The serfs were expendable. With luck, they would trigger any defenses that had been prepared.

Sure enough, the serfs were still two hundred feet away when the ground exploded in front of them. None were killed, for the explosion went off prematurely, but several horses were terrified and turned tail in the opposite direction, ignoring the panicked instructions of their riders and even bucking a few out of their saddles. The torch-bearing serfs mimicked the horses out of sheer fear until Randolph froze their flight with a few forceful commands.

It was clear to Randolph defenses had been laid in expectation of this calvary squad, but the extent of those defenses was still unknown. He didn't believe those explosions were magic, but they were some kind of new weapon he'd not encountered before, which meant it might as well be magic. Did the blast go off prematurely, or was it a kind of trap to lure them closer?

As he mentally debated the possibilities, a cry went up to his right. Four unknown riders were racing for the cover of the forest about two hundred yards away. The sun had almost dipped below the horizon, so they had been masked by the shadows. The riders were whipping and spurring their mounts madly in an attempt to escape to the safety of the trees.

"Ready!" He called to his archers.

Then, he had second thoughts and stayed their barrage with a motion of his hand. The dark riders were already out of range.

Randolph was nothing if not a decisive leader. Following sheer instinct, he instantly chose their course of action, barking different commands to his various groups. The villains he wanted were fleeing for protection among the trees. Though the house remained an unknown risk, it would still be there when they returned.

Dividing his men into three columns of forty, they rushed the forest. One column would enter the woods to the left of where they'd seen the bandits, and a second to the right. He would lead a center column. Then, they would squeeze the bandits into their dragnet.

Chapter 28

*"That's something to be proud of
That's a life you can hang your hat on"*

~ Montgomery Gentry

Hardy pulled up on his reins and walked his horse back until he was even with Mark. Ty and Abbie also slowed their mounts and joined the huddle. Mark began issuing instructions.

"Abbie, you and I will run diagonally to the left from here at full speed. Hardy, Ty, you guys do the same, but to the right. Get outside their little searching grid. Then, dismount, shift, and find a spot behind them. We'll shift back in and start picking them off. Leave the serfs alone, they're here against their will. The rest are fair game."

They all nodded.

"Remember — make sure your sixth shift is made when you *leave* this time. You don't want your watch shutting down in the middle of battle. The rest of us would have to come rescue you."

Ty was fiddling with the settings on the face of his shifter. "When's our anchor time, Mark?"

"Good question." They'd be bouncing back and forth between this evening and some other time. They couldn't choose their own modern time because the shifters would shut down for at least twenty minutes whenever they crossed that many years.

"Everyone set your secondary time to exactly fifty years in the future from tonight. Abbie, stay close to me. Ready? Go!" He swatted Abbie's horse in the rear, spurred his own, and they were off like rockets.

They leaned forward as low in their saddles as they could, yet some of the lowest branches still threatened to sweep them from their saddles in a distinctly unglorified manner. Fortunately, the horses were more than capable of choosing the easiest and most clear path with little guidance.

The growing darkness shrouded them, augmenting the distress and nervousness their enemies felt. Lord Geoff's men had heard rumors of the mysterious bandits and their apparent superhuman abilities.

The sheer numbers of their band would give the enemy some comfort, but that comfort would be easily shattered once further attacks encrypted by darkness and the shifters began. Twelfth century soldiers would only be able to ascribe such things to the realm of magic.

A column of men crossed their path to the right. Mark slipped forward toward their line, while Abbie hung back. Her bow would prove to be an effective tool in combination with the shifter.

She waited until Mark made his move and was able to sling four arrows at the troop before she and Mark shifted out. Her arrows took out at least three archers and wounded a fourth. Mark snuck up on a man-at-arms from behind, dispatched him, and then wounded another before turning back. Staying in the same place for too long would be suicide against these numbers.

He raced back toward Abbie and was still in motion and already pushing the shift button when he grabbed her wrist.

Now, in the future, they could safely reposition themselves in peace. *The U.S. government would kill to get their hands on these devices,* Mark mused.

After shifting back into the battle, they were behind the mass of soldiers again. Mark smiled. This was just too easy.

He slipped up behind a couple of stragglers, ripped a man-at-arms from his horse and took him out. He drew his broadsword and sent another rider to meet his Maker. Hearing the ruckus, a third horseman wheeled his steed around to bear on Mark. He ducked under the man's hurried attempt to lop off his head and landed a blow of his own to the man's stomach. His sword accidentally turned in his hand, however, so instead of a cutting blow, it only knocked the air out of the guy. Thankfully, it had still been enough to knock the man from his mount.

Abbie loosed three more bolts, but this time she only wounded her targets. It wasn't ideal, but a wound would serve their purpose as much as a kill. Their goal was intimidation, not decimation. Mark ran to Abbie and took her wrist in his hand, interrupting the loading of a fourth arrow.

The remaining thirty men that made up the column on this side were now in a state of confused, undisciplined chaos.

They shifted out again.

The sharp clangs of metal on metal as blades struck armor, the thundering hooves, the bellows of bewildered warriors, and the heavy grunts of those same men as they fell were now replaced by the whisper of a quiet nocturnal breeze and the rhythmic chirping of cicadas under the stars. Other than that, the forest didn't seem much different fifty years in the future.

The next shift into the battle didn't go quite as well. Abbie was fine, but Mark's position would have landed him right in the middle of a horse and rider. His shifter, of course, automatically adjusted to compensate for this, and translated him to the right, but this forcibly ripped his grip from Abbie's arm. The secondary and much worse consequence of this misfortune was that he ended up directly behind another horse. That beast immediately panicked, having sensed a sudden, unexpected presence next to its back legs. It kicked out at the perceived threat.

Mark took a full hoof to the stomach and was momentarily crippled. He collapsed to the dirt, gasping for breath.

Abbie saw what happened and rushed to his side, neatly avoiding the frightened dances of both animals and the half-hearted attempt of one of their riders to grab at her. She threw herself on top of Mark and pushed his shift button for him.

For the time being, they'd reached their shift limit. His watch wouldn't be operative again for a full 24 hours. Whether it was all the shifting, the horse kick to the stomach, or a combination of the two, he wasn't sure, but Mark fell violently ill and vomited for several minutes straight.

Abbie looked on with mixed amusement and pity, but only for a moment before nausea got the best of her too and she had to remove herself to the privacy of a copse of trees.

Mark took longer than her to recover, but once they could both walk again, they walked east to meet Ty and Hardy. The four met at the halfway point.

"You've looked better, Mark," Ty commented.

Abbie couldn't keep a knowing smile from peeking through.

"What happened?" Hardy grinned that malicious little grin of his.

"Got kicked by a horse," Mark grunted.

Ty and Hardy exploded with laughter, and Abbie couldn't help but join in. Mark started to get annoyed, but the humor of the moment got to him too. He laughed for about a second before the pain in his stomach doubled him over. His obvious discomfort only made the others laugh even harder.

They set about making camp for the night. Mark and Ty gathered kindling and firewood. Soon, they had a decently-sized blaze going. Hardy scouted the perimeter just to be sure no unsuspecting countrymen or travelers would surprise them. Abbie took charge of preparing dinner, and the aromas that flooded the air tantalized with promised culinary delights. She was either a really good cook, or they were just really hungry.

They ate, bantering lightly for the better part of hour. As the evening cooled, the atmosphere took on a more mellow tone. Mark reclined, allowing his stomach room to digest the feast.

After a time of wordlessly staring into the fire, Ty spoke. "So, what exactly are we doing here, Mark?"

"We're getting justice." He tossed a stick into the flames.

"How far do you want to take it?" Hardy interjected. "I mean...we can't defend the guy against the whole of England."

"Lord Geoff will get the message soon enough. He'll give in."

"It just seems like there's a lot of people dying so Smith can keep his land," Ty replied.

"I'm surprised, guys — surprised at both of you. What's the matter? Losing your nerve? This guy's a merciless dictator who's willing to kill children to get what he wants. We can't stand by and let a guy like that have his way with those fated to be at his mercy."

"Whoa, buddy. Calm down. Don't get us wrong. I can't speak for Ty, but I know you're right. Just wondering out loud is all."

"Yeah. Fighting's in our blood. I can't stand these unaccountable oppressors any more than you. I just thought there might be an easier way."

"And what would that be?"

"Don't know."

Abbie had held her silence throughout the discussion, but now she interrupted, for she could stand no more.

"I pray, gentlemen, that fighting would not be in your blood, nor dear to your heart! I am not so naive as to believe that killing is not sometimes required. Injustice *must* be met with force at times, or the world would certainly perish, but one should never relish nor enjoy the acts he must perform to redeem those injustices. The taking of life...any life...should be done faithfully, yet always with trepidation and sorrow, not glee."

Mark flushed at the rebuke — which had not been so gentle.

A moment later, Abbie stood abruptly and stormed away, her figure disappearing into the blackness between the trees. After watching her go, Mark rose and followed.

He found her underneath an old oak, staring up at the stars. The hood of her cloak had fallen back, revealing her auburn tresses in the pale moon's light. The curved, black outline of the top of her bow was visible above her shoulder. She looked like some kind of elfin, female Robin Hood.

"Your words were well deserved," he admitted, repentant.

His eyes caressed her cheek, but his hands remained at his

side.

"They were too harsh, I fear. I am sorry."

"They weren't too harsh. You hit the nail on the head. It's easy to forget the men on the other side have families too. It shouldn't be fun. You're right."

Abbie gazed up at the bright moon. Her smooth skin almost gleamed blue under its light. Mark caught sight of a large gash in the tree behind her head. It appeared to be an old wound, for it was well swollen over with new bark.

A tear rolled down her cheek.

What was he doing? Why was he was letting himself fall in love with this woman? His mind screamed to be careful, recalling well his latest romantic failures, but his heart wasn't listening. His heart was foolish, too easily forgetting former wounds at the wrong times.

"Mark," she whispered, "I held vigil over my village for years. I had to kill many Wampanoag to protect my people. I know what war is. I've done it. I've lived it. I'm not some pacifist, I'm just tired of killing."

Mark nodded.

"Can we just wound them tomorrow?" She asked.

"You were already doing that earlier tonight, weren't you?"

"Yes." She looked him in the eyes.

"I'll tell Ty and Hardy. They'll go along. We're just trying to make Geoff's men feel vulnerable for once anyway."

A smile lit her face like a candle. For the first time, her eyes seemed to hold true warmth for him, and it melted him. Instinct pushed him to kiss her, but he held himself back. She would not be open to such things from him; her culture was much more conservative than his.

"Abbie, you believe in God and all that...I was wondering...I mean doesn't the Bible say 'Thou shalt not kill'? How do you reconcile your beliefs with your defense of your people?"

"Dah taught me to read the Scripture. It says 'Thou shalt not murder', not 'kill'."

"Murder, kill. What's the difference?"

"To murder is to lie in wait for someone, maliciously wishing to take their life. On the other hand, killing is not always wrong. Sometimes, it is required. Scripture teaches that killing for self-defense or in the case of war is justified. Also, God requires us to take the life of a murderer. He commanded this in Exodus right after He said 'Thou shalt not murder.' Murder is always selfish, but killing may be necessary to protect others."

"I've never heard it explained like that," Mark agreed, "I'll go tell Ty and Hardy about the new plan."

"Thank you, Mark."

He still felt a strong pull to kiss her, but didn't allow himself.

It was a beautiful night. Why ruin a moment of intimacy with a rejection he'd force her to make?

He left her in contemplation under the moon and made his way back to the warmth of the fire.

"Guys, tomorrow we're only going to wound, aim for extremities. No kills if you can help it."

Hardy cocked an eyebrow, surprised, yet knowing.

"Are you kidding me?" Ty demanded, kicking at a fallen log they'd used for a bench. "Unbelievable! *Man*...here we go again! Hardy, stay away from *this* girl, all right? Last thing we need is a repeat of Laura."

Mark blushed. "It's not like that."

"Yeah it is. So, what are we *supposed* to do if we're in a tight spot, just keep nicking 'em?"

"Don't be ridiculous. If you're in danger, all bets are off."

"At least we've got that then," he spat sarcastically.

"Relax, Ty," Hardy said. "That's fine, Mark. We'll do it."

Abbie returned to the fire, and they told stories for another hour or so before turning in.

Ty had cooled off by then. Hotheadedness was not one of his normal traits, but the soldier in him bucked hard when an order contradicted some of his most basic training. *You don't wound an enemy, you aim to kill.* Anything less could come back to bite you — and hard. Mark and Hardy understood this. In fact, they felt it too, which is why they didn't blame him.

He was also angry because he didn't want another woman splitting up their team like Laura had.

The next day was spent lying around the campsite, trying to occupy themselves with mindless tasks to pass the time until evening. At last, the shifters became operational again.

They decided that, this time, all four of them would stay together and focus on the center column. So far, that group of soldiers had remained unscathed, and since that's where the leader was, that needed to change.

They entered the scene in front of the enemy's charge, Ty and Hardy on the left of the column, Mark and Abbie on the right. Abbie stayed at a distance from the rushing horses and sent her arrows into the arms and legs of all opportune targets.

The rest of them chose to get much closer, slashing with broadswords at men-at-arms and archers alike, seeking gaps in the mail of any armor. Each was able to wound three or four men before having to shift out and take a new position. They shifted in a second time, repeating the effort with similar moves.

On the third shift into the scene, Mark stayed his hand and simply sunk the tip of his sword into the dark earth, leaning on its hilt.

The enemy was in full retreat. These medieval mercenaries had no taste for a battle with unseen phantoms who could strike without warning from any direction and disappear just as fast. Heck, modern mercenaries would flee from a battle like that.

Suddenly, Mark sensed an unexpected presence behind him, and Abbie shouted his name in warning.

Mark wasted no time trying to turn. Instead, he threw himself into a side roll and popped up in a ready crouch.

A sharp blade slashed into the tree where Mark's head had been, slicing deep into the bark and sticking in its flesh.

Mark recognized the tree. Abbie had been standing in front of it the night before, fifty years in the future. He'd seen an old scar on the tree that night. Now, he knew what blow had made it.

The sword's bearer was the leader of these columns of soldiers, a tall, stately knight. His face was snarled in fury. Long, reddish locks of hair bounced recklessly as he struggled to wrench free his sword. The man was strong, but the sword had gone deep. Still, he had it free in a few seconds.

He wore no armor save the same mail that all the others wore over a brown leather tunic. His weapon was simple in style. When it came to intimidation, however, the power and skills in his arms more than made up for any lack of fancy trappings or symbols carved into its hilt.

Still crouching, Mark raised the tip of his own sword, pointing it at the man's face.

"What is your name?"

"Sir Randolph DeCleary. 'Tis good you know it, seeing he is about to end your miserable life."

"Mark Carpen. Pleased to meet you." He straightened, slowly, to face his enemy on equal footing.

"I've no care to know the name of a thief," DeCleary spat.

"I am no thief."

"Thief, bandit. You fight the Earl's men, which makes you an outlaw. Same thing."

"Seems the thief is the one who would steal a man's life while his back is turned."

Randolph curled his lips in distaste, but his eyes were ferocious as he raised his blade high to attack. "Why don't you flee back into the darkness, you coward?" he snarled.

The knight swung. Mark parried effectively, but the sheer force of the blow sent shudders throughout his arm. This was going to be a hard fight.

Surely, Mark could defeat this man by out-thinking him. He was strong, but that meant he would be slow and methodical. If Mark were swift, he could take him.

His thesis shattered as the man pulled back his weapon and redirected the attack with a speed that seemed to rival lightning, yet the force behind it was no less than the first. Mark was barely able to move his own sword in time to block the blow.

Again and again the knight swung. First at Mark's head, next at his feet. Then, he would lunge for his belly. Mark found himself jumping, ducking, and twisting as much as he parried. Randolph's sword was like quicksilver, darting here and there, hammering tremors wherever it struck. The man's skill was completely unexpected. Mark knew he'd be lucky to get in even one offensive blow and he was tiring far too quickly.

Swords don't look heavy, but now he knew differently. This kind of fighting used muscles he hadn't even known he had.

A brief hole opened in Randolph's defenses, and Mark took a desperate shot for the knight's feet. DeCleary had been expecting this though. In fact, he'd set it up on purpose. Deflecting the attempt with ease, he countered with a vicious swipe of his own at Mark's ankles. Leaping onto one hand, Mark kicked out with both feet at the knight's stomach.

It was the only satisfactory blow Mark had landed and thankfully, it sent DeCleary sailing onto his back.

Mark stood wearily. The fight had taken more out of him than he'd realized. He partially rested his weight on the hilt of his sword once more, as he had been doing right before the fight began. Seeing his companions were just standing there watching the whole thing unfold, he waved them in.

"Hardy, Ty. Little help?"

The fallen knight grunted and jumped to his feet. "Have you no honor, you coward?" he spat.

Mark cocked an eyebrow and stared at him. This man thought about battle in a completely different way than he did. Mark had been trained to win at any cost. This man had been trained to sacrifice his very life if honor demanded it.

"What I find dishonorable," Mark replied sternly, "is a man who fights for evil in the name of honor." Motioning to Ty, he said, "Knock him out, but don't kill him."

Ty feigned an attack and as Randolph turned toward him to face it, Mark advanced. Randolph turned back halfway, ready to defend two fronts simultaneously.

"You are a brave one," Hardy muttered as he slammed a log into the back of Randolph's skull, who collapsed neatly to the earth.

"Tie him up," Mark ordered.

"That *was* a bit cowardly, wasn't it?" Ty asked mischievously.

"I've got no problem admitting the guy was better than me with a sword. We're not here to prove anything. We're here to make sure the Smith family keeps their property and isn't murdered in the process. Just get him trussed up. It's time to meet Lord Geoff."

Chapter 29

August 4th 1100, Colchester, England

Lord Geoffrey de Mandeville was a man used to his luxuries. As the Earl of Essex, though the title was still not officially his, he held rights to one of the most important and most densely populated earldoms in all England. He'd fought alongside William the Conqueror against the Saxons at the Battle of Hastings in 1066 and had been one of his most important supporters. Noblemen like Geoffrey were given lands by William after the conquest of England was done, lands taken from the estates of the vanquished Saxons.

Geoffrey, however, had been closer to the king than most. He'd been given the important lands of Essex just outside London, including the city of Colchester, which was the oldest city in England. King William had also made him Sheriff of London and Middlesex, and Constable of the Tower of London, very important and prosperous positions.

William died during the siege of Mantes in France in 1087. While on his deathbed, he apportioned his estate between his three living sons. That he had not named his oldest son, Robert Curthose, as the new king, and instead bestowed the crown on Robert's brother, William Rufus, was no surprise. Years before, Robert had flown into a rage when his younger brothers, William and Henry, dumped some nasty bedpan water on him from a balcony. He physically scuffled with his brothers over the prank and when his father refused to punish them for it, he mounted an armed insurrection against his father, the Conqueror, in order to steal the crown from him. The rebellion quickly failed.

William disinherited Robert and the young man spent the next decades in exile in Normandy. In addition to this bad blood, the king saw a lot more of his own character and personality in his second son than he did the older. Rufus had always been his favorite, so he made him the new King of England before he died.

Robert had not been completely cut out, however, as his mother had pled with William to not abandon him. In the end, William left his estates in Normandy to Robert, giving him the title of Duke. The youngest son, Henry, had received a large sum of gold with which he was to buy land.

So, William Rufus became the second Norman king of England, and at first, Lord Geoffrey, along with most of the other nobles, was glad. Rufus did think and act a lot more like his father than Robert. Robert was the weakest of the three brothers and nobody wants a weak king.

Still, there was a problem. Rufus was greedy. Greedy to the extreme. He taxed his kingdom like no other king before him had. He employed Robert's former aide, Ranulf Flambard, to find new and creative ways of taxing his nobles and the people. Flambard, unfortunately, turned out to be very good at his job. The taxes Rufus imposed on his kingdom were wide-ranging and heavy.

Rufus purposely left a number of key church offices vacant for long periods of time so he could collect the income for the accompanying properties himself. Rufus cared more about the gold in his pocket than he did people's souls.

The high and burdensome taxes, combined with his ruthlessness, his contempt for English culture and anything not Norman, his perpetual animosity for the church, and rumors about his homosexuality, insured that William Rufus soon became one of the most reviled kings in English history by nobles and commoners alike.

And Lord Geoffrey de Mandeville had an extra reason to be irritated with Rufus. The young king repeatedly placated him with promises of the title of earl, yet he never would make it official. Geoffrey was tired of waiting.

The king treated him like a child, not the noble earl he actually was. Refusing Geoffrey a title he so obviously deserved was a repeated slap in his face, and an unwise way to treat a man as important as he.

There were enough subjects living in Essex that he could raise an army of several thousand within a couple of weeks if needed. Maybe even four or five thousand if pressed hard enough. The king could wage a war without him, but Essex was key to any force he wished to put into the field. The number of serfs available to Geoff for general labor were also numerous.

Geoff also had one of the only stone castles in southern England. Granted, he had to recognize that he partly owed that to the king. Rufus had allowed Gundulf, Bishop of Rochester, to be his architect.

Gundulf had also built the White Tower in London for Rufus' father, William the Conqueror, and was the most reputed builder in the kingdom. Still, Rufus' father was actually the one who commissioned both Colchester Castle and the Tower, but at least Rufus hadn't removed Gundulf from the project once his father was dead.

That Geoff wasn't an earl in any official sense yet did not stop him from using the title. It was only a matter of time. Especially now that Rufus was dead and his younger brother Henry was king. Especially since Lord Geoffrey knew a little more than he should about that wonderful event.

The official story going around was that William Rufus had been killed by *accident* while on a hunting expedition in the New Forest.

It was no accident. It was also no accident that the murder had occurred in the New Forest and on a hunting trip. Robert Curthose's illegitimate son, Richard, had been killed in a different *accident* on a hunting trip in the New Forest, almost exactly one year before in 1099. That accident had also been no accident. Rufus had flown into a spontaneous and momentary fit of rage at his older, exiled brother, and killed his brother's son out of spite. All the gentry of England knew what had happened, but it was said to be an accident. A number of others had perished similarly in the New Forest recently. Geoffrey knew that was the reason for the location and context of Rufus' murder.

Henry, Rufus' younger brother, wanted to be king. He'd garnered the support of enough of the nobles who despised Rufus to execute his plan in safety, but there was still the matter of his older brother Robert. If William Rufus was dead, Robert would want to claim the crown for himself. Fortunately, Robert was still en route back from the Crusade in the Promised Land. Henry knew that if he struck fast, he could assume the throne with little or no opposition.

They blamed it on Walter Tyrell, though of all those in the hunting party that day, Henry, William of Breteuel, Gilbert and Roger de Clare, Walter Tyrell, and Robert Fitzhamon, Tyrell was the only one who was not a member of the conspiracy to remove their regent from office through violence. It was said Tyrell accidentally shot the king in the chest with an arrow when a stag for which he was aiming suddenly crossed their path. The truth was Tyrell was nowhere near the king in the forest that day. It was Tyrell's servant, Raoul, D'Equesnes, who'd fired the fatal shot. Two days later, Tyrell had already fled the country, some said for Normandy.

Geoffrey knew that Henry had orchestrated the whole thing. He'd paid Tyrell's servant, D'Equesnes, a great sum of money for the deed. Most of the noble families in lower England not only knew what really happened, but they were tacitly on board with the plan as well.

Lord Geoffrey de Mandeville's condition for keeping silent was that he be given the title of earl as soon as possible, along with a few other considerations. The other nobles required an immediate lowering of taxes and the imprisonment of Ranulf Flambard, architect of the heinous tax system. Henry would be crowned tomorrow and he'd fulfill that promise shortly after.

As Constable of the Tower of London, Geoffrey was in charge of keeping this new and important political prisoner locked up, which lent him even more prestige in the eyes of the rest of the nobility.

Yes, the future looked bright indeed. He would soon be an earl for real. Finally. Taxes would be lowered. His new and beautiful castle was finally finished. They had a different king, one who was indebted to many for his new position, including Geoffrey himself. It had been a good week so far. With one exception, of course.

Lord Geoffrey kept the enormous fireplaces in his castle constantly blazing with timber brought in by the peasants to keep the chill from his aging bones at night, even in August. Animal skins covered the floors of his private chambers and the great dining hall. Tapestries dressed the stone walls in bright reds, purples, and golds.

His most favored men-at-arms and knights slept along the floor of the dining hall, though he limited the number of those he "favored" in order to inspire greater service. The best portions of food he reserved for himself, his children, and his wife, whenever she was in good standing with him that is. He himself dined on delicacies nightly.

By far, his favorite aspect of being a lord, however, was the power he wielded, the rights he had over those subject to him. Every man in Essex worked the majority of the week for his benefit. He could order men to prepare him a feast, or head off to war, depending on his preference. While he tended to leave the more homely women in the villages alone, no pretty young maiden made it to her wedding night untouched by his hands.

He lay upon his enormous bed, which was draped in finely woven covers, contemplating the days' events. The glow of torchlight illuminated the room darkly with wavering flickers of orange light. Normally, he would have been dreaming about some young vixen he'd spotted on the road, what she'd be like when he got her into his chambers, but tonight he was completely vexed with a matter of a different sort.

It would be wrong to say that he was fearful of these bandits that were attacking and eluding his men. Angry, without a doubt. Also, a bit concerned, but not really fearful. How could three or four bandits take on over a hundred armed soldiers and escape unscathed?

The answer should be: *They can't.*

Yet, they had. Randolph reported during this last attack they'd been assaulted from all sides, which had to mean many more men than just three or four.

Still, Randolph could have been embellishing to protect his inadequacy. Geoffrey missed Clyde of Dorchester. He didn't know Randolph DeCleary like he'd known Clyde. Clyde had been as close as his right hand for years. That was another reason to curse these bandits. They'd killed one of his best men.

Then, there were the reports of magic. He'd spoken with a number of the survivors himself, when Randolph wasn't around of course, and the fear which shone in their eyes was testimony enough they weren't lying about what they'd seen. The invisible arrows that struck men in the head and killed them when no archer was in sight. Mysterious explosions which killed man and beast alike with no apparent cause. *Were* these bandits magicians?

He would not allow a troop of peons to put the fear of God in him. No serf or bandit would force his hand. He was lord of this realm. Essex would stand. He would find out who these men were if it were the last thing he did and then he would crush them. And if he couldn't crush them, he would crush their families. They would pay, one way or the other.

Rage began its drum-like pulse, building and throbbing within his veins. No one got the best of Geoffrey de Mandeville, not even the king. Much less a group of nobodies. *Commoners.*

It occurred to him he could ask King Henry for help, but he was shaking his head before he even finished the thought. When the king called on *him* for help, his stature increased, but to call on the aid of the king because of a few mere bandits would be humiliating. He had to take care of the situation himself.

He was smiling contentedly, considering the many ways he would exact revenge on this band of ruffians, when a crackling sound to his immediate right interrupted his reverie. It resembled the way dry wood pops in a hot fire. This sound was followed by the sudden presence of cold steel pressed against his throat.

The earl froze. One move and his life could be forfeit. If someone dared violate the sanctity of a nobleman's private chambers, they would undoubtedly not hesitate to finish the deal by dispatching him.

Slowly, he twisted his head to the right to view his assailant. With difficulty, he avoided slicing his neck against the pressure of the blade.

A stranger stood by his bed, holding a broadsword against his throat. The man looked the part of a knight, but what knight would do something as bold and as dangerous as this? This particular knight looked very angry.

"Are you Lord Geoff?"

"Qu'est-ce qui se passe?" The Norman language was Geoff's primary language and the one he reverted to in an emergency. Geoff could not comprehend how this man had gotten in, or even who he was.

"Speak English, you old fool. I'll ask *again,*" he pressed the tip further, "Are you Lord Geoff?"

The earl nodded slightly, afraid to move against the blade. The man lifted it away slightly so he could talk.

"I am. Who are you?"

"Mark."

"Sir Mark?"

"Titles." Mark spat contemptuously. "Titles mean nothing. Is it not *I* who holds a sword to your neck, *Lord*?"

"What? You would hold contempt for nobility?"

"You don't have a noble bone in your body, worm."

The earl's face reddened, and he trembled with rage. An insufferable impotence overcame him, though he determined to shake it. He was at this bandit's mercy for the moment, but if given a chance...

"Robert Smith is a freedman. He paid you for his freedom, yet you've attacked his family and would press him back into service as a serf."

"I do not have to answer to the likes of you," Geoff snapped.

"Is it true, or not?"

The earl glared at Mark, doing his best to burn holes through him with nothing more than the power of his hatred.

"We have killed your man, Clyde. At least, that is what I am told his name was. Not to mention numerous soldiers. We decimated that little army you sent last night. I sent DeCleary back to you as a gesture of good will, but we will not be so merciful in the future. Our demand is simple. Rule your lands with justice and leave the Smith family alone."

"You demand? You *dare* demand something of me?"

Pensive, Mark reconsidered. He dropped his sword to his side and stepped back a step. Lord Geoff nimbly leapt to his feet to take full advantage of the opportunity. He was unexpectedly agile for an older man. Mark motioned toward the door with his sword.

"Go ahead. Open the door, call for help."

The earl shook his head. "You'll attack me from behind."

Mark stepped further back. "No, I won't. Go ahead."

The noble hesitated, but then made a mad dash for the door, ready to fling it open. Behind him, Mark shifted out of the bed chamber and reappeared between the door and the earl.

Mark placed a hand on his chest and shoved, sending him flying backward onto the bed. He raised his sword until its tip rested on the man's throat again, just above his Adam's apple.

"As you can see, we have capabilities of which you cannot conceive, and against which you have no weapon. You can send any size army you wish, and we'll make them turn tail every time."

"We?" The earl gulped.

"*We.*"

Mark dropped his sword back to his side and let the man sit up. He wanted the weight of the moment to sink in before he continued. He needed the man's full and undivided attention, and from the looks of it, he had it. Lord Geoff's face was paler than

Macbeth's ghost.

"This is my last warning to you. Leave the Smith family alone and rule your lands justly or I will return and kill you. Of that, you have my promise. Will you acquiesce?"

The man had just...*appeared*...right in front of him. He'd jumped across the room *without moving*. And the strange crackling sound that accompanied his movements — Randolph had been telling the truth. *These men were magicians.*

"You are...a wizard. How much? I would buy this talent you have. Teach it to me. I can pay you in gold."

Mark sent his foot into his groin as hard as he could and then slammed the hilt of his sword down on his shoulder. The earl's clavicle audibly snapped. Geoff howled in pain.

Mark ordered him to shut up, at which point, the wretch switched to a muffled whimpering.

"I am not kidding, *Sir Geoff.* The next time we meet won't be as pleasant. Do we understand each other?"

Geoff feebly nodded. Anything to get rid of the stranger.

Mark turned and called over his shoulder as he walked away, "Don't think the coast is clear just because you don't hear from us. We're always watching, be it a year, or twenty years from now."

Mark moved his finger toward his shifter, but then paused, stopping short of pushing the button.

"Know what?" he said, looking back up. "I changed my mind. You're coming with me."

***

Mark never thought the sight of a half naked man would make him happy, but to see Lord Geoff shivering and miserable in the moonlight brought a smile to his face for the humiliation Mark knew he was about to endure.

Mark forced the earl to accompany him on a shift to the far side of a nearby village in the middle of the night. He'd torn the bottom half of his robes completely off and thrown them into a darkened copse of trees nearby, leaving the man exposed to the cold night air.

"Home is that way." Mark pointed to the path leading right through the center of the village.

"You can't be serious."

"Oh, but I am."

"But why? Why would you...?" John's eyes flitted back and forth, searching the darker ways which skirted the village.

"Why would I purposefully embarrass you this way?"

"Yes."

"It'll be good for you. Heck, it'll do us all a good turn to see you put in your place for just a little while. Don't bother trying to go around the village. I'll just bring you back here and make you do it again."

The man gulped. His life, he could risk, but his pride? Losing that was the only thing that truly scared him.

Smacking his backside with a stinging slap from the flat of his sword, Mark let out a whoop that would be sure to stir most of the sleeping residents of this small community. The serfs that Lord Geoff drove so mercilessly were about to get a little levity at their master's expense.

Geoff yelped from the pain and jerked as he began a desperate scramble to get through the village before anyone could see him.

He didn't make it. Lanterns were lit and their glows spilled onto the street as puzzled denizens opened their doors one by one to see what was going on.

As they came to recognize the crazed, midnight rooster rushing down their street as fast as his naked feet would carry him, their initial stunned silence was broken by a female's cackle, and that quickly erupted into vociferous whistles and catcalls from all.

Mark looked on with true satisfaction. The Earl of Essex would have trouble garnering sufficient respect for a while.

Chapter 30

August 25ʰ 1100, Essex, England

The summer evening was pleasantly cool. They enjoyed the tremendous feast Mrs. Smith had prepared in gratitude for all they'd done. Now, sitting behind the Smith home around a warm cooking fire, they relaxed with the family. One couldn't help but be taken by the clarity and beauty of the stars twinkling in the dark expanse overhead as they chatted and cut up. The table at which they'd dined looked like a rustic picnic table. Around the fire, they sat upon horizontal logs and crude wooden stools. If it weren't for the clothing, the language, and a few other details, it could have been a scene from a modern camping trip.

Mark hadn't thought it possible, but with this meal, Elisa Smith had outdone even herself. The spread she'd laid out for them tonight had them licking their chops even more than the first breakfast she'd prepared. He had half a mind to return to this time more often just for the cooking.

Three weeks had passed since Mark's little visit with Lord Geoff, and the earl hadn't ventured outside his castle since that night. A lot of the villagers had witnessed the man in his full embarrassment, streaking naked at a mad dash through their town. Chuckles and mockery were still circulating throughout Essex. It would be a while before Geoffrey de Mandeville lived down the jokes and rumors.

Tonight, they celebrated, for it appeared Mark's ploy had worked. Perhaps Lord Geoff would leave them alone after all.

Robert Smith approached bearing two large wooden cups of mead. He gave Mark one, kept the other for himself, and sat down on the log next to him. Hardy, Ty, and Abbie had all been similarly supplied. Hardy and Ty were clearly enjoying their drinks. Abbie only sipped at hers, but she was having as good a time as anyone.

The taste of the mead was surprising. Mark had expected a beer-like ale, yet this golden drink tasted more like a sweet wine. Robert explained it was made from honey.

"I cannot express our gratitude for all you've done, Mark."

"No need." Mark waved dismissively.

"Of course there is! You've all put your lives on the line for my family. You fought Lord Geoff, and for the life of me, I've no idea how, but you won. He's left us alone for nigh three weeks now."

"We'll see if it lasts."

"We pray an' hope it will. Regardless, always we shall be grateful. I don't know what I did to merit such favor from the good Lord that He sent you to us, but I do praise Him for it."

Mark blushed, thankful the darkness hid the heat rising in his cheeks. He was uncomfortable receiving such thanks and probably always would be. He didn't do what he did to get thanked. There was just an overwhelming sense of duty built into his very nature which would not let him act to the contrary. He couldn't stand to see injustice go unchallenged. Hardy and Ty were cut from the same cloth, even if they feigned protest at times. He believed Abbie was too. Hadn't she secretly defended her village against the Wampanoag? Still, Mark hadn't completely figured her out yet.

One of the teenage Smith boys took up a musical instrument that looked like a pear-shaped fiddle. The boy launched into some lively tunes and in spite of the fact it only had three strings, it sounded pretty good. Mark didn't recognize any of the songs, but the cheerfulness infused in their notes was infectious.

Elisa cut in. "Darling, do you mind if I ask Sir Mark to dance?" She asked her husband.

"Uh...I'm no knight, Elisa," Mark corrected.

Robert shook his head, grinning. Grabbing Mark's hand, Elisa hefted him up. The strength imbued in her petite arms surprised him. She placed his hand on her waist, resting her own on his shoulder, and they began a lively dance, circling and bouncing to the rhythm of the fiddle. The rest of the family cheered and clapped as they twirled.

Soon, Hardy and Ty were up and dancing round and round with the two smaller Smith girls. Everyone laughed at the sight of these huge men trying to not overstep the small gait of the little ones.

After a time, Elisa excused herself and switched to dance with Hardy and then Ty. Mark went to Abbie. He extended his hand to her.

"Care to dance?"

She blushed, but rose, taking his hand with no comment.

They began a dance that moved at a much slower pace than that of the others, moving not in time to the music, but like slow ripples on a calm body of water. Abbie turned her gaze to Mark, letting him search her eyes as she searched his.

He was stupid for letting himself be so obvious. Why did he have such little control over his heart? He fell head over heels so easily for these women that came into his life. Too easily. He'd fallen for Abbie the first time he'd seen her in that dream.

Tonight, she was as beautiful as ever. Her fair skin was the color of light cream, cool like porcelain. She was pure, and he loved her spirit. He loved the way she was comfortable with a weapon, yet would not permit war to strip her of tenderness. She didn't let the horrors of battle harden her heart with bitter memories. In his experience, it was rare person who could do that.

Questions of what she was thinking sped through his own

thoughts. In her eyes glowed an affection, a warmth. For just a moment, that warmth shone for him, and he was glad. But then it was gone, as if an invisible door had swung shut.

Attempting to regain the moment, he reached up to stroke a lock of hair from her forehead and tucked it behind her ear. She started ever so slightly at his touch, not from excitement, but from the unexpectedness of it.

They danced a little longer, even for a few moments after the music had stopped, for they hadn't been keeping time to it anyway. She thanked him for the dance and politely excused herself, entering the house to sleep.

Mark watched her go, ignorant of the others watching him. His heart ached. Something within was unsatisfied.

It was loneliness unabated.

***

Their plan hadn't worked after all.

Mark shifted forward a couple of years to verify Lord Geoff was continuing to cower in his castle, but he wasn't.

The earl had bidden his time for the first year or so and, during that time, had left the Smiths alone. Mark had apparently instilled enough of the fear of God in the noble to last that long, but when Geoff hadn't seen or heard anything from Mark and friends for a while, he'd grown bold again.

One year later, in the black of night, Geoffrey sent a group of armed soldiers to the Smith home. They torched it while the Smiths slept and blocked the doorways so none could escape. Their friends, Robert, Elisa, Robyn, and all the other Smith children, had been burned alive.

The earl hadn't waited even a year to exact his revenge on the villagers who'd mocked his nakedness. Within a month after Mark's departure, the man had begun exacting his price from all those he connected with any rumor or gossip about him. His soldiers rounded up hundreds of women from families indiscriminately and brought them to his castle where he systematically violated them over a series of weeks. Men, he killed in front of their families. He cut out the tongues of several women and one man. He even hanged a twelve-year old boy, just like he'd almost done to Robyn that first day in the barn.

Fury and guilt raged in Mark at the news. Fleetingly, the promise he'd made to Abbie about avoiding killing when possible ran through his mind, but just as quickly he pushed it out. She would not expect him to keep that promise, not under these circumstances. Heck, she'd want justice as badly as he did.

Warning the earl a second time wouldn't last. Lord Geoff was an evil man and he needed to go. Had he hesitated because the man was a "noble"? They certainly hadn't hesitated with the knights and other soldiers they'd killed. The difference was they'd engaged those men in a battle begun by them, not by Mark. Over the years, the others Mark took out had been murderers and rapists who were about to commit their crimes.

This would be the first time Mark "assassinated" some-body for bloodstains which had not yet appeared on his hands. What was the difference, really? What was the difference if Mark killed a murderer who would kill one minute later, versus one who did so a month later? The only difference was time, and Mark knew what a fleeting illusion time could be.

It still felt like playing God in some respects though.

Yet, Mark could not stand by and let this man victimize anyone else. He just prayed this would not turn out to be one of those events fate would prohibit him from undoing. Ty offered his help, but this was something Mark wanted to do by himself.

September 2nd 1100, Colchester Castle, England

It was night. The nobleman's chambers appeared just as they had the first night Mark had threatened him. Darkened, but with a few candles lighting the room. The earl lay in bed, snoring peacefully. Tomorrow morning, the first act of revenge would be taken against the villagers by this sleeping monster.

Mark took a few steps toward the figure. Suddenly, there

was movement behind and on both sides of him. Three men-at-arms had been standing vigil, hiding behind tapestries. It was a trap for an intruder, an intruder like Mark. Each man held a broadsword pointed in the direction of his neck. One of the men called out, and they slowly advanced.

Lord Geoff sat up swiftly. He'd been awakened by the noise.

"Ha! You thought you would surprise me, thief! Tis *I* who have you." The earl grinned from ear to ear. He looked ready to lick his chops, like a cat ogling a mouse whose tail is caught in its paw.

Nonchalantly, Mark pulled a silenced pistol from a hidden holster. Taking his time, he aimed and fired at the soldiers in turn, striking each between the eyes. A soft *psst* was the only sound between the thuds of their falling bodies on the stone floor.

Geoff stared wide-eyed at the sudden death of what must have been some of his top soldiers, his face whiter than ash. Fear had truly entered him this time, and a bit of drool showed at the corner of his mouth.

He stammered, "Uh...I...uh...why? This is not right...I've left them alone. I have! I have not touched those people!"

"But you will."

"No. No, I won't. I swear it!"

"Yes, you will. Tomorrow, you will begin torturing and killing the villagers for laughing at you. A year from now, you'll have the Smiths burned alive in their home."

If the man's face could get any paler, it did as the rest of the blood drained from it.

"*How*...you can't know that!"

"Oh, but I do. I told you, we know everything."

"But, it's not true. I haven't done it. I won't do it. I promise!"

"You are an evil man, and there is only one thing to do with a man like you." Mark raised his pistol.

The earl screamed like a woman and thrust his arms in front of his face. Mark remembered Abbie. He remembered her words, her spirit. His flesh wanted to take pleasure in removing this garbage from the world, but his heart wanted to obey the spirit of what Abbie had asked. When he pulled the trigger, he felt true sorrow for the act, as necessary as it was. He felt sorrow that the nobleman had brought this on himself, and that he'd put Mark in this position, but there was no choice. Mark felt sorrow, but not remorse...and certainly not guilt.

The door burst open and sudden light outlined the large form of Randolph DeCleary, Geoff's newly appointed chief knight. He'd heard the scream and come running.

The knight surveyed the scene in the candle-lit bedroom. He saw his three fallen comrades and the bloody form of his master lying crumpled on the bed. Instantly, he charged Mark, sword drawn.

But Mark was tired of killing.

So, he just shifted out.

Chapter 31

He was back at the Smith cottage once more. Abbie, Hardy, and Ty were with him, as well as the entire Smith family. Instead of warmth and joy filling the cottage as before, stress and fear now permeated the cold air of the early winter morning.

Cloth bundles and leather saddlebags lay scattered around the feet of the former serfs. They were moving out. Their problems had not ended with the slaying of Lord Geoff. The earl's son, William was now ruling Essex in his father's place. William laid the blame for his father's murder directly at the feet of the blacksmith, his family and the mysterious bandits after hearing Randolph DeCleary's report. The new, young earl hesitated to strike, however.

He was afraid to attack without more support after what had happened to his father. Many of the townspeople were spooked, having heard reports of magic men who could vanish at will. Lord William had appealed to King Henry himself for aid, and it was probable the king would give it, considering one of his noblemen had been murdered in his bedroom.

The dreary morning reflected all their spirits.

"I'm sorry to have brought this on you, Robert," Mark said wistfully.

Smith shook his head. "You saved my son's life and put yourselves at great risk to help us. Were it not for you, we'd all be dead or slaves. There was no other way this could turn out."

"We can *still* fight. Your family doesn't have to go," Mark offered.

"Would you even fight the king?"

"If need be."

"He'll bring thousands of men, Mark."

Mark pressed his lips together, saying nothing.

"It's enough killing, Mark. Why should any more die? Just so we can keep this land? If these men want the land so badly, let them have it, I say."

"It's not about the land any more."

"I know, I know, but if we can just disappear somehow, change our names, we'll be okay."

"What will you do? Where will you go?" Mark was genuinely concerned for this family. He felt responsible, as if their troubles were somehow his fault, though he knew they weren't. Lord Geoff would have murdered the man's children one by one until he'd enslaved the rest. At least, Mark had ensured the children were still alive for the time being. And he'd removed a tyrant. Perhaps his son would at least be a bit more timid.

Robert sighed and looked out the window.

"We shall become *hoode*. We'll go where no one knows us. We'll change our names. If we're careful, we should be safe."

That was a word Mark hadn't heard before. "I'm sorry, I don't know that word. What does *hoode* mean?"

Robert looked to the ground, searching for synonyms. "Uh...criminal...someone who is outside the law."

"You're going to be *outlaws*? That's no life for your family."

"There are communities of *hoode* in some of the forests. We shall live with them. It will not be too bad a life. They aren't all bad, many are just fugitives like us. We shall be free again. I might even pick up some smith work from the other *hoode*."

"You'll always be looking over your shoulder."

"Life does not always give us a choice."

The man's mind was made up. Mark didn't blame him, it was the only decision left to him in a feudal system like this. Mark was just frustrated by his own impotence to fix the problem.

Abbie hoisted a couple of the bundles onto her shoulder. Hardy and Ty followed suit, grabbing saddle packs to help Robert load them onto his mule.

Once the family was loaded and ready to go, everyone said their tearful goodbyes. Elisa was a good woman, a strong woman. She was taking her exile in stride. Robert was a lucky man.

Last of all, Mark said goodbye to young Robyn. He took comfort in knowing that, if nothing else, they'd saved this young man's life.

"Goodbye, Robyn Smith. It was a pleasure knowing you." Mark said.

His father interrupted, "We are Smith no more, my friend. *Hoode*. His name is now Robyn *Hoode*," he said, winking conspiratorially. "We must begin getting used to our new names."

The full import of who young Robyn must be hit Mark like a slap in the face.

Robyn Hoode.

***

October 4th 2013, Boston, MA

Late afternoon light gilded the rooftops in lonely warmth as the sun drew nearer to the tops of the building in its descent. She'd come up here to think, to get away from some of the modernity in the building below.

She was not only suffering severe future shock, but culture shock to boot. She did her best to hide it from the others. They'd been overly kind and considerate, attempting in every way to make her feel at home.

She came up here a lot, staying away from the roof line as Mark had warned her. These isolated sunsets let her escape, even if just for a moment.

If she squinted just right, instead of asphalt roofs lined by brick kicker walls, she could see the thatched roofs of her village, plumes of cooking smoke curling up before the sun, and imagine her *dah* sharing the view next to her.

She missed him. Too much at times.

What *was* God's will for her? Was she supposed to have come here to the 21st century? What if she was supposed to be back at home?

"So, this is where you got off to." Mark had come up behind her.

Abbie turned and smiled. "Yes, I came up here to think."

"Sorry. Didn't mean to interrupt."

"Oh, that's okay. I was about to come down anyway."

"Abbie, you really shouldn't get so close to the roof line. We've got a truce with Rialto, but you never know."

"I know. I try to stay out of sight."

Over the past decades, Rialto had made sure Carpen's headquarters was constantly under surveillance by normal "mortals", i.e. men without shifters. It usually required no more than two or three hired thugs at a time who were given an apartment on the second floor of the opposing building. These thugs took shifts watching and noting any activity at the head-quarters visible from the outside. They were armed but had orders not to fire unless given new orders. For the time being, at least while the truce was in effect, they simply watched and reported.

If the truce were ever broken, Rialto would send his men back in time to specific moments where the three men had been seen together in public and take them out simultaneously. Frustratingly, there had been virtually no appearances of the men outside the building. They were using some unknown method for entering and exiting which he had not yet discovered.

His hired investigators, however, had no understanding of his grand scheme. All they knew was they were supposed to watch the place and tell him if they saw anything. Rialto paid them a good bit of money for basically doing nothing, so they didn't complain.

The particular thug up at bat at the moment was Tony Cardoza. He'd grown up in Brooklyn. His parents had divorced at an early age and he'd dropped out of school before reaching the 10th grade. He'd dabbled in drugs and their sales to wealthy suburbanites for a time before he got hooked up with the mob in an official capacity.

That had been fun, but this job beat all. Working for Rialto, he made as much money or more than he'd ever made then, and he wasn't doing anything illegal that could send him to jail.

Still, it was *boring*. There were days he thought that if he had to sit in front of this window for one more minute staring at some brick building which might as well be empty for all the activity going on, he'd have to slit his own wrists just to end the boredom. But then he would remember the pay, bite his lip, and sit up a little straighter. It was only eight hours or so per day, after all, unless Ringo showed up late that is, which unfortunately he did all too often.

So, when he saw the tall figure of a man standing on the roof of that building, excitement coursed through him. At last.

Something *different*.

Something was going on other than an empty, brick wall with windows you couldn't see through.

The sight set his finger to itching. He was inspired to *do* something different. Seeing something different required doing something different. The cocaine rushing through his veins didn't help.

C'mon Tony, you're going to screw up this cush job.

He couldn't help it. The temptation was too great. He raised his rifle.

Abbie let out a little scream as something slammed into Mark's chest and knocked him backward. Blood poured from a large wound under his back and from a smaller one in the front.

Reacting instantly, she leapt from her chair and crouched low. She scrambled to the two foot brick wall which marked the edge of the roof and dared a peek over it.

There was a man visible in an open window of the second story of a building across the street. He was peering out like a fool to evaluate his success as a killer. Her blood boiled at the sight of his ugly, leering maw.

A whirring from behind her caught her attention. Mark's

watch was loosening from off his wrist. That could only mean one thing. Her heart rent at the thought. She scrambled to his fallen body.

Without thinking, she slipped the watch on her own wrist. Whirring once more, it constricted itself. She'd seen him work it enough times to know how to operate it.

She dragged him to the other corner of the roof behind a low wall where neither of them would be visible to their former selves. Then, she grabbed his lifeless wrist and shifted his body back in time with her to a few minutes to before the shot struck home. She didn't know why she brought his body along, but she couldn't just leave him lying there.

She peered over the roof line again and saw the ugly man preparing to shoot.

Mark had gifted Abbie with a long, black, cylindrical carrying case, the kind businessmen normally use to transport large blueprints or artwork. She popped the cap off and withdrew her longbow. In spite of the century, she preferred it to a gun and never went anywhere without it.

The would-be killer never saw the silent missile as it sailed through the open window and struck his throat.

Confident the gunman was out for the count and would now never take the shot, Abbie returned to the other side of the roof. Behind her, Mark's body had disappeared as if by magic.

She breathed a sigh of relief.

Mark stood in the same spot as before he'd been killed. Now, his mouth hung agape, as if he'd been interrupted in mid-sentence, and his eyes were full of confusion. Abbie had just disappeared from the chair in front of him and reappeared on the other side of the roof.

The shifter was back on his wrist. Off of hers. The way it should be.

"Abbie...uh...why do you have your bow out? What happened?"

"It's nothing," she answered, "Why don't we get off of this roof? As you said, it's probably too dangerous."

Chapter 32

I wake up in tear drops, they fall down like rain
I put on that old song we danced to and then I head off to my job

"These Days"

~ Rascal Flatts

April 14th 2014, Swansea, MA

"Mark..."

Her fingertips brushed the skin of his cheek lightly, sending tingles down his spine.

They stood in an isolated copse of birch trees, their trunks bright, like tall, white sentinels of the forest. Warm sunbeams shone through their lime-green leaves as they flitted and danced in the breeze, and the small clearing was carpeted with the short blades of a plush, vibrant grass.

Abbie had invited him here. She'd left a note asking him to meet, with specific directions leading him to this hidden hollow among the birches. She was already waiting when he arrived.

He tried to remember her as she'd been when he'd first met her, but it was difficult. Today, she wore a tan leather autumn coat, a silk white blouse, and jeans. Her current attire bore no resemblance to the dress of Puritan New England. Then, her hair would have lain long, falling evenly across her shoulders. Now, it was pulled back into a pert pony tail and held in place with a red scrunchie. Not a very sophisticated look, just straight forward and simple, like everything else about her, which was a big part of her attractiveness.

Why had she invited him here? This place was close to

where her village had been back in 1675. His nerves fluttered as his mind debated whether this invitation would end in the breaking of his heart or the beginning of new joy. That she had something serious to tell him, one way or the other, was not in doubt.

"Mark..." She dropped her hand, pulling her eyes from his.

He reached for her fallen hand and took it in his own. "You said that already."

"Mark, I...I want to go back home."

Her words hit him like a ton of bricks. He'd always feared the feelings he had for her were not reciprocated. She'd never allowed the momentary, romantic sparks between them to fan into the flames he desired. He had tried to chalk her reticence up to her conservative upbringing, but apparently it had been more than that.

"Why, Abbie? There's nothing for you back there. What about all the good we're doing with these shifters?"

Reaching up, she touched his cheek again, smiling as she gazed into his eyes. "There's no doubt *you* are doing good, Mark. You're a good man. It's just not for me."

"Don't you want to help people?"

"Of course I do, but I don't believe the Lord wants me to live in this century."

First Ty, now her.

He was sick of this God talk. God had taken his children from him.

"If God wanted me to help you," she continued, "He would have given me a shifter too."

"What are you worried about? Being a burden to us, having to depend on us for safety? Don't. We'll never abandon you. I'll never abandon you."

"I know, Mark. That's not it."

"What then? Just because we don't have another shifter doesn't mean God doesn't want you to help us. I mean, think about my dreams. Why did I dream of you so much? Why was I led to come and save you? Didn't God give me those dreams?"

She ignored the last question. "It's not only that I don't have a shifter. I feel...well, I should say, I *know* what God wants me to do. He's spoken to me very clearly."

"God *spoke* to you?" Mark's tone was more than a little sarcastic.

"Not in my ear. In my spirit."

"How do you know it was Him?"

She laughed lightly, not mockingly, but with gentleness. "You are an adorable man, Mark. A good man. I know you have feelings for me, but...I cannot return them. I do not belong in this time...in your time. I belong back where you found me, with my people."

"But..."

"You cannot come with me, Mark. You belong here. You are doing what you were destined to do."

He blanched at her phrasing. Destiny was a traitorous word. He loathed that word.

"What will you do? Where will you go?"

"I will find a new village, a new home. I'll be fine. It's home to me there."

She saw him resisting the tears welling in his eyes. One escaped and she wiped it away with her finger, breaching his emotional dam. Quickly, he turned his face to hide his pain as more followed.

Grief built within like an ocean swell before a hurricane. The wounds deep inside, the wounds of his wife's abandonment followed by Laura's caustic infidelity had never really healed. If he didn't maintain control now, Abbie's leaving would hit even deeper.

He would not let another woman break his heart. Steeling himself, he sucked back the tears, wiping away the remnants with his sleeve. If it hadn't been for his history, he never would have been so sensitive to Abbie's rejection. Truth be told, he never would have let himself fall for her so easily if it hadn't been for his history. Abbie had been the perfect image of loyalty and purity, the two things most lacking in his ex-wife and Laura. That's why he had desired her so much.

He straightened and felt his heart harden. Like an iron fist slowly tightening its grip, the grief was squeezed from his core, leaving only inanimate cold in its wake.

She saw the change. Concern leapt into her throat, yet she could do nothing. When you have just hurt someone, any attempt to soothe their pain feels more like rubbing salt in the wound than a healing ointment.

She'd tried life in his time, in this century, and it didn't fit. She'd tried shoving herself into it like a foot in a shoe two sizes too small. Or maybe two sizes too big in this case.

She'd enjoyed working with Mark, and Ty, and Hardy. It *was* good work they were doing. Work not to be ashamed of. Yet, it left her strangely unsatisfied. She knew in her heart that she was not made for this century, that she must return to the life God had made for her in the time of her *dah*. For God's purpose, whatever that might be.

She liked Mark. You could even say she loved him — but as a sister loves a brother. Perhaps, with time, he could convince her to transform their relationship into a romance, but it would be short-lived. They were not made for each other. They were not a good fit. And as much as she was not made for this century, he was not made for hers. The watch on his wrist was proof of that.

She held out her hand. "Will you take me back now?"

"What about the others?" he whispered.

"I've already said good-bye to them."

He gave her the best smile he could muster.

"One last shift then."

Mark took Abbie's hand and depressed the magical button. They felt the shift and then they were a little over three hundred years in the past. The biggest change in the scenery was a little cottage which stood about two hundred feet distant. Abbie's home.

She'd known the lines of the local terrain so well she had oriented herself home without any historical landmarks to help, just the lay of the hills as a guide.

He held her hand longingly and then released it. Stretching her arms around him, she said good-bye with a hug. Then, she stepped away and walked toward home. After a moment, she turned back for a final look.

"Mark?"

"Yeah."

"Seek God."

He couldn't nod, he couldn't shake his head. He just stared and then flashed a quick wave good-bye. Then, he shifted out.

Chapter 33

When I go, don't cry for me
In my Father's arms I'll be

"All My Tears"

~ Jars of Clay

July 18th 2027, Boston, MA

Mark clenched the paper in his fist, crumpling it so hard it almost tore. He reread the newspaper article for the third time.

Body Found by Boston Common

Ty Jennings, 42, was found dead late last night near the Boston Common. About 2:00 AM, Jeff Williams, 47, of Worcester, was walking his dog along the sidewalk when he spotted Mr. Jennings lying on the sidewalk.

"He was just lying there," the computer programmer explained, "It was terrible. I've never been so shocked in my entire life."

Police interrogated Mr. Williams for several hours but released him soon after, stating the investigation was still ongoing.

"Whoever did this is still out there," said Sgt. Matthews of the Boston Police Department. "We're following a number of leads at the moment."

Mr. Jennings had been shot once in the head. It is believed robbery was the motive, though it is unclear what he was doing in the area so late at night.

Mr. Jennings has no known family in the Boston area.

Ty was dead.

After Abbie left, Mark had grown curious about the future. He and his team frequently traveled through the past, but for the most part, they'd left the future relatively untouched. On his own, he'd decided to change that and began exploring different years in the future.

For some reason that no one yet understood, not even their physicist Bobby Prescott, nobody could shift past the year 2029. 2030 and beyond were out of bounds. Whoever tried experienced a strange bouncing sensation and ended up right back where they left.

Of course, Ty thought God was limiting them. In his mind, for some reason, God was not letting them view too much of the future. Hardy and Bobby thought it was some technical limitation of the shifter. Mark didn't know what to think and had resigned himself to a state of agnosticism about a lot of things. He'd learned by now that what he didn't know about life far outweighed what he did know.

Mark first traveled to the year 2029. He wanted to know what the future held in store for them, assuming he could find records. A simple search on the internet revealed Ty's death certificate, which showed the cause of death to be homicide.

He next traveled back to 2027, the day after Ty's death, looking for the story in the *Boston Herald*, and sure enough, he'd found it in the crime section.

Who could have done it and why?

First of all, who could have gotten the drop on Ty? Surely it couldn't have been some street punk. There was no way Ty could have been taken out by an amateur, unless the surprise had been complete.

Mark activated his shifter. There was an easy way to find out.

***

July 17th 2027, 1:47 A.M., Boston, MA

As with any operation, Mark's first objective was to simply observe. Observe the target and the events as they unfold. Take careful note of any details that might affect the outcome of any potential intervention. Then, once the situation has been understood and all tactical considerations have been explored, shift in to intervene and change the undesired outcome.

Protocol would be no different in this case. During their work together, Mark had already seen Ty die on several occasions, but either Hardy or he had always shifted back in time to save him. And Ty always did the same for them.

Still, somehow, this time felt different.

Mark was nervous — *very nervous*. He had no good explanation for Ty's death certificate existing two years in the future from now. Both he and Hardy had always been close by. If something had happened to Ty, they should have jumped in to reverse it right away. Why hadn't that happened? Where was he? Where was Hardy? Mark could find no death certificates for either one of them, just Ty.

Butterflies floated spasmodically in his stomach. He felt nausea. Palpable fear that this might be one of those unchangeable events, like his children, lurked in the corner of his heart.

Ty was walking up the sidewalk now. His friend strolled at a casual pace, entering and exiting the yellow pools of light cast down by the street lamps overhead.

It was Ty all right, but not *quite* the same Ty he knew. This Ty had a lot of gray peppering his hair. He looked to be 25 to 30 years older than the Ty of Mark's time, yet 2027 was only 15 years in the future. Maybe he hadn't aged well.

As Ty drew closer, Mark caught a glimpse of movement behind some bushes lining the sidewalk and understood what was going to happen.

A dark form rose from the shadows as Ty reached a spot in front of a large shrub. The pistol in the hand of the shadowy figure bore a silencer. From this distance, there was no sound to be heard, just the image of Ty falling limply to the sidewalk.

Mark felt sick.

He was about to shift out of the nightmarish scene when he remembered he hadn't identified the killer yet. He waited while the dark form emerged from the shadows behind the bushes. The man entered the glow of the streetlight, glaring down at his fallen victim.

A scream of rage almost escaped Mark's lungs, stopped only by sheer determination to not give himself away. He knew *that* face. It was the face of a killer he would never forget. If Mark had any enemy on earth it was this man.

Alexander Rialto.

He vomited onto the ground, shaking with fury. The stench of his regurgitated lunch strangely calmed his nerves and strengthened his resolve. This would not stay this way. It could not. It would not. *He would make sure of it.*

***

May 5th 2014, Boston, MA, ChronoShift Headquarters

"The two of you look like someone stole your Girl Scout cookies," Hardy laughed.

It was Monday morning, time for their regularly scheduled debrief, but Hardy was the only one smiling today.

Mark and Ty were both sullen. Mark was staring at the table with his arms crossed. He was clearly in no mood for jokes. Ty had his elbows on the table looking pensive, chin resting on folded hands, eyes turned down. Mentally, he was somewhere else and hadn't even heard Hardy.

Mark still reeled from his weekend trip to the future where he'd witnessed Ty's murder. He stole a glance Ty's way. He hadn't told his friend what he'd seen yet, and he probably wouldn't. He needed to try and resolve it on his own first. If he couldn't, then he'd decide whether to tell Ty or not. In the meantime, Mark would bear this burden, this weighty knowledge, by himself.

Maybe they'd subconsciously avoided visiting the future until now for this very reason. The past was the past. They already knew what had happened in the past. When they traveled back to the past, mentally, they were still living in their present, not knowing *their* future. But if they traveled to the future, that future was not only the world's future, but their future as well. Once that Pandora's box was open, how did you close it again? How do you resist peeking at what's going to happen, and then how do you forget what you learned if you don't like what you saw?

"I know what's bothering me, but I ain't got a clue about Ty," Mark said.

Ty looked up, his mind landing back on earth upon hearing his name.

"Sorry, what?"

"What's up with you, man? What's the matter?"

"I've got to go kill a friend."

"What?"

"Whoa. What do you mean?"

"You know I've been traveling back to 'Nam now and then, saving my buds during the Tet?"

They both nodded.

"I got curious to see what they did with their lives after that, after the war, so I researched them. In the original version of history, all of these guys died — along with me, of course. I wanted to see if any of them had done something good, you know, something really good.

"A couple got killed again in later phases of the war, so I went and saved them again, but most made it back to the US and just led normal lives. You know, working hard, raising families. One guy became a neurosurgeon, another became a missionary. A few did some other remarkably good things. One guy saved a couple of kids from getting killed in a car accident."

"That's great!"

"Yeah, but it wasn't all good."

Ty's eyes welled with tears.

"One guy...this one guy...he...uh...he became a child molester," Ty finally spat out. "At least four different children were victimized, and he even killed one of them." A tear fell down his cheek, and he wiped it away.

Mark and Hardy both cringed. It was clear why this was eating at him. That kind of thing was one of their worst nightmares.

"Man, you can't control what these guys do with the life you save," Hardy argued.

Ty slammed his fist onto the table. "It's my fault!" He exclaimed. "*I did it.* If I hadn't saved the guy, those kids would be fine!"

There was nothing to say. Logically, he was right. Morally, philosophically, who could judge?

Ty placed his hands on the table resolutely. "I've got to go back and snipe this guy while he's still in 'Nam. I've got to look the guy in the eye and kill him."

"This is unreal," Hardy said.

"You know what's worse? John was my bud, not like a brother or anything, but we looked out for each other. I swear to you, there was no sign he was like that when I knew him back in 'Nam." Ty's eyes were pleading for affirmation that he'd done no wrong.

"I'm not sure what I'd do in your shoes," Mark said, "You weren't wrong to save him. You couldn't know."

"So, you'd just let him wander the streets, hurting more children."

"Absolutely not. What do we do every day? We take out guys like this several times a week. I just meant...its gotta be a hard thing."

"You want one of us to do it for you?" Hardy offered.

Ty sighed, "It's my mess, I'll clean it up."

After the meeting adjourned, Ty pulled Mark aside.

"Mark, what if I can't do this?"

"You mean you think you won't be able to pull the trigger?"

"No. I mean, are we justified assassinating someone who hasn't committed any crimes yet." Ty rubbed the top of his close-cropped hair with one hand.

"Could you stomach letting him molest a child before you felt 'justified'?" Mark asked scornfully.

"Of course not."

"What's the difference between this case and when we take out some gang banger right before he whacks somebody? Neither's committed the crime yet, but we know they're going to."

"I don't know."

"I don't either, but I do know I'd rather take the risk of becoming a murderer than I would letting a child get molested."

"Good point."

"Good luck."

"C'mon," Ty laughed for the first time that day, slapping Mark on the back. "You know I don't believe in luck."

Chapter 34

February 7th 1968, Vietnam

Ty squinted through the rain as it drizzled down his wet brow in rivulets. He was trying to catch a glimpse of his target through the dense foliage without giving his own position away.

He'd lain in this jungle the entire night, soaked to the bone, which brought back memories of his time here, back when he'd still been a jarhead. His prey's patrol would leave camp before daylight. Around dawn, they'd be ambushed by VC. Instead of shifting in to strike, he'd spent the night exposed to the elements because he wanted to be in place without having to scramble at the last minute. He didn't want the VC to catch sight of him either. The Marines on patrol would be on high alert, expecting an attack from any side, and they'd be armed to the teeth. One stray noise or accidental movement on his part might invite a shoot-first, ask-questions-later situation.

He dreaded what he was about to do. Ty had not fully reconciled himself to the idea of executing a man years before he committed a crime, though he had to admit Mark's logic in this case was pretty good. What was worse, this man was a friend...*had been* a friend, at least. John was a United States Marine... a fellow Marine for goodness sake. Ty was about to do the unconscionable, murder a fellow Marine in cold blood.

God had seen fit to take John's life once before already. It had been Ty who'd intervened, saving him. Ty had been the interloper, butting in, usurping God's sovereignty. That fact alone brought Ty some level of comfort in his decision to do this.

Then, there was no more time to think. The ambush had begun, and his target appeared in his sights. Marines were scrambling for cover behind trees and in gullies. There would be a small window of opportunity for Ty to complete his mission before John reached shelter. Ty would have one shot, then he'd have to shift out immediately since the kill could draw return fire from either side.

He settled himself, placing his eye on the rifle scope. Thick raindrops co-mingled with a tear of frustration. He squeezed the trigger, applying even pressure as he'd been trained.

A dry click softly echoed — then nothing. The rifle had misfired. A jolt of sudden joy rushed through him. *Should he try again?*

His moment of hesitation had allowed John to make it safely to cover behind a tree, but it didn't matter. Ty understood. He packed his stuff and shifted out.

***

"What happened?"

"Rifle misfired."

"You've got to be kidding."

"Nope. God intervened, so I called the snipe off."

"Just because your gun misfires doesn't mean God intervened," Mark snapped.

"It did in the past...for you," Ty rebutted.

"That was different. I tried a lot harder before giving up. Not just one shot."

"I *felt* it."

"What do you mean you 'felt it'?"

"I mean, I sensed it. I understood that God was telling me not to do it."

Mark clenched his fists. "So, you're just gonna let those kids get hurt?"

"Didn't say that. I didn't say I felt God say 'never'. It was more like a 'wait'."

"I swear, you and this God stuff. I'm about sick of it."

Ty shrugged, which reminded Mark of Hardy in their early days together, so the gesture irritated him even more.

"When then? How can you be sure you'll get to him before he hurts the first kid?"

"The trial was public record. I'll get the time frame out of the transcript."

"How do you know there wasn't another child who never came forward?"

"I'll make sure of it."

***

Golden light layered the street in a warm, late afternoon glow. The sun would be down in about an hour and children up and down the block were trying their best to squeeze in a few last moments of play as mothers began calling them in to dinner.

Higher end town homes lined one side of the street, their beige, stuccoed facades butting up against one another like a residential sentry line. The other side of the street was a large grassy field, which, for the time being, was still empty of development of any kind.

The BMW didn't look overly pretentious, being an older model, but Ty knew his prey well enough by now to know the man wished it was this year's model. He'd watched his habits for several days in a row. He had no children of his own, thank goodness. The wife would not greet him at the door. She'd be waiting inside. Ty didn't get the impression their marriage was the best of matrimonies anyway.

He waited till the vehicle had parked and his former friend had stepped out onto the pavement before emerging from around the corner.

"Hello, John."

The ex-Marine spun, clearly startled by the unexpected voice. His eyes narrowed, then widened in surprise.

"Ty? My gosh, I haven't seen you since 'Nam. What are you doing here?"

"Can you do me a favor?"

"Sure, bud. What's up," he asked is a hushed tone. "Anything for another grunt."

"I need to talk to you." Ty beckoned with his hand.

John walked closer to him, clearly puzzled by the whole thing.

As soon as he was in range, Ty grabbed the collar of his shirt, twisting it roughly. He slammed his forearm into the ex-Marine's throat, throwing him back against the garage door.

"Ty," he gurgled, straining against the unexpected attack, "What's the matter with you? What's going on?"

Ty's tone was as serious as he'd ever been in his life, flat and deadly in its directness.

"John, you don't know this, but I saved your life back in 'Nam. Just believe me when I say that with absolute certainty. You'd be dead if it weren't for me."

"Uh...okay..."

"Shut up! Your life depends on *you* now. I *know* what's going on in your mind."

"What do you mean?"

Ty slammed his head against the garage door. Withdrawing his arm, he rammed his fist into the side of John's head, dazing the man. "Shut up, I said. I know what you're thinking about doing with certain children."

The man paled visibly.

"I should kill you right now, I really should. But," he grimaced through gritted teeth, "I'm going to give you *one* chance. I *will* know if you molest anybody. Believe me, I will *know*. Be assured of that. And if you do, I will kill you. I will come back and kill you. This is your only chance. I won't warn you again. Do you understand me?"

John nodded weakly, blood dripping from his nose and lip.

"I hope you do."

"John? Are you out there?" A woman's voice called.

His wife hadn't seen them yet.

John stared at Ty with lifeless eyes. His expression was a mixture of shame, disbelief, hurt, and anger.

Ty stepped back several feet and made a showing of the shifter on his wrist until he was sure John saw it. Then, he shifted out. He hoped the image of him disappearing in front of the man's eyes with a magic watch would be sufficiently strange to intimidate him into good behavior.

Chapter 35

Like we ain't scared and our boots ain't muddy, but no one laughs,
'Cause there ain't nothing funny when a soldier cries.

"Letters from Home"

~ John Michael Montgomery

It wasn't.

The warning had given John an extra six months of life as the guy waited that much longer before succumbing to the evil in his heart.

So, Ty borrowed the corporate jet. He intercepted John after work one evening, put a hood over his head, knocked him out and shoved him into a van. Then, they drove to the local airstrip where Ty shuffled him into the back of the jet. The pilot flew them to Vietnam, but he would never see John, nor even know he was on the plane.

The man's wife would never see him again. They would find his car abandoned in the parking garage where he'd left it. Ty was actually blessing this man in a way. Now, he would be remembered as the husband who'd never come home from work, the Marine who'd fought bravely in Vietnam for his country. There would be no lives ruined, no memories of an evil child molester to taint his legacy and haunt his wife's regrets.

Once back in 'Nam, Ty transported him unconscious to a very specific location. It was an isolated place, a place where he knew the bullets would be flying back in '68.

Ty yanked the hood from his head and woke his former friend with a few lights slaps and some smelling salts under the nose.

John blinked repeatedly, eyes hurting from the sudden

brightness of the sunlight. For the first time, he saw the face of his abductor, but no surprise registered.

Ty stood John at attention. His hands were still tied behind his back, and his feet were bound together. Ty sat down on a rock limply, gun in hand.

"You wanna say anything?" Ty asked.

"I didn't do anything!" John declared.

"You will."

"You can't know that," he pled.

"Yes, I do. Do you want to pray?"

John nodded. The resoluteness in Ty's eyes evaporated any hope he might have had. He bowed his head and closed his eyes. His lips moved fervently. After a moment, he lifted his head again.

"I don't want to do this, John, but you've left me no choice. You were supposed to die in 'Nam and now you will. Are you ready?"

John nodded.

Ty lay flat on his belly at John's feet. His former friend remained standing. Ty gripped John's ankle with his shifter hand and then moved them both back to '68.

The bullets were flying indeed. Ty had shifted them into the middle of a huge firefight between VC and regular U.S. Army. He would wait until he was sure the job was done.

A stray bullet struck Ty in the back of the calf, but it was only a flesh wound. After about four or five seconds, though it seemed an eternity, a bullet finally slammed into John's chest and he staggered. A second bullet slammed his head back, and his lifeless body collapsed to the ground.

Ty shifted out and cried.

***

Mark lay on his stomach in the cool grass letting the night breeze blow softly across his back, forehead resting on his forearm, oblivious to the stars in the clear sky above and the lights of Boston all around. He was just listening to the night sounds of the park, feeling the wind on his skin and in his hair. He'd been this way for a good thirty minutes.

Rialto was below him, at the bottom of the hill Mark was on. His enemy waited with murderous intent and soon he'd carry out his evil plot.

After a long while, Mark finally sat up and checked the weapons he'd brought, which were a sniper rifle, a pistol, and a grenade. He tried to swallow a lump in his throat as he went through the motions of making sure each gun was clear of obstacles and fully loaded.

A basic mistrust of God had developed within him. He had no hope this would work. Images of his children raced through his mind, which he batted away as fast as they came to him, but their effect was deep. He hadn't been able to save them. God had become capricious and cruel to him, giving him the shifter, a tremendous and miraculous gift which could be used to change the past, but never allowing Mark to use it to save his own kids. He didn't believe he would be able to save Ty now either.

Half-heartedly, Mark set up his sniper rifle. It was almost time. He didn't want to look. He didn't want to see Ty coming down the sidewalk again. He ignored his friend and limited the scope of his sight to his target only.

Why wait? Mark pulled the trigger, not really aiming very carefully. It clicked harmlessly as if empty. He knew it wasn't. It wasn't misfiring.

He pulled the trigger again, and again, and again. Each time, no explosive retort sounded, no bullets sailed Rialto's way. The man still sat comfortably, waiting in ambush. The hated being was at peace when he should be dying.

Tears streamed down Mark's cheeks as he pulled the pistol out his bag. He stood and pointed it down the hill. Empty clicks were the only result as he pulled its trigger over and over. Disgusted, he threw it to the dirt and reached for the hand grenade. Desperate resignation gave way to fury.

He ripped the hand grenade up and grabbed hold of the

pin, ready to lob it at the enemy.

The pin wouldn't come out.

It was as if someone had super glued it inside the clip. Mark was bordering on temporary insanity now, forgetting all training and caution. He stepped on the grenade with one foot and began tugging with all his might on the stupid little pin, but it would not come out.

He chucked it toward Rialto, pin intact, but it bounced worthlessly off a tree and came back to him. Enraged, he tried to charge down the hill, screaming bloody murder, but he was frozen in place, and no sound would come out of his open mouth.

He didn't want to see it again. He turned and sat hard on the soil, fury expended. Quietly, he began collecting his tools and weapons and packed them back in the duffel bag.

Chapter 36

For Randolph DeCleary, life was no longer the promising dream it had once been when Lord Geoff was alive. Geoffrey de Mandeville's son, William, was now lord of the lands of Essex and constable of the Tower of London in his father's place. Rumors abounded with regards to King Henry officially naming William de Mandeville the first Earl of Essex. Geoffrey had taken to using this title before the king had given it, believing it was his right, and thus out of spite, the former king, William Rufus, had delayed giving it.

Now that Rufus was dead and Henry was king, and since the support of Geoffrey de Mandeville had been instrumental in securing the kingship for Henry, it seemed the coveted title might actually be given. Such a silly thing, titles, Randolph mused. Being an official earl wouldn't put any more money in William's pockets.

Still, William was clearly less than competent when compared with his father. He was young and impetuous, given to revelry and other indiscretions. He was not sufficiently reverent or even concerned when it came to affairs of state and his opinion was easily swayed by the more sophisticated of the nobility, yet he was not wise enough to discern their motives were not always in his best interest. He was a schemer, like his father, but without the skill to pull it off as his father had.

All of those things could mean a turbulent future for William de Mandeville and anyone associated with him, but that was not what concerned Randolph the most at the moment.

Randolph's first and foremost problem was that William

blamed him for his father's death. Randolph had become Geoffrey's right hand man after Clyde of Dorchester had been killed, but William the son didn't trust him. William had heard the stories of the magical bandits. He'd seen the strange and unexplainable circular wounds in his father and the three men-at-arms who'd been guarding him, but still, it was Randolph alone who'd come down from his father's bedroom reporting the murder. William hadn't necessarily disbelieved Randolph's story about the magical bandit disappearing from his father's bedroom after killing him. What motive could Randolph have? What fantastic weapon had he used and where was it? Still, he didn't quite believe Randolph wasn't complicit somehow either.

So, Randolph DeCleary, one of the best warriors in eastern England, was relegated to the sidelines. He was clearly *not* William's trusted right hand. What was worse, William wouldn't even include him in discussions of any official business. It was humiliating being treated like a simple man-at-arms for hire when his prowess as a knight was so well-known.

All of this meant Randolph was seriously reevaluating his plans. His future in Essex looked dimmer and dimmer by the day since Geoffrey's death.

It was never an easy thing to change fealty between lords, and rumors of Geoffrey's strange death and Randolph's role in it had already reached the ears of most of England's nobility. Most lords would not want to take a chance on him in spite of his reputation.

Perhaps his best bet lay northward. The lords whose lands bordered the Scots were constantly battling their Celtic neighbors and usually short on good fighting men. Those lands were not as prosperous as the southern estates, so his lifestyle would certainly become more dreary should he be forced to serve there.

He could always enter the service of one of those northern lords for a few years and then, once he'd distinguished himself again through battle, return to the south. He might even be able the service of the king himself.

wall on which Randolph sat was an ancient one, low

and grey and uneven, full of moss-covered stones. Ignoring the clear blue sky overhead, he twirled the tip of his sword in the dust at his feet, doodling in the dirt with the point as he contemplated his options.

A sharp crackle, like a muted bolt of lighting singeing the air, sparked directly behind him. He'd heard that sound before.

He'd heard it a number of times that night in the forest when the bandits had routed his forces. He heard it when the bandit Mark had disappeared from Geoff's bedchambers, leaving the lifeless earl behind.

Instantly, he was in motion, swinging his sword up into a perfect arc to attack before the crackling noise had even ceased. He spun smoothly on the ball of one foot, knowing his blade would slice through the neck of this bandit without even having seen him yet. It would have too, had the bandit not been standing five feet out of reach.

Randolph halted his movement, holding his sword out-stretched with its point aimed at the man's throat. He did not recognize this man as one of the bandits he'd met before, but that meant nothing.

"*Hwo artou? Hwat wolte?*" He growled.

The use of Middle English was a detail Alexander Rialto had forgotten and thus overlooked. Communicating with De-Cleary would be more complicated than he'd ideally want, at least at first, but Rialto would still get the message across somehow. He always did.

***

May 5th 2014, Washington D.C.

Rialto's team now numbered seven. Stanley Graves and Vincent Torino had both worked for the mafia before he recruited them. Graves was the better planner and thinker of the two, Torino was an assassin, a calm and assured hunter of men.

Hugh Plageanet was of a different sort. Rialto had recruited him simply because the man was so mean. A plantation owner from the mid-1800's in Georgia, Mark Carpen had killed Plageanet's father, basically ruined his life, and then tried to kill him too. Plageanet didn't need any motivation to get back at Mark, in fact, it would be hard holding him back until the moment was right.

Randall Cook was his fourth recruit. Back in 1814, he'd been the purser aboard the HMS Huntingdon. Cook had shanghaied Carpen and Phillips from a tavern, forcing them into service in the British Navy during the War of 1812. They'd escaped, however, knocked the man unconscious, and then marooned him in modern 2013.

Cook wasn't as revenge-oriented as Plageanet, but the sailor still had a serious chip on his shoulder with regards to Carpen. Cook's best asset was his burliness. The man was a rough and tumble street fighter who would barrel his way through any situation. The icing on the cake was that he had no ethics to speak of. What he did have was street smarts.

Laura was the seductress. She was very pleasing to the eyes, of course, but her cunning and wiles were the real reasons he'd sought her out. Where a man might opt for brute force, she would manipulate and tease and lure, using her femininity as a weapon. Not to mention she had her own history with Carpen. He suspected her talents would prove to be very useful.

Finally, there was the shining knight, Sir Randolph DeCleary, who owed his professional downfall as well as the severe pricking of his personal pride to Carpen and company. His physical prowess as a medieval knight could make him useful in older historical settings, but Rialto planned on using guns whenever possible anyway, so that wasn't the real reason he'd pulled him in. No, he'd taken a gamble on Randolph because of the history he had with Carpen. There was a certain confidence in the man, a steeliness which would strengthen the team as a whole. Of all those to whom he'd given shifters, Randolph DeCleary showed the most leadership potential, but that actually worried Rialto more than it pleased him.

He'd had to learn a bit of Middle English just to speak to the man initially, which annoyed him, but it was worth it. He'd had Laura spend a couple of weeks teaching Randolph modern English so they could all communicate and the knight picked it up pretty fast.

Rialto called this team of his to a meeting at the same abandoned warehouse as he had Torino and Graves once before.

They belonged to him now. Sure, they would become wealthy and they would have their chance at revenge with Carpen, which would satisfy most of their wants, but the idea of freedom for them was in the realm of myth now. They would have no choice but to do his bidding when he required it.

At least, that is what he wanted them to think. Stanley Irvine, his resident physicist/technician created another fake shifter, and Rialto blew it up with a remote triggering device during the meeting so they would be sufficiently cowed. Neither Graves nor Torino blanched when it exploded. They'd been through this little drama once before.

Nevertheless, both men gritted their teeth in anger. Rialto had given them tremendous power in the shifters, but there had been a price. They were his slaves.

A curt scream escaped from Laura's throat when the watch exploded. She reddened, embarrassed to show weakness among this group of ruffians. Cook jumped at the unexpected noise, and Randolph nearly fell out of his chair. Interestingly, Hugh Plageanet didn't move a muscle, though he was the closest to the explosion.

Rialto waited until they'd simmered down before continuing.

"You know our enemy." He tossed enlarged photos onto the table in front of them. "They are Mark Carpen, Ty Jennings, and Hardy Phillips. They've hurt each of us. As I speak, I'm sure you can almost taste the sweet revenge in your mouth, but you will be patient. Regardless of how angry you are, you will *not* act without my permission. The time must be right. The attack must be well planned."

"Why do we have to wait?" Cook blurted.

"Graves, Torino, and I have already battled these guys once. That time, we supposedly had the advantage. We had weapons at our disposal they had not yet developed *and* we had the element of surprise, yet the fight still ended in a draw. Not only do they have shifters like us, but each of them is a highly trained, former special forces soldier. Plagaenet, Cook, De-Cleary, not being from this century, you don't know what that means really, so just trust me when I say they are better trained fighters than any soldier you've ever known and in a one-on-one fight, they could beat any one of us into an inglorious pulp."

"I have already bested this Carpen once in a fair duel of swords," Randolph DeCleary interjected, "Had his friends not intervened, I would have destroyed him. I can do so again."

Cook spat on the concrete floor.

Rialto's expression showed moderate surprise. "I *am* impressed, but here in the 21st century we fight with guns, not swords. I assure you, you will not best them in an exchange of bullets.

"Anyway," Rialto continued, "I believe our superior numbers will be enough of an advantage we can take them, but our plan must be perfect. We must kill all three before any one of them can rescue the others. If we kill two and miss the third, that one will be free to shift back and save his friends before we kill them.

"We've been through a battle like that already, and it's no walk in the park. We no longer have the element of surprise or an advantage in technology. Since then, I'd be surprised if they hadn't built up their defenses as well. We do have Laura, who's an insider. She knows their habits and how they think.

"Our plan must be flawless in design and in execution. Once they're dead, we'll be free to rule this world as we see fit.

"Last item. When we do take them, it is *extremely important* that you do not kill them until I'm there."

"Why?" Plageanet growled.

"Because when a man wearing a shifter dies, the shifter

becomes highly unstable and will kill anyone close by if it is not handled properly," Rialto lied, "I'm the only one who knows how to handle the shifters. Any other questions?"

There weren't.

Rialto stood. "Enjoy yourselves. Get rich. Do what you want. Just stay away from Carpen and friends for the time being. Make sure you shift back to this year once per day at this time. You've each got beepers and I'll page you when I need you."

Unbeknownst to them, he'd also affixed a unique and tiny GPS locator on the underside of each of their shifters. He could locate their position realtime anywhere on earth via satellite during the past twenty years.

He left them stewing in their thoughts.

***

Sir Randolph DeCleary observed the others around the table.

He didn't like what he saw.

The eyes of the men Rialto called Graves and Torino were lifeless, black and beady like rats. They were dead men walking, ruthless and without mercy. Paid assassins.

He'd met sailors before and this Cook fellow fit the bill to a tee. He appeared simple, stupid, and generally unimpressive, at least to Randolph's eyes. He had the look of a London commoner accustomed to frequent brawls in the local tavern. Randolph didn't even perceive in the ruffian the discipline of a simple man-at-arms.

A cold shiver ran down his spine as he appraised Plageanet. This man was not necessarily physically impressive, more wiry than thick, but in his eyes shone a cruelty that was unmistakable. Something evil lurked deep within that man and Randolph didn't like it.

Laura was the kindest of them by far. She'd spent a significant amount of time teaching him what they called modern English. He referred to it as crass English. It certainly didn't have the style, the flair, or the subtleties of his home tongue.

He found her to be easily frustrated during the lessons. She was an essentially selfish woman and patience was not one of her virtues. Still, he appreciated her effort, even if it'd been commanded by Rialto.

More than exotic, her appearance was almost alien. All the noble women he'd ever known, intimately or otherwise, had pale countenances. The peasant women of England who worked in their fields were a bit browner, having been darkened by the sun, but even they were nothing like the color of this woman. He'd seen a Moor once, a man brought from the far South whose color was as dark as coal, but she was not that dark either.

Her color was like a honey brown stallion. He'd heard of such women in Spain or Italy, or among the Saracens, but had never seen one, though those women were said to have raven black hair. Hers was golden brown.

The violet color of her eyes had surprised him the most, for he'd neither seen nor heard of a woman with such coloring, and when she'd appeared to him one day with green eyes instead of purple, a sparkling vibrant green the likes of which he'd never seen either, he'd decided she was some kind of witch.

Soon, he'd realized her appearance was not so unusual. Many of the women of this time, this "modern" time as Rialto referred to it, had strange and unusual coloring, and even odder clothing. Clothing which revealed more than it hid, advertising a lack of chastity he found simultaneously maddening and disgusting. An English woman would be publically scorned for such manner of behavior. Though he was growing more accustomed to the customs of this time, her appearance still fascinated him.

Aside from that, there was nothing he liked about this group of people. None would hesitate to stab him in the back if it suited their purposes, and they'd probably smile while they did it.

Desire for power, gold, and fame undoubtedly burned in his heart as well, but he still held a modicum of honor which he would not relinquish easily. These people were not honorable.

They had no code, no chivalry. Yet, he was trapped neatly, like a fox with a leg in a snare, and he had no choice but to follow. The object around his wrist held him prisoner more fastly than the Tower itself.

If left to his own designs, he'd go back to *his* England and use this "shifter" to acquire gold. A lot of gold. And knowledge. Knowledge was power. Then, he could purchase land and finally become a nobleman. With this device, he could become the greatest landholder in all of England, maybe even king.

Plageanet broke his reverie.

"Why do you suppose he wants to be there when they die?"

"Yeah, there's something up with that," Graves agreed.

Cook stood and spat again. He left the room. Torino eyed his back darkly as he went.

"Mark told me once that the only way to get a shifter off your wrist was to die," Laura said, "He didn't say it would explode though. He said it just loosened and fell off the person's wrist."

"What exactly *is* your relationship with Carpen, woman?" Plageanet sneered.

"*Was*...not is. And it's none of your business," she replied coolly.

Randolph interrupted, his strong accent holding fast the attention of the others. "Does it matter? We are forcibly in Rialto's service. If we disobey, shall he not do to us as he did to that?" He pointed at the remains of the destroyed shifter.

Sullen villains are the worst of all enemies, for one way or the other they would seek out the revenge that burned within them on somebody, and that somebody would not necessarily be the one who had provoked it.

Chapter 37

May 9th 2014, Boston, MA

Their round table had become so familiar. Mark ran his hand along the edge, sensing the rough spots and dents under his fingertips. Ty had made one of the larger dents playing pool, he remembered. A few months ago, he'd slipped on a break and sent the cue ball sailing through the air right into it.

Hardy was shooting billiards by himself at the moment. Ty and Savannah were already seated.

"Hardy, you'll probably want to sit down for this," Mark said.

One look at Mark's face and Hardy put down his cue and took a seat.

"You look like you've seen a ghost," Hardy commented, "You finally going to tell us what's been eating at ya?"

"Yes."

They waited, expectantly.

"We're going to break the truce with Rialto."

Ty grimaced. "Why do you want to start that up again?"

"We're going to kill him and every last one of his crew."

Savannah gasped, "Why, Mark? I thought the truce was working."

"Yeah, what's up?" Hardy pushed.

Mark didn't want to tell them. He stared at Ty. He longed to spare his friend the pain of knowing how he'd die, of knowing Mark couldn't stop it. Deep down, Mark was seriously worried about the whole situation, what horrible ends might await them all.

They were alert now and boring holes in him with their

eyes. He was going to have to tell them.

"I shifted to the future."

"How much into the future? Past 2030?"

"No, I still bounce off of 2030 just like you guys. I went to 2029 — to see what I could find out about our futures."

"And?" Hardy was growing impatient.

"I found a death certificate for Ty dating 2027. So, I went back to 2027 to investigate. I...uh...found out how Rialto gets his shifter. He kills Ty." Mark leaned his elbows on the table and started to cover his face with his hands. Then, he changed his mind and instead steeled his expression, while pressing his knuckles firmly into the table top. His gaze turned vacant, staring off into space as he recounted what happened.

"He takes the shifter off your wrist, Ty, and puts it on his own. I watched him do it. I watched him do it too many times. I tried to stop him. I tried everything I could think of, but that invisible force kept stopping me. I can't stop it."

Mark's eyes shimmered. Savannah began to cry. Hardy's fists were clenched so tight they burned white.

"You're not suggesting we give up, are you?" Hardy demanded "You want us to just leave it like that? Let Rialto kill Ty?"

"Of course not," Mark responded. "We're going to do everything in our power to stop him. This truce is off and we won't rest until we've won."

"What about you and me?" Hardy asked. "How did Graves and Torino get their shifters?"

"I don't know. There was no record of death certificates for either you or me in any year."

The anger and emotion was strong in the room, with the exception of Ty himself. The others were too caught up in the distress of the moment to notice the look of peace on his face.

***

Hardy lay 300 feet away on top of a low two-story building. Through a lot of footwork and a few well-placed bribes, they'd figured out where Rialto lived. Right now, Hardy had a great view of his front door. He also had a sniper rifle.

Mark kneeled on the roof of a five-story building about a block away with his own rifle. The black tar under his knees was so hot he kept having to change positions once a minute or so. He couldn't imagine how Hardy was tolerating the boiling roof under his stomach while lying in wait.

In preparation for this mission, Mark had asked Bobby Prescott if he could develop electronic jammers for them that could be carried in their pockets, and Prescott had come through with flying colors. They each had a small jammer now.

If activated during a shift, the jammer would create an indecipherable amount of static noise that would mask the fluctuations from their shifters and make Rialto's detectors useless. In other words, they could shift without fear of Rialto knowing where they'd gone.

As soon as Rialto appeared in the doorway, Hardy would take him out with a single shot. That would not be the end of it, however. Either Graves or Torino would shift in behind Hardy and try to kill him *before* he shot Rialto. Mark hoped both men would.

He had Hardy's back and he'd take out anyone who shifted in anywhere near his friend. If both Graves and Torino tried to gang up on Hardy, Mark would take them both out, allowing Hardy to finish Rialto off in peace. Boom, boom, boom. Done.

All three men would be out of the picture permanently with no one left to save them. The war would be over.

If only one of Graves or Torino shifted in, Mark would still take that one out. In such a case, he would carefully clean up any traces he'd left of his presence and leave — without shifting. His position was far enough away from Hardy they wouldn't be able to determine his location accurately with only one shot fired.

Then, he and Hardy would reposition themselves on the roofs of other buildings and wait for the third man to make his appearance somewhere. However it played out, they hoped to finish the war once and for all right here. They'd used this strategy once before and it had worked fine. That time, however, they'd been on defense. This time, they would be the aggressors.

Ty remained behind for security reasons. If Mark and Hardy didn't make it back to the next debriefing, Ty would leave a note in Mark's mailbox for him to find before they embarked on this mission warning him not to execute. The plan seemed foolproof. Mark's only worry was that Murphy's Law usually had a way of mocking "foolproof" plans.

A shimmering appeared to Hardy's right. It was the beginning of a shift. Another shimmering appeared to his left. Mark evaluated this in a fraction of a second and noted the time. His elation at the thought of being able to get Graves and Torino together in one fell swoop was interrupted by the unexpected sound of another shift behind himself.

In that same second, Rialto appeared in the doorway below Hardy. Two figures surrounded him. Somehow, either he or Hardy would miss one of their shots, allowing someone to escape and get behind Mark.

Crap, here we go again. Were they about to enter another lengthy chase through time?

Twisting and flinging himself to the side, Mark saw it was Vincent Torino, a veritable assassin if there ever was one. The pistol in the man's hand was held with the confidence of an emotionless professional who'd taken life too many times before. The distance between him and Mark was only about twenty feet, but Mark doubted mafia experience would trump his own training. He could still finish this here.

The static of another shift caused Mark to pause. A burly figure appeared, a strangely familiar and completely unexpected figure. It was Randall Cook, the purser from the HMS Huntingdon back in 1814. Mark shook his head in disbelief, even as the burly sailor charged.

***

Ty was alone back at headquarters. Mark and Hardy had left a while ago to execute the new plan. Operation Rialto Round-Up was how Hardy had dubbed it. Savannah had gone out to run some errands.

Ty would remain in the protective confines of their building until Mark and Hardy returned. He was their safety net and couldn't take a chance on getting himself killed on some other task.

He was taking the news of his own death fairly well, considering. Mark had written his reaction off as more of Ty's weirdness, as usual. Hardy had learned long ago not to comment. Ty couldn't explain, but knowing when and how he would die didn't really bother him. It actually brought an odd peace to his spirit. Being more of a glass-half-full kind of guy, he viewed the news as assurance of another 15 years of life, which was much more than he'd had before Mark had saved him in 'Nam.

He'd just begun a game of solitaire when the intercom buzzed. *Was Savannah back already?* Why was she using the intercom?

He pushed the button to talk. "Yes?"

"Ty? It's me, Laura."

"*Laura?* What in the world do *you* want?"

"Can I come up? I need to talk."

"Mark's not here."

"That's okay. I doubt he'd want to see me anyway. That's why I need to talk to *you*, Ty."

"I don't know..."

"*Please.* I feel really bad about the way things ended between Mark and me. Hardy too for that matter."

Ty paused and then finally hit the buzzer to let her in. "Come on up," he relented.

A minute later, she was on the second floor with him. Ty certainly understood why Mark and Hardy had both wanted her. She was a beauty, whatever a man's tastes might be.

"Speak, girl. You got one minute."

Sheepishly, she fiddled with a gold bracelet on her wrist as if searching for the right words. "Like I said, Ty. I feel really bad about..." She swiftly drew a taser from her purse and squeezed the trigger. The prongs flew through the space between them and plunged into Ty's chest.

"...having to do this," she finished.

Electricity coursed through his body, spasming every one of his muscles.

I never should have trusted her was the last thought to run through his mind before he collapsed to the floor.

Bending over his inert form, she examined his watch. The face of it had turned red, indicating it had gone into "inoperable" mode. *Interesting.* The electric shock had shut it down. She hoped she hadn't damaged it permanently.

She went back downstairs, opened the front door to let Randolph in, and led him up to where Ty lay.

"What now?" she asked.

"We wait for Rialto. He said he wanted to be here when we kill him."

Chapter 38

Cook slammed into him, driving an elbow into his stomach and knocking the wind from his lungs. Mark's plan was going bad fast. Desperately, he tried to draw breath, but couldn't. Torino would have shot him by now if Cook hadn't gotten himself in the way so rashly.

As winded as he was, all Mark could do was shift out. Thankfully, he had the presence of mind to activate the jammer in his pocket before he did.

Torino shouldn't be able to track him, assuming the little devices Prescott had made for them worked correctly. Unfortunately, since Cook had landed on top of Mark, he came along when Mark shifted.

Cook had a full ten seconds to land as many blows and kicks as he could while Mark got his wind back. Fed up, Mark swung the butt of his rifle into Cook's face and knocked his attacker back. He stood and followed it up by ramming the rifle into the sailor's stomach. The final blow was a full swing of the weapon, as if it were a baseball bat, into the back of his neck. Cook fell limply to the roof. Angry determination pressed Mark's forearm hard into the unconscious man's throat as he dragged him toward the edge of the roof, fully intending to throw him over the knee wall.

Then, he spied the silvery shifter shining on Cook's wrist. The sailor certainly hadn't had one back in 1814. Somehow, the man had hooked up with Rialto and was working with him now.

If I kill him, somebody will shift in, save him, and the battle will go on.

He knew leaving Cook behind was the best bet to elude them. He didn't like the realization, but there it was.

Right now, Rialto didn't know where Mark was. Mark just needed to evade so he could get back to Hardy. This fight could wait for another day.

Releasing the choke hold, he chopped down on the back of Cook's neck once more for good measure to make sure he stayed out of commission for a while.

Using the jammer again, he shifted to yet another time and made his way to Hardy's rooftop. He guessed about where one of the figures had phased in behind Hardy and tried to shift in right behind that man.

Bingo! He'd only been off by about a foot. Two more of Rialto's men surrounded Hardy, and in the moment Mark arrived, his friend was still turning to face them. He wouldn't be able to do much. Both men already had their pistols aimed at Hardy's head.

Mark recognized Graves as he brought the butt of his pistol crashing down on the back of Graves' skull. The second goon was another newbie. His cruel, ugly sneer was uncannily familiar, but Mark couldn't quite place where he'd seen him before. His more immediate concern was the gun in the guy's fist.

Mark's bullet hit the man in the leg, eliciting a loud howl from the unexpected pain.

"Shift!" He called to Hardy. Hardy would know to use his jammer. They'd agreed in planning that jammers would be standard procedure in a battle like this.

Once he was sure Hardy had gotten out, he shifted out himself to a time different from Hardy's. They'd meet back at headquarters. The sinister guy he'd shot in the leg didn't even have time to recover and re-aim before Mark was gone. The whole ordeal took about five seconds.

He was frustrated — and more than a little concerned. Rialto was still out there. Their mission to end this war once and for all was a complete failure. Not only that, but Rialto had at least two more thugs working for him now, thugs with shifters, *thugs that Mark apparently knew*. Rialto had superior numbers, which meant besting him would now be infinitely more difficult.

He brooded all the way back to the office. They'd lost the element of surprise. It wouldn't take much of a brain for Rialto to figure out Mark had jammers now. Someone had designed the shift detectors for Rialto, and that same someone could make him jammers too.

Mark slammed his fist on the console of his car. They'd lost every advantage they had in that battle, and with nothing to show for it. And the truce was off.

Where had all those extra guys come from? Where had they gotten their shifters? How many shifters did Rialto have? He'd watched Rialto steal Ty's shifter and slip it on his own wrist. Until now, he'd had the sneaking suspicion that Graves and Torino had procured their shifters from his and Hardy's dead bodies, but he couldn't find any death certificates to prove it. Now, he wasn't so sure. Rialto's team had at least five different watches, so where had Cook and this other man gotten theirs? And who was that last man? Mark could swear he knew him from somewhere.

He slammed on the brakes and twisted the steering wheel sharply to the left, sending his vehicle into a sliding u-turn. He was going to Washington D.C.

***

The sharp point of the Italian's angled nose was just as prominent as ever, but this version of Rialto had much less grey hair. Mark even saw a modicum of kindness still remained in the younger Rialto's eyes, but Mark would have no pity.

There was more than one way to skin a cat.

He'd driven to Washington D.C. and shifted back to 1990 when Rialto was still a rookie agent with the IRS, before he ever had a shifter, before he had even ever heard of Mark Carpen.

For several evenings, Mark tracked Rialto from work to home, looking for the best point of attack. This "innocent" Rialto had no reason to suspect he was being stalked.

The tax agent had a bad habit of cutting through a particularly narrow and dark alley on his way home each night to his apartment in Georgetown. Mark chose an especially dark evening to execute his plan.

He waited in the recess of a doorframe which was partially blocked by a dumpster, dressed in solid black.

At the ideal moment, Mark emerged from the shadows like a nocturnal panther ready to pounce upon its prey. The sight of the automatic pistol drained enough blood from Rialto's face that Mark could see him paling even in the limited moonlight.

"Wha...What do you want?"

Mark did not answer. There was nothing to say.

"Here...t...t...take my wallet, take whatever you want," he stuttered.

Mark squeezed his trigger several times in a row, and joy swept through him as the explosive retorts of bullets successfully fired rang in his ears. No misfire had occurred this time, and the acrid aroma of burnt gunpowder smelled so sweet. Only five feet separated the men. There was no way to miss.

Yet...Rialto still stood. Why was he not down? Mark fired again, and again, and then two more times. Rialto took a step back, almost stumbling over himself, and screamed curt shrieks of bloody murder with each successive shot before racing for the other end of the alley. He didn't appear to be wounded.

Disgusted, Mark slung his weapon to the pavement where it clattered to a stop against the brick wall of the opposing building. He'd worn gloves, so there would be no prints.

It was time to shift out.

Alexander Rialto stumbled in mid-run and almost crashed to the sidewalk, more from an excess of adrenaline than any injury, though he did feel a stinging sensation in his side. Reaching down, his hand came away bloody. Terrified, he stopped and ripped his shirt up to inspect the damage.

Relief came like a flood. It was nothing more than a crease in his skin, a long, shallow bloody cut. One of the bullets had narrowly missed causing some real damage.

How that man had missed at such a close range, and after so many times, he had no idea. How many shots had he fired? Six? Seven? He'd lost count in his panic. All that mattered was he was safe and the guy hadn't followed him. He was even more relieved to see a police cruiser parked a little way up the street.

**

"That you, Hardy?"

"Yeah."

The stink of Boston's sewers wafted around them, its nasty little tendrils periodically assaulting their noses. The smell seemed a little worse today than usual, though the underground entrance to their headquarters was in a section of pipe currently not in use, and the paths they blazed in these forgotten tubes tended to stay far away from actual refuse and sewage.

"I've been thinking, we need to get some air freshener spray for when we come in," Hardy said. "This stench is in all my clothes."

"Yeah, good idea. I'll ask Savannah to pick some up."

"Why, 'cause she's a girl?"

"No, because she's the office manager."

"Get 'em yourself, man."

"Why don't you get them?"

"Fine."

Irritation still lingered from their failed plans as they ascended silently in the elevator. Just one more of the many safety features Mark had installed in their secure facility was a top-of-the-line elevator which made almost no sound as it operated. They fully expected Rialto would invade their inner-sanctum sooner or later, so they did their best to stack the deck in their favor.

Door hinges were well oiled, squeaky floorboards were immediately replaced. In addition to all the electronic security, there were a plethora of hidden cameras throughout the edifice, and numerous secret passageways and hiding places. The only people who knew about these things were himself, Hardy, Ty, and Savannah.

If either Laura or Randolph DeCleary had shifted into their time anywhere near the headquarters or the remote sensors, Mark and Hardy would have been alerted to the unfriendlies by a silent alarm long before they got to the upper floor.

Yet, since Laura and Randolph had simply walked in, no alarm was triggered. The alarm sensors couldn't detect a shifter when not in use as the shifters were normally passive devices. They emitted no traceable signal unless activated.

So, when the elevator doors opened, Hardy and Mark were quite stunned to see Laura and Randolph DeCleary standing over Ty's inert body. Uncharacteristically, both men stood motionless instead of jumping into action. Perhaps if it had been anybody but Laura standing there, or Randolph DeCleary for that matter, who they never expected to see in this modern era, they wouldn't have been taken off guard so completely.

Yet, there they stood, frozen in place, unbelieving, watching the woman they had both loved, or at least they thought they had loved, standing over the body of their dear friend, and they couldn't tell whether he was alive or dead. Laura held no visible weapon, but Randolph wielded a gun in his left hand.

Mark blinked several times as if trying to clear his eyes.

The elevator's doors had been so silent, Laura and Randolph were still unaware of their presence.

"Laura?" Mark was incredulous.

Randolph whipped around. Forgetting the gun in his hand, he reached for a sword on his hip which wasn't there, a habit which now cost him any advantage.

Mark drew his own pistol and shot Randolph square in the chest without taking his numbed eyes from Laura. Randolph flew back a few feet and fell. He didn't get up, but there was no blood. Body armor had stopped the bullet, but not the concussion of it. The shock had knocked the ex-knight out.

"Laura?" Mark repeated. "What's going on?"

She smiled, lifting her tan, slender arm for both to see. An all-too-familiar, gleaming silver bracelet adorned her wrist. It should have looked large for her size, but instead seemed a perfect fit. A perfectly nauseating fit.

The magnitude of her betrayal shocked Mark speechless. He shook his head, disbelieving, not willing to believe.

Being the more cynical of the two, Hardy accepted what he saw without reaction. This would have to be dealt with like anything else. "What did you do to Ty, Laura?" He asked.

"He'll be all right," she purred. "I just tased him." As she slinked her way toward them, sashaying her hips seductively, it was all Mark could do to keep from falling under her spell again. She was incredible.

"Stop right there, Laura." Mark turned the pistol on her.

"Aw, you wouldn't shoot little ol' me, would you?" Her smile might have charmed the pants off a cobra or maybe even the Cheshire Cat himself.

"One of us will," Hardy blurted. His gun was out and pointed on her heart too. It was one of the few times Mark had ever seen him looking emotional.

Mark sighed. "Why did you tase him, Laura?"

Unlike Hardy, all emotion had strangely left Mark. A cool indifference had taken roost. "What are you doing here? And what are you doing with DeCleary?"

She clammed up. The distinct clarity of purpose in their tone proved they were serious about shooting her. Her seductive act deflated like a blow-up toy pricked with a pin. Slouching, she hefted herself onto a table, staring at them indifferently while she chewed some stale chewing gum she'd probably had for over an hour.

"Let's have it, Laura."

She refused to speak.

"You ungrateful wench! We gave you everything! If you didn't like me, you had Hardy. Was there anything we didn't buy you? I saved your life for crying out loud! How could you betray us like this? Working for Rialto? How could you break in here and hurt Ty?" Mark's fury welled up like some uncontrolled beast, flashing and slashing fiercely.

Then, just as quickly, it dissipated. He couldn't guess what was going through her mind. He'd never been able to.

"I didn't *break* in, Mark."

Thankfully, Ty was beginning to stir. He hadn't been truly unconscious, just incapacitated. Groggily, he struggled to roll over and lifted himself into a chair. They wanted to help him, but doing so would have cost them position.

"H...H...Hey, guys," Ty croaked like a frog on its last legs. "I let her in."

Mark frowned, but understood how she'd gotten the drop on him. He wouldn't have had reason to be wary.

Randolph was moaning and rolling around now too.

"They're waiting on Rialto," Ty managed.

"Is that so?" Sarcasm dripped from Mark's words. He motioned with the pistol. "Gather your friend and get out of here. You disgust me."

To her credit, for the first time, she looked hurt. She slapped Randolph's cheeks until he was fully awake and then helped him to his feet. She wrapped his arm around her shoulder and neck, lending support as they walked.

They stumbled toward the door just as Savannah was coming back in.

"What's going on?" she asked. The tension and injured men made it obvious something dramatic had just happened.

Laura stopped just outside the doorframe and turned her face back toward Mark, her gaze not quite meeting his. "It's not like you think, Mark. Rialto's got a lot of control."

"Everybody's got a choice."

"It's not like you think."

"Get out," he ordered.

Chapter 39

The tension in the room was palpable. The pool tables and cues were untouched, no one lounged on any of the couches. Each face was etched with a similar expression of stern concern. The only bright spot in the otherwise dreary morning was the smell of the warm pastries Savannah had brought.

Ty was okay. The taser had hurt like the dickens, incapacitating him for a few minutes, but he'd shaken it off. Some of his muscles still spasmed every now and then.

This building was their castle, their safe haven. It was the only place they could feel safe now that the war was on again. Here and only here, the enemy could not break in or sneak in. The only way they could get in at all was through subterfuge as Laura had done, and Mark had already laid down a new standing rule that *no one* outside the four of them was allowed inside the building at any time. Period. At least not without serious discussion beforehand.

Mark asked Savannah to temporarily move her things into the building for safety reasons, and she agreed. He'd build her a nice private apartment in one of the upper floors until they could work something else out.

All too easily, he could envision Rialto snatching her off the street, holding her hostage in order to get at them or secure a way into the building. She was to check in at certain times per day so they'd know if anything happened to her. Mark gave her certain code words to use under duress if she called or emailed and was being held against her will. If she thought she was being followed, Mark instructed her to simply not check in with them at the prescribed time and they would find her.

He, Ty, and Hardy would all have to live in the building

as well. At least, until the Rialto problem was solved. They didn't need more than one perimeter to defend.

"How can we possibly stop seven of them, Mark?" Ty asked.

"I don't know," was his quiet, pensive answer.

"I'll tell you how. We'll take them down one by one," Hardy declared.

"Including Laura?" Mark raised an eyebrow.

"She's left us with no choice, hasn't she?" Hardy grimaced.

"You're right...she hasn't," Mark admitted, "I know how you felt now, Ty. Having saved someone's life only to have it come back and bite you in the butt." Mark tossed an empty paper cup at the trash can. It bounced off the rim and hit the floor. "The trick is *how* do we do that, Hardy? If we just kill one, two, or three of them, the rest will shift back to undo it. We've been down this road before."

"What if we ring an area with small explosives that would be triggered by an unfriendly shifter?" Ty offered. "We could lure one of them into a place, take that guy out, and then the explosives will kill anyone who shifts in to save them."

Mark shot the plan down. "Too dangerous for us. Plus, they would just shift in farther away and use rifles."

It was a brain-bending conundrum, the likes of which no warrior in history had ever had to contemplate. They harnessed all their creativity, yet still drew a blank. It seemed an unsolvable puzzle.

Finally, Mark ended the meeting. "I'm going to go see Bobby Prescott and see if he can come up with any new tools we might use to gain an advantage."

***

The tension in Rialto's boardroom was born not of pre-occupation but animosity. They'd failed, which meant he blamed his people regardless of any culpability of his own.

"There is no excuse for this!" Rialto ranted, "You had them in their headquarters and failed. Now they know you work for me!"

Laura was defiant. She ignored his distasteful remark about her working for him. As true as that may be, she didn't like believing it. "We had Ty down and out," she replied, "We were waiting on you to get there to finish him off, *like you requested,* when Mark and Hardy showed up. If you hadn't let them get away, we'd be done."

"Why *did* they get away, Torino? Why didn't you two follow Carpen and finish him off? If you'd done your job, Phillips couldn't have escaped."

"The detector didn't work. We didn't know what time he shifted to."

"What do you mean it didn't work? Was the battery down? You can't turn it off."

"I don't know what happened. Carpen shifted and when I checked the detector, instead of a date and time, it had some kind of nonsense error symbols."

"Did you break it? They're supposed to be indestructible. Give it to me." Rialto held out his hand.

Torino gave him his detector. Rialto ordered him to shift in and out.

"Look," He held it up to show him, "It's working fine."

"It wasn't then."

"Irvine, what do you say?"

Stanley Irvine squeezed the bridge of his nose without removing his thin-rimmed glasses and closed his eyes in concentration. These meetings made him nervous. These *people* made him nervous. He'd been involuntarily sucked into this mafia of sorts, and the things lurking behind the eyes of the others made it clear to him he wasn't likely to get out very easily.

"I couldn't say for sure..."

"And if you were *pressed* to say," Rialto pushed.

"Instinct tells me they may have developed some kind of jammer. It wouldn't be too hard to do. Create a small emitter that mimics the electro-magnetic field emitted when they shift, but adds random fluctuations to that field, making it impossible for the detector to interpret."

"Could you make some of those for us?"

"Sure."

"Why hadn't you mentioned this possibility before?" Rialto demanded.

"Uh...it didn't occur to me it would be needed."

"You're lacking, Irvine. Seriously lacking. I don't want to be caught off guard like this again. Do I make myself clear?"

Having found his scapegoat, Rialto visibly calmed.

"People, we've lost the element of surprise, but we've still got superior numbers. We'll match their technology again soon. The truce is off. Once we're ready, we'll attack, and this time we'll succeed."

"Alex," Laura purred, "We did learn something interesting."

"What?"

"When I tased Ty? It turned his watch red. I thought it might have been the electricity from the taser that shut his shifter down."

It took a minute for what she'd said to register, but as it did, along with all the corresponding possibilities, a genuine grin broke out on Rialto's face.

Chapter 40

If we were lost in fields of clover,
would we walk even closer until the trip was over?
And would it be ok if I didn't know the way?

"Would You Go With Me?"

~ Josh Turner

Hardy didn't like being cooped up. Not at all. In fact, he couldn't stand it. If he were in the field, that would be a different story. He'd once laid virtually motionless in a sniper's nest for over 18 hours, only moving once. He could stand being confined inside a small building for days on end if his mission were clear, and it was necessary for surveillance reasons.

In this case, however, Mark was talking about an open-ended, self-imposed confinement until they could figure something out. Not that he was questioning Mark's leadership. Mark was absolutely right. They needed to stay out of sight and in a strong defensive position until they had a viable plan. It was just the vagueness of the timetable which rubbed against his ADD-leaning personality. Well, Mark and Ty could lock themselves up, but he had other plans.

The cottage was a lot like he remembered, but there had been some changes made since he last saw it a year ago. The home was humble, yet quaint and inviting. The thatched roof's vibrant color had dulled after months of exposure to the elements. The log walls were now covered by roughly hewn planks of wood, stacked horizontally, one above the other. A window had also been added, and Hardy noticed a bit of blackened discoloration at one corner of it. The charred wood told him it had probably been scavenged from one of the burned-out villages nearby.

He wasn't sure if she was home. If not, he'd just wait. She'd be back sooner or later. He raised his hand to knock on the door in spite of the lack of activity he sensed. The door swung open before his knuckles could even touch the wood.

"Hello, Hardy," she smiled.

"Hello, Abigail."

"Come in. Have a seat. I've already put some tea on. Saw you coming." She withdrew back into the house.

Indeed, she had two places set for tea, as if she'd been expecting him. It took a moment for his eyes to adjust to the dimmer light inside.

She looked the same. Beautiful, pure, full of life.

"I hope I'm not intruding," he said.

"Not at all. Tis good to see you, to be sure."

"We've got a situation in 2014. Rialto's got us bottled up..."

"Surely you've not come to ask me to return with you," she cut him off.

"No, no," he laughed, "Relax. That's not it. Mark's got us locked up inside headquarters until we can mount a counterattack, and I'll go stir crazy if I have to stay cooped up. I was hoping I could stay here for a time until we get things sorted out in the future. I'd be no trouble, I swear."

Her laughter was light, like a bubbling brook. "Certainly! You are always welcome here, any of you. It would not look right though, us living in the same house. We'll set about building you a cabin next door right away."

"That sounds like a lot of trouble. I don't think I'll be here that long. I'll be shifting back to headquarters during the day and staying here at night. Perhaps I can stay in a nearby village?"

"Nonsense. I'll stay with a friend in the next town. You can have my house till you've got your own place."

"I feel bad putting you out like that," he murmured.

"It must be bad — the problem with Rialto, if you're taking such drastic measures."

"It's not good. He's got at least six time-shifters with him now, besides himself, including good ol' Randolph DeCleary. You remember him from our little 'vacation' back in medieval England."

"I surely do."

"We're outnumbered."

"God will see Mark through, of that I am certain." She took a long, slow sip from her cup of black tea.

"I'm not so certain Mark believes in God," Hardy replied.

"And you?"

"What about me?"

"Do *you* believe in God? Isn't that why you're really here? To learn about God?"

The blood rushed to his cheeks. "I told you, I need a place to hang out."

"You're blushing. Surely there are lots of places and times where you could hide. Why did you come *here*? Am I not right in what I suggest?"

"Maybe."

"Don't worry, we have plenty of time." Her smile was soothing.

***

He spent a lot of time working on a home of his own. He hated putting Abbie out of hers. From time to time, he'd shift back and check in on Mark and Ty. They were curious about where he'd been hanging out, but they didn't pry. They knew he wouldn't do anything that would jeopardize security.

He didn't return to the future every day after all. Sometimes, he'd spend weeks in the 1600's before shifting forward. Yet, for Mark and Ty, he'd only be absent from headquarters for however long he wished for them to perceive. It was fantastic. He was on an extended vacation, if you could call frontier life a vacation. His shifter made it possible to live two completely different lives, disconnecting centuries so they no longer progressed chronologically, at least with respect to him.

The pristine untouched Massachusetts woods were gorgeous. The crisp air was fresh. The sky looked bluer than any you could see in modern day. Even the birds seemed to sing louder. Maybe they were happier. They certainly didn't have to put up with cars, noise, or pollution. No cell towers, no power lines, no billboards, no trash, nothing to blemish the landscape. And Abbie made very good company.

He felt bad about taking time off from their normal operations. He could be out there saving people's lives and instead he was taking it easy, kicking it back in the 17th century. He needed some time off, he reasoned. Plus, they weren't doing normal "save" operations right now in 2014, not until they sorted the Rialto mess out.

He built himself a structure which was essentially nothing more than a line shack. It had a small fireplace, a smaller table, and enough room for a single bed. There was no point in dedicating a lot of effort to it, as he spent most of his time visiting with Abbie in her cottage or out hunting. Once he'd finished his shack, he threw himself into bettering Abbie's house for her.

She'd already replaced the ropes that held her roof up with less perishable iron chains, but Hardy set about building her a real roof, one that wouldn't have to be supported by chains from above. She sincerely appreciated his efforts, but resisted when he'd expressed a desire to add rooms to the house. She didn't need such a fancy place, she said. So, instead, the two of them set about improving her garden, planting new vegetables, expanding its size.

At night, she would read to him from her well-worn Bible, one she'd inherited from her father when he passed. He didn't want to admit it to himself, but that was the real reason he was so content spending all this time back here. Well, *she* was the real reason — but the evening Bible-reading was a big part of it.

He'd never before entertained a belief in God. Not that he'd necessarily been a committed atheist or anything, just an unofficial agnostic. He'd always believed that if there were a God,

He must have simply wound the universe up and then let it go, watching it unwind like some giant, cosmic sport. Otherwise, he couldn't reconcile the evil he saw in the world with the possibility of God.

His parents were New England Catholics and had raised him in that tradition, but he'd shrugged off the formality of their belief system as soon as he'd hit his teens. He'd convinced himself that if there were such a thing as God, then He couldn't be known, and He certainly wasn't like the God everyone claimed they knew.

Still, two things shook up his deeply ingrained convictions, or lack thereof. The first was meeting a person as good as Abbie. She was pure — truly a good person. If he'd ever met anyone who could be called "righteous" it would be her.

He'd already met evil on the battlefield a thousand times over before Mark had found him, and since then, he'd personally witnessed it again and again burning in the eyes of countless vicious criminals before he dispatched them. He saw it incarnate in the person of Alexander Rialto.

To meet someone like Abbie, however, was a first. She was a direct contrast to all the selfish, evil people he'd ever met. That blatant difference between good and evil before him forced him to recognize there was something more to the world than what he'd been willing to admit. Maybe something spiritual *was* going on behind the scenes, motivating people, influencing events and minds in such a way people could see the effect, but not the cause.

In spite of Hardy's argumentative digs at Ty to the contrary, the second thing that had shaken Hardy's belief system was the obvious interference they'd experienced from time to time when trying to alter history. Clearly, Mark could not save his kids. Ty had not been able to save a few of his buddies. None of them were apparently allowed to change any major historical event.

The operative word there being *allowed*. Unless there was some yet undiscovered natural force of the physical universe which kicked in automatically to prevent chronological paradoxes they couldn't predict, and of which Bobby Prescott, their resident physicist, couldn't conceive, Hardy had to concede the force preventing them from changing certain things was an intelligent one. Which could only mean that God had not just wound the universe up and let it go, but was still actively involved.

Abbie had been right. Being restricted to headquarters in the future was just an excuse for coming back here. He'd really wanted to spend time with Abbie, to learn from her, to learn what she believed. His heart was hungry for answers.

Those simple hours they spent every evening reading from Scripture, the gentle intonations of her soft voice as she read, the way she answered his questions without judgment and posed pointed questions of her own at just the right moment, it was transforming him, bringing him to a new state of being.

She'd asked him the night before last if he was ready to follow Christ, but he'd deferred. She was a dedicated Christian, but it was a big leap from admitting there was a God who was actively involved in the daily life of people to believing that Jesus was His Son. There were still too many doubts, though Abbie was an expert at deflating his seemingly important questions with little pricks of truth.

He probably would be ready someday, he guessed. It was likely only a matter of time at the rate he was going. Just not yet...

Chapter 41

Today, Hardy was worried.

Abbie had left on a hunt early yesterday and had not come home all night, nor was she back this morning. She'd slept overnight in the forest before, but she'd always told him before she did that. This time, she'd said she'd be back before nightfall.

Something was wrong. Hardy loaded a knapsack, slung it over his shoulder, and headed down the path she'd taken.

Three hours later, he found signs she'd backtracked and tried to hide it. She wouldn't have done that unless she'd thought someone was following her. She'd done a good job of it too. If he weren't an expert tracker himself, he never would have seen it.

He soon discovered the reason for her actions. A couple of moccasined footprints crossed her trail a few hundred yards further on. The natives had been following her.

She hadn't been able to shake them and later took more drastic evasive maneuvers. An hour further down the trail, he found a hastily constructed booby trap which had already been sprung. She'd cut and sharpened some short sticks and tied them in series to the end of a low tree branch like spikes. She'd pulled that branch back, hooked it on another branch, and then set a trip line across the path which would release it when kicked — into the legs of whoever tripped it.

Somebody had triggered the trap, because drops of blood ran in a line across the tops of the dried leaves, showing where her stalker had staggered on. The outlines of the footprints matched the type of moccasin typically worn by Wampanoag, which wasn't really a surprise. The height of the trap indicated Abbie hadn't really wanted to kill, just wound and slow down. It had most likely struck the stalker in the thigh.

Hardy would have to be on guard against booby traps himself now. He could end up her unintended victim if her pursuer successfully bypassed one. Sure enough, about thirty minutes later, he spied another nasty-looking trap.

This one was more serious. Aimed at neck level, this spiked branch was intended to maim, at a minimum. Deftly, he undid the hazard and moved on. He decided it would be safer to continue following on a line about ten feet to the left of the actual path she'd walked from here on out.

There were no more booby-traps, however, before he found her. She lay face down in the dirt in a small clearing directly ahead of him, her body distended unnaturally. An ugly arrow shaft protruded from her slender back.

He raced to her side, oblivious to the possible danger of attackers still lurking in the bushes.

None apparently were, as the afternoon air was not stirred by any new airborne missiles.

He was too late.

They'd slaughtered her mercilessly. There was more than just the one arrow in her back. Another jutted horizontally from her arm, and a third stuck out from her foot.

He estimated she must have gotten off a few shots of her own because she normally kept seven to eight arrows in her quiver, and now there were only five.

It was just one more killing to the Wampanoag. One more death in the war between them and the settlers of Massachusetts, but it was the rude destruction of a precious friend to him.

Hardy was not one in whom passion boiled easily, yet as he held her pale, limp body in his arms, its fiery stirrings titillated his blood into a fury he hadn't known before.

He vowed then and there to make them pay for this. He would kill every last one of 'em.

He just prayed this wasn't one of *those* cases.

Please, God, help me fix this.

***

One day earlier

The grey mist parted briefly, and she caught a glimpse of the shadowy figure as it flitted back and forth between the distant trees and brush. Curt, muffled cries echoing in the cool morning air accompanied it wherever it went.

Abbie had left home quite early this morning in search of quail, turkey, or whatever other game she might find. A good tracker knows when they are being followed, and she'd noticed right away. In these times of war, she had no doubt as to the nationality of the man, and surely it had to be a man, on the trail behind her. Of course, he had to be Wampanoag.

She'd set a few traps hoping to warn him off, or at least slow him down, but he'd avoided them and closed in further. She should have stopped to mount an ambush, or made some kind of attempt to dig in and defend herself. Instead, she'd stupidly walked into this clearing and was now exposed and vulnerable.

She'd walked in a trap of her own making. Imitation bird calls sounded from the brush on all sides. Her follower had not been operating alone.

He had creatively herded her into this clearing where his friends waited in ambush, and she was hopelessly surrounded.

She notched an arrow and dropped to her stomach in the grass, which really didn't provide much cover, but it was better than nothing.

That was when she first saw the shadowy figure.

One Indian had stood, ready to release a shot her way, when the strange form appeared suddenly, slaying the would-be attacker, and then disappeared just as quickly. The thin grey fog that ebbed and flowed with the breeze made positive identification impossible from this distance, yet she suspected it must be Hardy. Who else knew she was out here that could appear and disappear at will?

The shadow darted silently between groups of hidden Wampanoag, eliciting without mercy weakened death cries from those it attacked. She moved closer, wiggling her way through the grass, partly desiring to help, partly wanting to confirm it was indeed Hardy.

The sound of static from the path behind her followed by a heavy thud startled her. She whipped her head around and saw the shadow man had just killed the Wampanoag who'd been following her.

It *was* Hardy.

She got a good look at him before he shifted back out, though she'd never seen such tight anger in his face before. Mark, yes, but not Hardy. Hardy was always so much more at ease.

When she reached the far side of the clearing where most of the fighting was taking place, several shocking realizations hit her at once. First, she had apparently been surrounded by a war party of about thirty to forty painted warriors lusting for white blood. If it weren't for Hardy and his unnatural ability to shift through time, she most certainly would have been killed.

Second, Hardy was not quitting. He was like a man possessed. The warriors were already in full retreat, fleeing as fast as they could from the deadly phantom. Yet, he did not let them go, but pursued them in whatever direction they ran.

A warrior in his early twenties rushed to escape the killing ghost and twisted in a panic at the sound of static behind him. He stumbled, fell back, and raised his hands helplessly in a fruitless gesture to fend off the phantom, his face morphed with fear. Hardy dispatched him.

He should stop. The will to fight had left the warriors.

"Hardy!" She called.

He didn't waver. Another warrior fell and the phantom vanished once more.

As soon as she saw him appear again, she yelled louder, "Hardy, stop!"

He paused and turned toward her. She didn't recognize the distant, pained torment in his eyes.

"It's okay, Hardy. Stop. They're leaving. I'm safe."

She understood they must have originally killed her and he'd found her body. That was the source of the ferocity in him now, which was thankfully, and finally, melting away.

He came to her.

"I've been fighting for four days," he mumbled to no one in particular.

Of course, he could only shift six times before his shifter shut down. As many times as she'd seen him shift just now, he must have spent several nights sleeping in the damp forest waiting to resume the attack. Abject weariness showed now where the anger had been.

She laid her fingertips lightly on his cheek. "They're gone, Hardy."

"They'll be back."

"No, they won't. Let them go."

Bending down, he kissed her softly on the lips.

And she let him.

Chapter 42

Randall Cook wiped a strand of greasy hair out of his face. "So who are we gonna test it on, Cap'n?"

Even in modern society, the man avoided baths far too often and he stank. Rialto never thought he'd have to make rules about hygiene, but it was getting out of hand. "I thought we'd test it on you, Cook," he replied dryly.

"Uh-uh." He shook his head vigorously. "I ain't vol'teerin' for no electric'ty test."

"Plageanet?" Rialto motioned to the former plantation owner, who stepped up behind Cook and promptly slammed his weapon into the back of the sailor's skull. Cook collapsed to the floor unconscious.

"There ya are." Plageanet looked disdainfully upon the fallen man before turning away.

Graves and Torino stood like silent sentinels in opposing corners of the room. They weren't about to let anyone sneak up behind *them*. Laura merely watched, a blank facial expression denying any observer insight into the thoughts running behind her eyes. DeCleary had refused to participate; he wasn't even in the room.

Rialto dragged Cook onto two metal plates Stanley Irvine had designed just for this test. He'd asked Irvine to study the taser and any way they could use electricity to make a shifter inactive. He knew that tasers had a potential of anywhere from 50,000 to 400,000 volts, but Irvine had explained that voltage wasn't as important as amperage when it came to electrocuting somebody, and that when a person was being tased, only about 2 milliamps would be flowing. It was enough current to cause a lot of pain and incapacitate, but not to kill.

So, they designed a plate system where they could test the actual amperage necessary to shut down a shifter, and Cook was now on them, fully clothed to match the electrical conditions that would likely be present when they needed to use such a set-up. They attached electrodes at different points on Cook's skin to measure the current flowing through him.

Rialto flipped the switch allowing electricity to flow through the plates and then slowly turned a knob which controlled the voltage differential between them. They immediately registered .5 milliamps flowing between the electrodes on Cook. Rialto stepped it up from there. There was no need to cause his man any more pain than necessary. Laura's job was to monitor the shifter and signal as soon as the face of it turned red.

She did at just a little over 1 milliamp. That didn't seem like a lot, but there it was. He shut the over-sized equipment off.

"Wake him up," he ordered.

Plageanet threw water from a glass in Cook's face. It was a good thing Rialto had already turned the shock plate off.

The sailor began to roll about, cursing.

"When he's got his senses back, tell him to take a bath," Rialto called over his shoulder.

***

September 12th 1675, Swansea, MA

The romance proceeded unusually, and Hardy had not expected anything different. For starters, Abbie called it a courtship, not a romance, or dating. She had let him kiss her, but just that once, and the kiss had been almost platonic in nature. Still, it lingered in his mind like none other.

He was in love with her. She did not deny having feelings for him as well, but informed him flatly that things could not progress until she was sure of his religious piety. In the back of his mind, he'd always known it would be this way. He knew she was waiting for him to shrug off his agnosticism once and for all and make a final decision to follow her Lord. She'd made that perfectly clear.

Still, he resented it. He shouldn't, but he did, even though he understood her and her reasoning. The idea of making such a tremendous decision under pressure to continue a "courtship," well, it just rubbed him wrong. *If* he were to make such a decision, he wanted it to be genuine. He would decide independently of her, of his desire for her, and he would decide such a thing when *he* was ready.

"Hardy, I hate to ask...but I need help."

"You?" He laughed. "You never need help."

"It's my young cousin, Nathaniel. Metacomet attacked a small hamlet nearby and little Nathan was killed. I just found out. He was only seven."

"I didn't know you had any family left here." He knew her mother, father, and brother were all dead.

"I've a few scattered here and there. Nathaniel is the son of one of my first cousins. His parents died of the fever a few years ago. Some neighbors took him in."

"This war has really been devastating, hasn't it?"

"Thankfully, Metacomet and the Wampanoag are beginning to lose more than they win. I spoke with one of the colony's officials a month ago. They think they'll have him on the run shortly, but he estimated we've lost almost half our brothers and sisters in Christ in this bloody war. They don't know for sure, but the Wampanoag may have lost as many as seven out of every ten. It's so senseless."

"Yet many times unavoidable."

"Will you help?"

He couldn't resist her large blue eyes. The beginnings of unwanted tears made them shine even more crystalline. "Of course, Abbie."

***

September 7ᵗʰ 1675, Hadley, MA

He was all too familiar with the scene. Puritan village. Indians attacking. From the first time when they'd saved Abbie's life to his latest foray with her to save fellow colonists from Metocomet's hatchet, Hardy had become an unwitting veteran of King Philip's War which took place three hundred years before he was even inducted into the U.S. army.

He sat with his back to the wooden wall of a home on the outskirts of the village. The battle had already begun. Hardy tamped the tobacco down in his rustic 17ᵗʰ century pipe and relit it, taking a deep breath of smoke. He reclined his head against the weather-worn planks, his posture relaxed.

Abbie was a bit more tense than he. The boy *was* her cousin after all, but this wouldn't be any different from other extractions, he reasoned.

The boy was fine for the time being. He was cowering in some brush about fifty yards away. Hardy could even see the Indian who would kill him walking slowly toward the little guy's hiding place. There was plenty of time.

Hardy laid down his pipe, steadying it to make sure it wouldn't tip over. He loved this Puritan tobacco. It had a certain kick to it modern tobacco lacked.

He raised his bow, notched an arrow, and centered his sights on the warrior's chest. He pulled the string back to his cheek and waited for the perfect moment to release.

Then, the string snapped.

Abbie let out a low moan of distress as she scrambled to get her own bow ready. While Hardy was busy restringing his bow, Abbie swiftly loosed three missiles at the attacker. Each shaft sailed true, only to veer off sharply at the last minute as if blown by some unfelt wind. That got Hardy's attention. Abbie was not one to miss.

Tension now coursed through his veins. This was not

going to be an easy extraction after all. Abbie dropped her weapon and ran to rescue the boy, but she tripped on a rock and slammed shoulder-first into the ground.

It was too late. Hardy grabbed Abbie and turned her head away from the carnage, covering her eyes with his hand. He immediately shifted them back to several minutes before the attack.

Distress in the eyes of someone you love is an excellent motivator and Hardy redoubled his efforts. Abbie was bordering on frantic. He'd never seen her like this, but this was family, and she was afraid. She was afraid this was *one of those times.* One of those times they didn't like to talk about, but one of those times where the unseen hand prevented their interference.

This time, when the boy hid himself, Hardy hunkered low and ran toward him, hoping to grab the boy and whisk him off to safety. However, the boy heard the noise of Hardy's approach and panicked. Without looking and fearing it to be an Indian, he ran off in the opposite direction. This accelerated the inevitable, driving him right into the hands of his killer. Hardy had a few more seconds to try something else, but his bowstring broke again and his rifle misfired twice. He shifted out of the unpleasantness once more.

He sat on his haunches with a solid thunk. He shook his head, not liking how things were shaping up.

"I don't think this is going to work, Abbie."

"Please," she pleaded.

"You've seen this before. You know what it means."

"*Please*, Hardy."

She melted his resolve to give up. It reformed into determination to succeed. He *would* do this for her. One way or the other.

He retrieved some additional modern weapons from his mini-armory stashed under his one-bedroom shack next to Abbie's cottage. He carefully noted the line of attack the Indian would take. Alone, so Abbie wouldn't see the boy's body, he shifted forward to just after the battle and located the Indian's footprints. One by one, he stuck a stick in each footprint to mark its exact spot, and then, holding the stick, he shifted to the night before the battle and buried landmines where the Indian would step. He buried seven in all.

Then, he and Abbie shifted into the middle of the fight once more. Together, they would fire on the warrior simultaneously. She'd use her bow, as that was all she was comfortable with, but he wasn't going to waste time with that. He'd brought a M240, an Uzi, and several pistols, which he planned to unload in rapid succession as needed.

One by one, each of his guns misfired. Out of the corner of his eye, he couldn't tell what kind of trouble Abbie was having, but she obviously hadn't succeeded either. Fatalistic resignation drifted back into his heart, but he dissolved it into dogged determination once more.

An audible click accompanied the warrior's first step on a mine, but as his foot left it, no explosion followed. A dud.

A hollow click from the second mine, and then, again, nothing. Disgusted with failure, Hardy began packing his gear back into his oversized duffel bag.

Suddenly, an unexpected explosion tore through the air. Little Nathan was knocked onto his back, but he was all right. The Wampanoag warrior was another story. There wasn't much left of him.

Hardy was so startled, he didn't react instantly as he'd been trained, though the sight of Abbie rushing to the boy's side broke his dumbfounded reverie. A few other warriors were drawn to their side of the field by the explosion, but Hardy took them out before they knew what had happened. In less than five seconds, Abbie was back at his side, cradling her young cousin in her arms. Hardy gripped her shoulder and shifted all three of them to safety.

He set her down under a tree. She was doing her best to soothe Nathaniel, stroking his hair and rocking him gently. Later, Hardy would need to shift back and disarm the remaining mines.

For now, his feet were rooted to the ground like the oak

tree under which Abbie sat. Stunned. He had not believed they would succeed. He'd been certain little Nathan's death would turn out to be one of those unchangeable events. All the evidence had pointed that way.

Yet...there he lay.

Breathing. Alive.

Hardy had not believed. Now, he did believe. Something about the unfolding of this drama pierced the last levee around his heart. He felt the floodgates open and he surrendered his last resistance.

The tears in her eyes had been unbearable, yet he'd had no hope. Then, the invisible hand holding him back had suddenly and mercifully released its grasp.

By itself, a landmine working as it should was no miracle, but it had not been chance foiling their efforts until then.

That force, that power, which till now had been insurmountable, controlled the destiny of the universe. He knew that they had not overcome the force, but that *it* had shown mercy. The force had shown compassion and love. And he knew within himself the force was no "it," but God Himself. He did not understand the hows and the whys, but submission was the only natural response.

"I'm ready, Abbie."

She nodded, smiling between sunny tears raining down her cheeks. She knew he didn't mean he wanted to leave.

Chapter 43

June 1ˢᵗ 2009, New London, CT

It was a work of art, this cold, sterile room Alexander Rialto had constructed. Devilishly simple in design, yet cleverly sophisticated in concept. The walls were poured concrete, six feet thick, with no way to break in or out. There were no windows and only one door, which was made of thick steel and reminiscent of that of a bank vault. It was sealed with massive bolts and a time-lock that would only open with Rialto's palm print, or in two years, whichever came first. The sensor pad could also sense a decrease in skin temperature if somebody killed him and then tried to cut off his hand to get in.

Inside were a series of narrow, finger-width vents lining the ceiling which could emit any kind of gas he wished to inject into the ventilation system.

Few explosives on earth could penetrate these walls or the door, and none that a person could carry.

His secret weapon was the massive magnetic field generating coils he'd buried inside all the walls, above the ceiling, and even under the floor. These coils produced strong electromagnetic fields that would cause increased electric current to flow within just about anything in the room. The currents produced were so strong they would instantly fry any sensitive electronic devices. Laptops, televisions, even cell-phones would begin smoking within seconds. The human body, on the other hand, was a natural resistor. Exactly 1.2 milliamps of current would flow through a person without any exterior source of electricity being applied.

In short, when he flipped the switch, whoever was

standing inside would experience a current of 1.2 milliamps, which was enough to make a person seriously uncomfortable, but not enough to hurt or stun them. It *was* enough, however, to permanently shut down a shifter said person might be wearing until Rialto turned the system off from the outside.

They'd tested it too. Everyone's shifter shut down once inside until they turned the generators off or they left the room.

He couldn't wait to try it out.

The plan was to get one of the goody-two-shoes trio to shift into the room while chasing one of Rialto's crew through time. Rialto didn't care which one of Mark's men it was. Any would do. They'd hold that one prisoner in the room until another showed up looking for him.

That someone would come looking for the guy was a given. The room was large on purpose. It measured 150 feet by 150 feet. Rialto had built it knowing Carpen's propensity to shift into a situation at a distance from their object of interest for safety reasons. However, 150 feet would be more than adequate to catch the followers even if they were being cautious.

Anyone who shifted into his giant room would be hopelessly trapped, unable to shift out. Once he had all three, it would be night-night forever for Carpen and crew. Even if he only got two of them, they could round up the last one without having to worry about his friends coming to save him.

It was a nasty little plan. He couldn't help but snicker as he set it in motion.

***

I'm not who you think I am, I slipped a stranger inside.
It helps the nights go quicker, but I diminish each time.

"Last Night I Nearly Died"

~ Duke Special

September 21ˢᵗ 1675, Swansea, MA

Hardy had come to enjoy working in her gardens, the sun warming his back as he planted and pruned. The scent of the moist earth on the early morning breeze always seemed to rejuvenate his spirit. It was incredible how effectively outdoor physical labor could reconnect you with your Creator. Today was another beautiful, peaceful day, and he was relishing it.

Until the unexpected voice paused his hoe in mid-stroke.

"What are you doing here, Hardy?"

Hardy straightened and slowly turned to face him.

"Didn't even hear you coming, Mark. You're still the best."

Hardy stood tense, visibly so, ready for anything. He'd been down this road once before when Mark thought Hardy had stolen Laura. Mark had gotten violent that time.

Hardy laid down his hoe, arms loose at his sides. Mark was his friend. The last thing on earth he wanted to do was hurt him again. Yet, how could he possibly explain all that had transpired between him and Abbie over the past months? How he'd been reborn. How could he explain in a matter of a few seconds everything that needed to be said, because that's all he would get before Mark slugged him.

He resolved to not fight back. If Mark got aggressive, Hardy would just shift away and find him later once he'd had a chance to calm down. He steadied himself to receive the punch that might be on its way.

Mark stared at Hardy for a long minute, the emotion

filling his eyes changing hues several times. Mark opened his mouth as if about to say something and then shut it just as quickly. He looked away, fixed his eyes on the ground, and then walked to Abbie's cottage where he knocked softly on the front door.

Abbie's surprise was evident when she saw Mark standing there instead of Hardy.

"Mark..." She began, not knowing what to say. There was no guilt, nothing of which to repent, yet a distinct discomfort draped the encounter. She had turned his advances down, and now he found her here with Hardy. That he would be hurt was not in question.

Mark raised his hand to silence whatever explanation or excuse she was about to offer.

"I just stopped by to check on you, see how you were doing." Glancing back at Hardy, he continued, "But, I see you're in good hands."

"Come in, Mark. Have some tea," she invited.

He hesitated, and then entered the house, ducking under the low door frame to do so. Abbie motioned vigorously behind his back, beckoning Hardy to come in too.

The three of them sat down together to share some home-baked cookies Abbie had made that morning, as well as a spot of tea. They discussed everything from the day's weather to the current situation with Rialto to how he and Ty were going stir crazy with cabin fever, but they conspicuously avoided the elephant in the room, Hardy's new relationship with Abbie.

"So, you've been here for months, huh?"

"Yeah," Hardy glued his eyes to the table, "I stay for a couple of weeks and then shift back to meet with you guys the same or next day after I left."

Mark stirred his tea with a spoon. His face was vacant, empty of expression. Finally, he managed a weak smile.

"It's fine, Hardy."

They both knew what he was talking about. Mark looked to Abbie, strengthening the smile a bit.

"I'd no claim on Abbie. I'm glad for you both, I truly am. Now I know I don't have to worry about her any more, cause you'll be here."

"You'll still come around for visits, of course," Abbie confirmed.

"Sure, sure."

It was obvious he was sincere, but saddened nonetheless. He'd expected a joyful reunion with Abbie today, only to receive a gear-wrenching, third-wheel surprise.

They chatted for a bit longer, and then Mark excused himself, standing from the rustic table.

"See you tomorrow?" He extended his hand to Hardy.

Hardy took it. "See you tomorrow. Tomorrow, your time."

Mark went out the door and shut it behind him.

Hardy reopened it, but his friend was gone. He'd already shifted out.

Chapter 44

June 1st 2014, New London, CT

The silver-nosed Acela speed train sliced through the crisp morning air like a lethal bullet on rails. It was the 6:05 commuter train out of Boston, on its way to Washington DC. Almost 300 people were on board this morning.

Alexander Rialto peered through binoculars from a platform that held a clear view of the only section of its track he cared about. Torino and Plageanet were the only two on his team whose lack of conscience was complete enough that could trust them with this job. They'd planted powerful explosives underneath the tracks at a junction just outside New London, Connecticut. It was 7:25 AM and being an express train, there was no stop scheduled for New London. The train was traveling at 150 miles per hour, its full speed.

At the critical moment, Rialto remotely triggered the C-4 packs buried under the track. The shock wave from the explosion thudded against his chest and staggered him. Almost simultaneously, he felt the ground rippling beneath his feet. It was an awe-inspiring sight to see 540 tons of steel hurtling out of control.

The train twisted in a sickening angle as its front end was lifted momentarily by the blast and then dove back into the earth, gouging a deep trench with its nose. A plume of dirt billowed before it, piling up over its front and then falling to either side in a continual wave. It was still going well over 100 miles per hour when it crashed into the concrete barrier separating the track from the Connecticut suburb. He'd chosen a curve for just this reason.

The rebar-reinforced concrete wall shattered before the train's impact as if a hammer had slammed up against a piece of glass. Train car piled into train car as the silver bullet passed into the neighborhood. It was not the five houses it destroyed as much as the drag of the earth which finally stopped it.

A shredded carcass of steaming metal remained, smoke and fire billowing from various openings. Painful moans and cries of shock and horror emanated from its body as well as several of the houses.

With purpose, Rialto strode to the wreck, inspecting his handiwork. The wails of the wounded were louder than he'd expected. One feeble, pale, bloodied arm stretched toward him through a broken window, pleading for help.

Calm down people, he wanted to shout. He fully expected all of this to be undone.

There it was, the object of his interest, the front power car. He'd been worried it would be buried under rubble, but the most that covered it was a pile of dirt. He crumbled some of the last bits of broken glass from its casing in a door and inserted his calling card.

A shriek of genuine agony pierced the cacophony of noise and sirens as someone inside awoke from numbness to the reality of their pain.

"Oh, do shut up," he muttered as he walked off.

***

"You see this, Mark?"

Ty held up the morning paper. They'd been out of touch with current events for the past few weeks with the exception of whatever they read in the paper.

Train Derailed,
Over 200 Dead

[New London, CT]

The Acela Express train derailed yesterday at about 7:25 AM just outside New London, destroying at least five homes before coming to a halt. The commuter train was filled to capacity with early-morning commuters traveling between Boston and Washington DC. According to the Connecticut State Police over 200 people on board were killed in the accident. Another 100 were injured, some critically.

"We do not believe this to be an act of terrorism," said Homeland Security Agent John Bryant, "though we will not rule out any possibilities until the investigation has been completed."

Several eyewitnesses reported hearing a large explosion right before the train derailed. A source inside the State Police department has indicated there was a large crater at the point of derailment. Many windows in the vicinity were blown out as well, which is further indication of an explosion of some sort.

The Boston Herald has also learned that a business card reading "Dark Shift, A. Rialto" was found at the scene, apparently left by someone after the accident had occurred. One witness saw a man approach the front of the train after the derailment who may have left the card.

Federal authorities are not commenting on the card or on any possible causes of the derailment at this time.

The article continued from there. Mark's hands clenched as he read of the casualties, crinkling the paper permanently. They knew what the cause was, or better said, they knew *who* the cause was.

They might be the only people on the planet who truly knew Rialto and what he was capable of.

It had become clear to Mark that there could not be an endless supply of time-shifters out there working for Rialto since Rialto had gotten his shifter from Ty and all of his recent recruits were people Mark had struggled with during his historical escapades.

Still, they couldn't explain where Rialto had gotten all of his shifters. Mark suspected that Rialto would kill him and Hardy at some point in the future and hide their bodies well. That would explain the lack of death certificates for him and Hardy, as well as how Graves and Torino had gotten their shifters, but the theory still did not explain the others. *Where had the other four shifters come from?*

It didn't look like they would have time to solve that mystery. They had to stop Rialto and they had to stop him now.

"You think it's a trap?" Ty asked.

"I'd bet on it."

They waited expectantly for Mark to lay out a plan. Military protocol had been drilled into them like a second set of DNA. Once he stated the plan, they would comment or recommend changes. In the end, he was like their unit commander and they would do whatever he decided.

"First thing we're going to do is disarm those explosives and stop this tragedy. Taking care of Rialto will be secondary."

"We gonna expose ourselves?" Hardy inquired.

"You got any other ideas? We can't let 200 people die. I'll disarm the explosives myself. I want both of you to take up sniper roosts on opposite sides and cover me. You'll position yourselves as far from the scene as possible, half a mile if you can. We need to make sure Rialto can't locate you, 'cause you're my only back-up."

***

Mark inspected the wreckage. It was a horrific scene. He peered inside one of the cars and saw blood splashed chaotically across its interior. How any man could be so callous toward innocent life, he could not understand.

The question that caused him the most struggle, however, was how *God* could allow such an evil man to have such power.

He made his way to the crater. It was huge. He never understood how the government could get away with such non-committal in their public assessments. This was clearly no accident, and Homeland Security had to know that.

Police were stationed outside the perimeter of the scene to prevent curiosity seekers from tampering with it. Evading them was easy, but he made sure he was out of sight before shifting.

First, he set himself up in an observation post. They needed to identify exactly when the explosives were placed on the track, and by who, but he guessed it would be sometime the night before.

Sure enough, around 5:00 AM, Vincent Torino approached the track carrying a duffel bag, not with the cowering insecurity of a thief avoiding scrutiny, but with the confidence of a man who knew he was immune to attack.

The assassin pulled a shovel from the duffel bag and dug out a significant hole underneath and around the track. He shoved C-4 sticks into the hollowed out area and attached an electronic device to them, which was probably a radio receiver that would trigger the explosion. After burying his handiwork with gravel, he faded off into the darkness.

"Anybody got a bead on Torino?" Mark whispered into his radio mike. Their comm system was encrypted and secure from infiltration.

"I've got him in sight," Ty replied.

"Stay where you're at till I'm done here, then follow him. Don't try to take him out, just find out where he's going and scope out who else might be around. This has got to be a set up to draw us out. Hardy, you follow Ty from a distance and keep him covered. Copy?"

"Roger."

"Out."

Mark concentrated on the track in front of him. He trusted his friends to watch his back.

The explosives appeared simple to disarm — unbelievably so. Wary, he inspected every crevice and crack several times, searching for a hidden tripwire or some other booby-trap, but he couldn't find any — which only worried him more.

Oh well, if I blow myself up, at least I'll save the train. Plus, Ty or Hardy would shift back and warn him off before touching anything if he did.

Holding his breath, one by one, he removed the leads that connected the trigger to the explosives.

Nothing happened. *Too easy.*

He packed up the trigger and the explosives in his own duffel bag and left.

He had no doubt that if they watched the news later today, there would be no mention of a train derailing and two hundred people would go on living their lives normally, never knowing the mortal danger they'd escaped.

Chapter 45

Torino moved through the streets like a silver fox. His stride was purposeful, yet not swaggering. It was the walk of a professional killer, a man who knew what he was about and had no desire to be noticed.

Ty followed at a safe distance. Hardy had the most training of the three in covert surveillance, but Ty was no slouch himself. Torino's apparent lack of concern that he might be followed was what worried Ty the most. Most likely, one of Rialto's other team members would be stationed along Torino's path waiting to ambush Ty.

He followed Torino all the way into town and then through it. The man was certainly going out of his way to walk a long distance. *Why wasn't he driving?*

The sun was dawning and a short burst of reflective glare revealed the ambusher up on the roof of a building across the street. It was a poor position for a sniper, but then their enemies' lack of training never failed to amaze him. If it weren't for the superior numbers of the other side, he and Mark and Hardy would have won by now.

Ty halted his pursuit and ducked into an alley. He approached the sniper's building from the back and stealthily ascended the stairs. Surprisingly, the door to the roof was well-oiled and made no sound when he opened it.

He slipped off his shoes and stepped softly toward his would-be attacker. The man never heard him coming. Reaching around the man's neck, Ty yanked him up and back, pulling his forearm hard into his throat. The sniper thrashed about helplessly until he fell unconscious. Ty didn't want to kill the guy, at least not yet. That would only attract other dark shifters to save him. No, he would tie him up for now and return to finish him off later.

He rolled the man over and shock throttled him. *Hugh Plageanet.*

Plageanet, the evil, disgusting son of the plantation owner they'd taken out in 1863. Ty double-blinked and rubbed his eyes. The last time they'd seen this piece of human garbage was when the younger Plageanet had entered his family outhouse to relieve himself. Mark and he had blown that outhouse to smithereens. How in the world had Plageanet survived? There had been nothing left.

There would be plenty of time to contemplate such mysteries later, he decided. For now, he had a mission to complete. He grabbed each of Plageanet's wrists and handcuffed them to iron rails imbedded in the concrete structure of the building. He also wrapped the man's legs up tight in a chain and padlocked it. The final touch was a strip of duct tape over his mouth.

Without a third party freeing him, little Hugh would wait right here till he got back.

Back on the sidewalk, Ty continued the pursuit, shifting back to a time when Torino had still been in sight. He was a little more relaxed now, feeling like he'd discovered the trap, but his guard was nevertheless up, wary, ready for anything else Rialto might have up his sleeve.

Torino arrived at an empty field outside of town. He left the road and disappeared into the wild, unkempt grass. There were no trees in sight, but the grass was tall enough by itself to make it difficult to keep Torino in eyeshot, though it also helped disguise Ty's pursuit. Torino's lack of concern about being followed still bothered him.

Torino stopped to look around, so Ty ducked out of sight behind a bush. Apparently satisfied he was alone, Torino hit his shifter and disappeared. Ty checked his detector.

Same day, five years prior. Likely just your typical "shift and evade" maneuver.

Ty knew how to get around that. He adjusted his own time display to five years ago, but thirty seconds earlier. He would arrive before Torino and scope out the situation. He'd have time to set up a nice little surprise, or simply shift out to report back to Mark, Torino never being the wiser.

Ty felt himself being pushed upward a bit as he arrived at the target time. That usually meant there was a floor or some other object below him which hadn't been present previously.

Unexpected walls suddenly surrounded him on all sides. Dull, grey walls. Something hazy obscured his vision and blurred his view of them.

He was in a room where there should be a field, and a strange gas, a bitter-tasting gas, filled the air. His lungs jolted from it at the first breath. A moment later, the blurriness in his vision grew worse.

His hand moved to his shifter, then stopped short. The face of it glowed red, inoperable.

Panicked, he ran toward one of the walls, desperately looking for a way out of this trap. The room was huge, much larger than he'd realized, and the exertion caused the gas to work even faster on his system.

He saw a door in the distance at the front of the room. It seemed to be the only way in or out.

He wasn't going to make it. His knees buckled before he could make a move toward it. The smoky gas overwhelmed his senses, thoroughly permeating his blood. The last thing he saw before losing consciousness was Vincent Torino as he shifted into the room, smiling.

***

Hardy didn't have trouble keeping up with Ty. In fact, he barely watched his friend as they made their way through the Connecticut suburb. His eyes were glued to the rooftops, windows, and the landscape surrounding them. His job was to make sure nobody got behind Ty and ambushed him.

He spied the sniper about the same time Ty did. He watched from a distance as Ty disarmed the man. Throughout the rest of the surveillance, he spied no one else waiting to get a drop on them, but something about the whole set-up still smelled rotten. He grew more and more concerned as Torino kept walking farther and farther out of the town. *Where was he going? Why was he on foot?*

He mentally willed Ty to be extra careful when Torino veered off into the empty field. There had to be a reason behind this odd behavior. They were either being lured, or Rialto's men were completely incompetent.

C'mon, Ty, what are you doing? Don't shift, he pled silently.

According to Mark's instructions, Ty was only supposed to follow Torino and then report back to Mark. Instead, it looked to Hardy like Ty was about to shift somewhere in order to keep up the surveillance.

His suspicions were confirmed as Ty disappeared. Now, *he* would have to decide if he would follow or just go get Mark. He reasoned he should be safe if he distanced himself far enough back from Ty's position. That way, he'd know what to tell Mark to expect if they had to go after Ty.

Seventy-five feet ought to do it. Close enough to observe, but far enough not to shift into the same trouble Ty had, assuming there was any. First, he circled the entire field to make sure he was not being observed. Then, he moved to about seventy-five feet away from Ty's point of departure and set his shifter to the time displayed on his detector. Ty had gone in about thirty seconds before Torino, but Hardy thought it safest to choose Torino's time.

The formidable concrete walls on all sides surprised him, and the gas was completely unexpected. Ty lay unconscious on the floor, and Torino stood over him.

The only visible door was flung open. Several men outfitted with gas masks and bearing machine guns entered. Torino made his way toward them. He stumbled just as the men reached him, apparently affected by the gas. One of them laid an oxygen mask over his mouth and they helped him to his feet and out the door, which swung shut solidly behind them. Bolts locked into place, echoing hollowly in the gas-filled chamber.

Hardy began to feel the effects of the gas as well. His head was swimming. The room was huge. Seventy-five feet hadn't been far enough away. He needed to get out of here. He wouldn't be able to help Ty without a gas mask.

He shook his wrist in disbelief, wondering if the gas was making him see things. The display looked red. It *couldn't* be inoperable. This was only his second shift, and he'd only gone back five years. He pushed the shift button.

Nothing.

He rocked his head side to side, trying to shake loose the growing cobwebs. The room was becoming confusing.

It spun and a knee hit the floor, a knee which was now operating independently from his mind.

That was the last thing he remembered.

***

June 2nd 2014, Boston, MA

Neither Ty nor Hardy showed up back at headquarters. Mark waited in the lounge alone, knowing something had gone wrong.

An antique clock Savannah bought a few months ago faced him from the mantle, ticking away the seconds like an eternal metronome.

If a trap had been sprung it was up to Mark to fix it. They would be depending on him.

Absentmindedly, he fiddled his fingers, lost in concentrated thought. They were clearly in a precarious position. Rialto had them outnumbered and equally matched in equipment. If he'd killed or taken Ty and Hardy prisoner, then all Rialto would have to do now was finish Mark off and the game would be up for the good guys.

The buzz of the intercom startled him, jarring his thoughts

together like the cars of the derailed train they'd just saved.

"Mark?"

"Yes, Savannah?"

"Two gentlemen are in the lobby waiting to see you."

Here we go, he thought.

"Rialto's men?"

"They claim to be Secret Service."

"Secret Service?" It had to be a ploy. "You're not in the lobby are you?"

"No, I'm inside. I've only spoken to them over the intercom."

That was good. The door between the lobby and the rest of their headquarters was virtually impenetrable. As long as that door was not breached, no one could get in, which is why he'd given Savannah explicit instructions not to go outside or open it for any reason.

"I'll be right down," he replied.

When he got there, he saw two men on camera. And they did indeed look like the Secret Service type.

He depressed the intercom's send button. "Can I help you?" He asked.

One of them held up what looked to be an official badge, but it was hard to be sure viewing it through the grainy camera image. "Secret Service," the man said, "We're here to see Mark Carpen." His voice was tinny over the electronic communication system.

"What about?"

"That's between us and him," The guy with the badge said.

"Put your badges in the security tray." Mark slid open a small, sliding box, similar to those used in a drive-thru at a bank. Both men placed their wallets in the tray and Mark pulled it back through the wall.

The badges looked authentic enough, but with Rialto's money, anything could be bought.

"You'll have to come back another time. We're busy today."

The men smiled at each other in the way only arrogantly confident government men can. One of them leaned over to speak into the intercom. "Sir, I don't know who you are, but this is regarding a matter of national security. You're either going to let us in right now, or we're coming in after you."

That made Mark mad. He'd had enough.

"Sirs, I have no idea who *you* are. That's exactly the problem. You can try coming in after me if you want, but the steel door between us is as thick as a bank vault. In the meantime, the door behind you is now locked."

One of the agents turned and tried it, verifying it was locked.

"Those small round black holes in the walls surrounding you are the barrels of eight different wall-mounted automatic weapons. Each of them is trained on you as we speak, attuned to your body heat, and I can activate them with the push of a button."

He did. The ominous sound of rounds being loaded into multiple chambers echoed through the small foyer.

"All I have to do is push a different button and they'll start spewing rounds. Not to mention the explosives buried in the floor under your feet. I'm having a pretty bad day so far — so don't push me."

The blood drained from the men's faces, their self-assurance deflated as surely as if he'd stuck it with a pin.

"Hold up your hands," Mark ordered.

Reluctantly, both men obeyed.

"Take off your jackets and roll up your sleeves. That's right. Push your sleeves really high. I want to see your wrists, and I want to see them good."

They did so. Neither had a shifter, at least not on their wrists. Mark turned to another screen. He'd installed a density scanner in the lobby for a situation such as this. It could scan people or packages for metal or otherwise dense objects using X-ray and other imaging techniques.

"Put your guns in the tray."

The agents complied once more, and Mark slid the tray back inside, confiscating the weapons.

"You've both got ankle holsters. I'll need those too, and you, on the right, you've got something shoved in your waistband behind your back. Fork it over."

One of the agents cursed audibly, but they did as commanded. They were not accustomed to being told what to do by a citizen, nor did they like it in the least.

Mark continued with the drill. "The front door is now unlocked. One of you can go back outside and wait. The other can come in."

The one on the right went out. The other stayed.

He locked the front door again. "All right. Take off all your clothes except for your boxers and then turn around." He was not taking any chances. "Socks too." The agent grimaced as he leaned down to take them off.

Finally, when the government man had followed all his instructions, Mark unlocked the vault door to let him in. Unclothed men often found it more difficult to fight as aggressively as they would fully dressed, plus it eliminated potential hiding places for a weapon the scanner might have missed.

As the agent entered, Mark kept him covered him with a .45, refusing to lower it for even a second. The vault door slid shut solidly after him.

The agent first looked to Savannah, who maintained her distance at the side of the room, and then Mark.

"What is the matter with you, man?" The agent was incredulous.

"Let's just say we have plenty of reasons to be suspicious."

"Are you Mark Carpen?"

"I am. What does the Secret Service want with me?"

"We don't. The President of the United States does."

End of Book 2
ChronoShift Trilogy

Acknowledgements

Authors often begin their work inspired in solitude, yet before a novel can be considered complete, it has been aided and touched by many hands, each contributing to its final excellence in their own way.

My sincere thanks go out to Jack & Barbara Mason, Lindsay Mason, Joel Odom, Daniel Server, Paul Wolak, Charlie Warner, and Lynda Bacon for taking the time to review my writing and for their endless offerings of encouragement.

To Fran Stewart, for her selfless and detailed copyediting, which clearly helped make *Chase* a better book. To Matt Smartt, a true artist, for designing such a phenomenal set of book covers, and for putting up with my nit-picky perfectionism.

To 12Stone Church, for opening up God's house to allow a writer a peaceful place to craft his work (And to Patti Reiland for keeping him supplied with endless amounts of coffee).

And finally, to all my friends and clients who have voiced their support and helped spread the word, may you receive a multitude of blessings as you continue the journey.

About the Author

Zack Mason loves the art of the word and the thrill of the story. He has wandered the countryside of Bangladesh, built churches in Costa Rica, roamed the desert in Arizona, hiked the Alps in France, and fought human trafficking in Atlanta. He has been a dishwasher, a house framer, a teacher, a waiter, a salesman, and a businessman, just to name a few. He currently resides with his family outside Atlanta, GA and plans to continue writing for as long as he is allowed to do so.

Want a peek at a Secret Chapter?

The author has installed a secret chapter on ChronoShift's website that can only be viewed there.

1. Go to www.Chrono-Shift.com
2. Use the same login give earlier in this book and click on "Search Archives".
3. Enter a search for "Oval Office Assault".
4. Follow the instructions.

Don't forget to look for the next installment of the ChronoShift Trilogy

Turn

Coming Soon - 2012

CPSIA information can be obtained at www.ICGtesting.com
Printed in the USA
LVOW040056190512

282293LV00003B/7/P